About the *A*

John Bishop was born in Heswall on the Wirral and now lives in Codsall near Wolverhampton. Originally an English teacher, he was for six years a College Principal in Erdington, Birmingham. A great-uncle who won the Military Cross in WW1 but never really recovered from his experiences aroused an interest in this 'war to end all wars' that only led to a second, more extensive one within twenty years.

John's first novel, *The Chinese Attack*, featured a neglected aspect of The Great War, the role of the Chinese Labour Corps, in which his grandfather was a sergeant, on the Western Front from 1917.

His second, *Love, Freedom or Death* (2013), also published by Matador, is a love story set against the resistance struggle in Crete in WW2.

Website: www.johnbishopauthor.wordpress.com

Cover design by Ian Byrne: contactbyrne@gmail.com

REFUSE TO FORGET

JOHN BISHOP

Matador
9 Priory Business Park
Kibworth Beauchamp
Leicestershire LE8 0RX, UK
Tel: (+44) 116 279 2299
Fax: (+44) 116 279 2277
Email: books@troubador.co.uk
Web: www.troubador.co.uk/matador

ISBN 978 1783063 130

British Library Cataloguing in Publication Data.
A catalogue record for this book is available from the British Library.

Printed and bound in the UK by TJ International, Padstow, Cornwall
Typeset in 11pt Bembo by Troubador Publishing Ltd, Leicester, UK

Matador is an imprint of Troubador Publishing Ltd

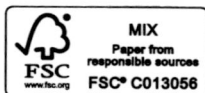

MIX
Paper from
responsible sources
FSC
www.fsc.org
FSC® C013056

In memory of those
described by Paul Fussell
in *The Great War & Modern Memory* as

'a well-meaning, trusting generation'

who marched away to secure our future
and of whom eight hundred thousand never came back.

One

September 1926

Twelve years on, almost to the day we went to Belgium! It was Lady Hester's funeral that brought back the nightmares. For twelve years I'd tried to push them out of mind – and succeeded, too, most of the time, especially after I was sent off to Arran in early 1915 to keep me out of sight. I thought forgetting was where safety lay, then.

If I brooded on anything during those first years it was never having got to drive the Wolseley again. Besides, I was set to labour so hard there – crofting makes working a country estate down here seem like child's play – that I had no time to ponder on our helter-skelter two months in Autumn 1914; then the news from the later years of the War put our little 'adventure' far into the shade. If anything, the bullishness of the 'Home Front' – yes, they still called it that, even in the Scottish Isles – made me share the returning Tommies' reluctance to admit to any knowledge of what I'd seen.

I shouldn't have come back for the funeral. I don't really know why I did. Curiosity? To find if anything had changed? To express some silent gratitude? Lady Hester had been responsible for my education, not that I realised that until recently. But she had opened my eyes, for what *that* has been worth.

I'd like to think it was to do with being near the centre of things, until the Strike was crushed. A hope that there was a stirring of hope again. Perhaps that lured me south just as the madness of the summer of 1914 had drawn me across the Channel at the first opportunity. In reality I suspect it was only more of the drifting that had settled on us all in the decade after the War. I always have been easily led.

At the funeral I saw at once that nothing *had* changed. Certainly

1

not the hypocrisy. I nearly turned and 'ran' for it, then. In most of the faces the mask of grief barely covered the gloating. They'd turned on Lady Hester when we came back from France, once some of the 'facts' came out, and now they'd driven her to an early grave. The surge of anger almost had me blundering in amongst them, wielding my fists. Until I remembered my own part in it all. My lie that had set it off.

That turned me cold. I could feel myself keeling over. The faint came on so sudden. It was the surprise as much as anything. I'd kept that recognition away years ago but it had swung back and hit me between the eyes. Teaching me a lesson for trying to forget.

A passing chap I didn't recognise steadied me and his 'Easy, old man' let me get a grip. I nodded my thanks but my head whirled with the questions. Was it really my fault? If I hadn't been too young would she have received so much condemnation? Didn't I do it for myself, with no concern for the consequences for others? There was no point in denying that. Or any of it. I could put up all sorts of reasons for why I did lie but in the end I wouldn't have missed it for the world. It was my choice to go. My responsibility.

I limped into the back of the church in a daze. By now a gammy leg was a war wound nobody bothered to notice. What an irony for me there. Not that the gentry had any interest in me. Nor did anyone else. Only then did I have my second shock. I began to scrutinise the congregation, in the church, though my view of those at the front was limited. Several of the villagers I remembered though no one recognised me. Hardly surprising, that.

Some of the toffs I'd seen on their visits to the House. But it was with a creeping panic I experienced a sense of isolation worse than I'd felt in my exile on the island: with the exception of Lady Helena, who didn't really count, of our small band, I was now the only one left.

The realisation swept me back those twelve years and nearly bowled me over again. Things began to unravel once more, replay themselves, like a moving picture show. This had happened on Arran but it had been sporadic and worn off during the winter. I'd spent the last decade evading the images, carrying a dull sense of shame that deadened the terror. What I'd have done if you hadn't caught up with me, or I was steered towards you, I'd like to say I don't know. But I do: kept on drifting, I suppose.

This time I've let the past re-run to take in properly what I'd been in the middle of. If anything, to tell you the truth, that process has almost been more unnerving than the reality. Being so young then the full implications passed me by in the excitement. Afterwards I'd thought I wanted to be free of the memories but now I see it's about more than me. It's about obligations.

★★★★★★

1914 ought to be the last of those glorious hot summers that seemed to fill my childhood. Then it was high hopes and the belief you were indestructible. At fourteen I'd 'shot up no end' my mum used to say. I was bigger than my dad and sent to take on the heavy jobs out on the estate that he'd begun to struggle with.

Except I didn't see it like that. I resented the drudgery, the being put upon. The heat seemed oppressive, my mum's voice always complaining. I felt I'd outgrown myself and longed for something to lift me out of the rut I was stuck in.

The thing I remember first about the year was the new motor car. A Wolseley tourer, it was. The family had had motor cars since I was little, of course – not that I had anything to do with them – but this one was special, even before we took it to Belgium. That year my dad was given the job of chauffeur. I think I was more pleased about it than he was.

Although I was big for my age I was more shy than a ten year-old. What I liked about cars – apart from the obvious thrill of their noise and power – was that you didn't feel they were weighing you up all the time. They'd catch you out, right enough, and try your patience but you wouldn't find yourself blushing with shame at something they'd made you do. You could lavish your time on them and they'd accept it. Even with horses you weren't always sure of that.

The spit and polish I gave that car, in particular, the Wolseley. The care with which I cleaned the seats, when I was allowed to, and soaked up all the knowledge of its engine's workings. The dream I had of actually going out for a jaunt. And the dizzy turn I had when the dream came true.

That jaunt on a Sunday morning in midsummer was, I grew to realise, when the wild escapades of that year all began. My life before it seems to belong to someone else. Who could have imagined the same would apply to the whole world? Something happened on that day after which there was no going back. At the time, no one understood and by the time they did it was too late.

I was hunkered down behind the front seats buffing up the leather that thoughtless boots had scuffed when Lady Hester's voice swept over me. It had a brittle, metallic twang. 'Butler, take me for a drive.'

My dad, I think he had the bonnet up, must have begun to prevaricate because I caught an imperious 'Now!' and before I could react the passenger door was opened, a wave of scent poured in and the door shut. I held my breath. The bonnet closed and I heard the starting handle being turned. Only when the engine surged with that smooth roar that always made the hairs on my arms tingle did I remember where I was. I couldn't move. Should I try to slip the door open and slide out? I doubted I could do that unseen. Could I leap out over the side as it moved off? The truth is I was in too much of a funk, scared I'd get my dad in trouble, to do anything. And then we were gliding away.

I sank to the floor, stifling tears and hardly daring to breathe.

'Where to, ma'am?' I heard my dad's voice. With luck she'd only want dropping at church and I'd be safe.

'I want a spin on the Downs,' came the reply and my heart stopped. I was stuck. And for how long? An hour? Two? My nose started to twitch and I held it tight in case I sneezed. This was no spin, more like a torment.

Lady Hester didn't speak — I don't think I'd ever heard her say much — and the silence above the purring of the engine didn't ease my nerves. My dad must have been nervous, too, because he crashed the gears a couple of times. After the third time I got another shock.

'I'll drive.'

'But Lady Hest…'

The car jolted and I almost banged my head against the foot of the back seat.

'Stop the car. I said I'll drive.'

As the car crunched to a stop on gravel I shuffled myself behind the driver's seat, hoping she wouldn't catch sight of me as she climbed in. Strange to think that, to look at her in public, you'd have taken her for the timid, retiring sort. To the servants she had another side: anything out of place and you were in for it. If seen, it wasn't her timidity I shivered about.

Doors opened and closed then my dad's panic-stricken instructions floated back. 'Now, with the clutch… p-press once, then…'

'Don't fuss, Butler, it can't be that difficult, can it? Start the engine.'

The engine wound up and spun. For one terrified moment I thought she was going to drive off alone but the passenger door opened and my dad got in.

'Now, let…' he began but with a huge jolt we shot forward, the engine cut and we jerked to a halt. My head did bang on the base of the seat and I saw stars. In panic I wondered if I'd cried out.

There was silence from in front. Had anyone been hurt? I heard an exasperated sigh from Lady Hester. If I hadn't been so wrapped up in my own plight, I'd have taken some satisfaction from that: the reward for treating a Wolseley like a servant.

'Just go through it again, Butler. Rather more frisky than Jemima.'

Jemima was her favourite mare. My dad took her through the procedure again and this time she asked questions when he wasn't clear. Which was often because, as he told me later, he was too busy thinking what Sir Brydon would do to him if he found out, let alone if she wrecked the thing. He'd forgotten all about me.

At the fourth attempt we set off. I was soon black and blue with all the buffeting. Those old roads over the Downs weren't made for motor cars and she wasn't the steadiest of drivers. It was the changing of the gears that caused most of the problems, as it always does. I lost count of the times the engine suddenly stopped. Each time the smell of petrol swamped over me and I began to feel quite sick. Any smugness I felt soon dried up.

Lady Hester wasn't the slowest driver, either, and the old girl – the motor car, that is – never needed much encouragement to go. Lady Hester certainly let her rip. It did cross my mind she might be after causing a wreck to spite Sir Brydon but by now I was less afraid of being caught, or even killed, than suffering from the fumes and feeling miffed at missing out on the thrill of seeing us racing over the empty Downs.

Except they weren't completely empty. I could see nothing, of course, but for flashes of sky. It was the blast of the horn I heard first and felt our sideways lurch along with the frantic neighing of horses. We bumped and crashed across uneven ground, the car slewing and the engine roaring. Lucky we were in open country, I recall thinking, or there'd have been a heck of a smash-up, but mostly I was bracing myself expecting us to go over at any point. Behind us I could hear angry shouts.

However, the jolting steadied, the cries grew fainter, I caught the scrunch of pebble and we slowed to a stop. We were back on the track. There were a couple of deep sighs from in front. My heart was thumping so much I feared they might hear it.

'I think you'd better take over, Butler,' Lady Hester said and my dad grunted and opened his door. I'm not sure I'd have been able to stand straight after that but it sounded as if they managed to change places. I must say that felt like a pretty decent piece of driving, and not just because it was a woman. Naturally my dad said nothing.

'Home, I think, Butler, if you could. And perhaps the less said about this the better. You know what I mean?'

'Yes, ma'am,' came the reply and my fear of discovery re-bounded with a start. If she saw me now my dad would be in for it good and proper. It wouldn't need Sir Brydon to wield the axe.

I'd hardly begun to wallow in this self-pity when the shouts behind us became louder again. The horsemen must be after us. And if they came alongside, from their height I'd be completely visible skulking in the back.

6

'Quickly, man, start her up,' Lady Hester rasped – back to her old self – and there were the sounds of hectic scrambling as my dad went for the starting handle. But the Wolseley was a beauty, fired first time as always and we shot away just as the first horseman, in full cavalry dress uniform swept from our left past my eyeline. His attention was stuck on the driver and at that angle I knew I was obscured. For the moment.

'Hold, you lunatic…' he shouted but I heard Lady Hester hiss at my dad, 'Drive on' and caught a glimpse of hooves as the horse reared to avoid the car's surge. I tensed for them to clatter on the car's boot and then the sounds of pursuit but apart from a few yells there was no more anxiety. Aside from the driving, of course. After the shocks he'd had my dad's driving was as jerky as Lady Hester's.

My head was buzzing. From the silence in front I expect theirs were, as well. Then Lady Hester spoke. Very matter-of-fact, she tried to sound, too but a waver gave her away. 'Take no notice of Douglas, Butler, he's all wind.'

'D–Douglas, Lady Hester? Not L–Lord Douglas…?'

'Good God, no. Haig. Douglas Haig. Cavalryman.'

The car swung a bit to the left. I hoped my dad wasn't going to go into a faint. He managed to splutter out:

'Y–you know the g–gentleman y… we almost hit, ma'a…'

'Brydon served under him in South Africa. Still believed he was dashing across the veldt, no doubt. No thoughts of listening for an engine coming over the hill.'

'B–but if he knows S–sir Brydon…'

A bitterness I'd never have suspected informed her dismissive answer. 'Oh, he's soared far out of Sir Brydon's sphere since then. And I'm sure he wouldn't have recognised me, the little woman. *I've* never been a lady of the Queen's bedchamber, after all.'

What that was all about, I hadn't an inkling. We made it back to the House without further incident and only when my dad had seen Lady Hester out at the front steps and driven round towards the motor house they'd made in the stables did I relax.

A bit too soon. When I opened the back door and staggered out I gave him his third near-heart attack of the morning. His face looked ashen. Yet it went even paler. 'You what? You been hiding in there all the time? You heard...? For the love of Mike... You little bleeder. What you think you were doing?'

'I was cleani...' was as far as I got before he cuffed me, unbuckling his belt as he did. By the end of the leathering I had weals on bruises and bruises on the weals.

However, after a few days, once he'd calmed down, he was glad of having someone to talk to about it. Helped get it off his chest. A bit like I feel now. We were even able to laugh over it. That, and the funny business in Serbia the same day, where it was the car's stalling that led to the Austrian Duke's getting shot by anarchists.

'We was lucky there,' my dad joked. 'If it hadn't been for that Haig chap was a cavalryman and the old Wolseley's spirit, we might have paid a price for it ourselves.'

I laughed too. A near motor car accident on the Sussex Downs and the assassination of that Archduke Franz Ferdinand in Serbia had nothing more in common than a joke about this new and thrilling form of transport. It never occurred to me until long afterwards that there was more of a link than I'd realised at the time.

But like most people I hadn't much interest in strange goings-on in faraway places. More exciting developments occurred at home. Like my learning to drive and getting to fiddle with the engines. Not on the Wolseley, at least not then. Sir Brydon collared that, and my dad, for his own use. Important business at the War Office, so it was said, though Carstairs insisted on calling it the Haw Office and laughing whenever the subject came up.

Carstairs was the Lumsden's chauffeur and he came over to remedy any problems my dad had with the engines. He spent most of his time muttering foul words under his breath but when I told him my dad wouldn't let me drive any of the cars because of the danger he seemed to warm to me.

'Danger? Pouf. It's the future, this, son. It'd be criminal to keep you in the dark.'

We came to an agreement. If I told no one, he'd teach me, not only how to drive the Model T but how the engine worked. Did I hesitate! I was in there like a shot.

Carstairs was what I called a proper chauffeur. Not like my dad, who'd sort of stumbled from being a part-time coachman into looking after the motors. Carstairs had even worked at building cars. In a factory. He could take an engine apart like nobody's business. And in me he found an eager pupil.

'It's like a woman, a motor car,' he told me after I'd jerked and stopped the engine on my first few attempts to drive. 'You gotta be smooth and gentle, then give it a whoosh.'

I hadn't a clue what he was talking about but I soon realised that the smoother your actions the better the car responded. As for the 'forbidden land under the bonnet', as he called it, my delight was almost too much and had him guffawing. I was mortified but once he stripped down the spark advance lever and the timer – the Model T has an electric starter – all that dissolved. I was in wonderland. In fact, one day we were so wrapped up in beavering away under the bonnet that my dad came back unexpectedly and caught us.

'What you doing, causing trouble, getting in his way?' he laid into me, though I think he was really pulling up Carstairs for encouraging me. The old staff never liked the newcomer chauffeurs because they thought they got above themselves with all their swanky ways. Carstairs didn't show any sign of being put down, though.

'Oh, no trouble, Mr B, just needed someone to hold the spanners and your lad was kind enough to help.'

Helping Carstairs wasn't a recommendation to my dad and it took some time before I was forgiven. This was when my mum took sickly and I could see how it was weighing down on him. I helped out as much as I could and one day he even brought himself to thank me. Something never heard of! Sensing my opportunity I told him I could help him more if he let Carstairs teach me about engines and how to look after them.

Either because I was persuasive or more likely because he thought it could save him from reliance on Carstairs, he agreed. Carstairs also jumped at the chance of being free from my dad's beck and call. I was sent off to my first lesson with dire warnings.

'You take it slow, you hear? No fancy business to show off. If you aren't sure what to do, you're to stop and enquire.'

That wasn't Carstairs' way.

'Ah, just suck it and see,' he said when I asked him how you knew what to do when you were stuck. The prospect of oil in my mouth didn't appeal but then again Carstairs never actually seemed to practise that move. It was all 'Give it another tweak and then try it.'

I certainly picked up a lot and my confidence grew. Soon I could do many of the routine jobs of maintaining Lady Hester's cars. For my dad, getting *my* hands covered in oil rather than his had its advantages. For me it was a dream.

I'm sure it couldn't really have been that idyllic. Looking back across this gulf makes it seem so. Life in our house was fraught. My mum lay in bed all the time and the young ones got on her nerves. The cottage never quite lost its smell of damp, despite the hot weather, and there was so much dust we had to keep down for my mum's chest. And the flies!

I don't think I noticed a lot, just got on with things as was the way. A bit like the rest of the country, now I look back on it, ignoring the developments in the big world. I don't know what excuse they had. I was too swept up with my new-fangled enthusiasm for the cars.

Even the events of the 23rd of July didn't come as a huge shock. Austria's ultimatum to Serbia. I only really realised it had occurred a few days afterwards. That sort of thing wasn't out of the ordinary, then. Trouble had been going on from time to time over there for years. 'Small war in the Balkans,' people used to laugh, 'They're at it again.' Nothing to do with us.

Then, suddenly, it became serious. Again, it was a car that made me sit up and take note of what was happening. One afternoon my head was under the bonnet of the Model T.

'Carstairs. Where the hell are you, Carstairs?'

I recognised Mr James's voice and hunched lower over the engine, hoping he'd not notice. It didn't work.

'Carstairs, is that you? Oh, hell, no. Who the hell are you?'

'Butler, sir, Mr B…'

'Never mind. Have you seen Carstairs?'

'N–no, s–sir. He's not come over today, sir. He said he was going up to London…'

'Was he, be damned? You're Butler's boy, are you?'

'Yes, sir.'

'He around?'

'No, sir, he's…'

'Know anything about cars, do you, Butler?'

'A little, sir, I…'

'Well, come and look at the Sunbeam. Can't get the bugger to start. There's a shilling in it if you can.'

He marched off and I followed him round to the front of the House. I'd not seen the Sunbeam before so I was a mixture of excitement and terror. The fear because Mr James was an officer in the Life Guards. He had inherited none of his mother's timidity to anyone. He was fully his father's son. Getting on the wrong side of his tongue would bring you a fair lashing.

A tall young lady dressed in yellow stood beside the car with a parasol over her right shoulder. Her eyes blazed with impatience. But my eyes were on the 16/20 – a bright green beauty. She looked eager for the road and I wondered how Mr James had failed to get her to start.

Carstairs' teaching proved its worth that day. He'd told me that checking the timing was the trick to get any engine started and though I'd never seen inside a Sunbeam I guessed at its layout. I fiddled a bit, trying to ignore the ribbing Mr James was picking up from his lady friend.

'I hope you won't have to run for the servants when this war starts, James,' she said and I remember thinking 'What war?'

'I haven't noticed you doing your own scrubbing, darling,' Mr James replied. 'And if there's a war you may have to look to it, so I shouldn't be so cheery.'

This sounded as if it rattled her. 'That talk's all nonsense, surely? We'll never go to war?'

'Before the summer's out, I'd say.'

'No?'

She wasn't the only one taken aback. I had to grit my teeth to stop my hand shaking. What did Mr James, with his inside knowledge, know that all the rest of us didn't?

'Oh, cousin Willy's gasping for a show. Been dying for one for years.'

'The German Kaiser?'

'The very same. Can't stand being the family dunce. Austria's declaration of war came like manna from heaven for him. Now Russia mobilising against Austria will enable him to play the big brother. Show his muscle. Still, if it gives us a chance to put his nose even further out of joint... We'll soon have him off his high horse.'

Her voice had a note of panic to it. 'Oh, James, don't, now you're teasing me.'

I hoped he was, too, but I wasn't so sure. The mention of horses reminded me that Mr James was a cavalryman. And of Lady Hester on the Downs. Horses versus motor cars would be no contest if it came to a war. Mr James's reply didn't make me any happier.

'Mark my words. We'll be hunting elsewhere come September. Any joy, Butler? You'll have to shape up quicker than this when the bugle sounds.'

'Try it now, sir,' I said, not daring to look him in the eye.

She started first time. I stood marvelling at my good luck and the Sunbeam's gloss. So much so that I forgot about the shilling until they'd driven off.

I went back to the Model T in a daze. If I did have a knack for this engine business, maybe I could get on in life. Work in a factory like Carstairs had. With the harvest coming up, that sounded like a decent prospect. I wasn't really cut out for being a farm boy. Growing up surrounded by nature only made me want to escape from it. And all the years on the estate hadn't exactly set my parents up in comfort. While a warm factory full of machines...

But what Mr James had said also stuck in my mind. For the first time I also started listening to people. What I heard was a strange mixture but it certainly fed my curiosity. And my growing frustration. Here was a chance of adventure that seemed certain to exclude me. How I longed to be part of it. I wasn't the only one. Any dissenting voices were ignored if not shouted down. More's the pity.

Two

'It won't happen, he's all wind, that one,' my dad scoffed when I mentioned Mr James's claim while describing the Sunbeam to him. 'Look around you. There'll be no war. Who wants a war? Nobody. Except a few young bucks that ain't got enough to do besides tearing round in fancy cars putting decent people's lives at risk.'

Who'd listen to my dad? He had his own motives. Not us lads in the woods, certainly. We were already drilling with 'rifles' we'd cut from branches. Curly Hopkins, who was eighteen but a bit simple and who'd been to summer camp with the Church Lads' Brigade reckoned he knew about drill and had us marching all over the place. Keeping in formation wasn't easy among the trees.

'You 'ave to keep in step,' he'd moan in despair. 'If you don't keep in step you won't 'ave no keeshian. You'll be like them Russian peasants of the Sarr's.'

I didn't know what keeshian was but I didn't want to be like a Russian peasant. Though with hindsight, in our only engagement we probably fought like them. That is, we ran away.

'Hey, look at these drips,' was my first warning. I blundered into Tom in front, who'd stopped and for a moment I couldn't see anyone ahead through the trees. Then I saw the Topham lads, bunched in the clearing ahead. We must have been so busy trying to keep in step we'd wandered into their den.

'I'm off,' Tom muttered as he pushed past me. He wasn't the only one and when I glimpsed their leader, Robbo Inskins, waving a club as he shouted "Charge!" I joined the flood. Curly seemed to have forgotten about keeping in step when you retreated but he certainly led the way.

While that put me off childish games it only increased my desire to be involved in a proper show if there'd be one. I didn't seem to have much chance of that.

'But I look eighteen!' I protested when my mate Robert laughed at me for saying I wanted to join up.

'Yeah, but you're not, are you? They won't just take you because you say so.'

Well, they did a good few in the event but at the time I only felt more humiliation. It wasn't fair and I stomped about in a fine old tizz believing I'd miss out on my chance. Who knew how far off the next one might be if I missed this?

Things did seem to be gathering pace. For a moment I thought it had already started. My dad had spirited one of the newspapers out after the servants' hall had finished with it and left it lying on the bench in the motor house. When he'd gone off in the Wolseley I sneaked a look. I nearly passed out. 'The Bloodshed in Dublin' was the headline. What? Were the Germans already there?

Then, further down the page, I saw 'War Clouds Lift'. What was going on? I could hardly read straight and it took me some time to calm down. The Germans weren't at the gates, as it were: all the fuss in Dublin was over that Carson bloke threatening to fight off the government's plans for Ulster. Who cared about that, they were always causing trouble.

The news from Serbia was almost as depressing to me. The paper claimed that Russia wasn't mobilising so there was no risk of the war spreading. It sounded as though we'd all miss our chance. I bucked up a bit when I decided that if it held off for four years I'd be old enough. But four years to wait? It was all too much of a bother.

The women's peace rally in the village on the first Saturday in August only made my confusion worse.

'They shouldn't be allowed,' Curly Hopkins said. 'It's unnatural. It's our duty to go and break it up.'

Since our 'retreat', as he'd taken to calling it, from the Topham lot, Curly had struggled to keep us in step. There'd been muttering about 'waste of time' and 'loony games'. Maybe he thought women would enable him to re-assert our discipline. As usual, he was wrong.

From the sound when we arrived plenty of other local men

seemed to have come with the same idea as us. Saturday night wasn't the most sensible choice if you wanted to make a peaceful point, I thought, but I'd had to keep my ideas to myself in case Curly stopped me going.

When I glimpsed the Topham lot across the other side of the Square and heard the chants of 'No surrender!' I wished he had. The smell of drink hovered around us and several of the worst tipplers were already tishy. I wasn't too happy at turning on women but if they hadn't had the nouse to start earlier before the crowd got going, I didn't feel much sympathy for them. Especially if they were going to try to spoil any chance of fun.

My irritation cooled when the car arrived. One of the new Rolls Royces. These couldn't be ordinary women. One of the four was even driving! They didn't seem to be put out by all the jeers as they walked through to reach the hay wain that was their platform, either. When they got there they made no attempt to speak over the chanting, just stood and faced the mob. I began to be puzzled at their game.

So was everyone else because the noise died down. The leading woman – they were ladies, really, you could tell not only from their clothes but the way they held themselves – had a smile on her face.

'Thank you, gentlemen,' she said. 'Our intention tonight is not to interfere with your enjoyment.'

'Bleedin' good job,' shouted someone to my left but the lady took no notice and carried on.

'We know you won't agree with us…'

'Too right, there,' a drunk called.

'But all we ask is that you listen and consider what we have to say.'

This brought some grumbling. She was being too considerate for those of us who'd come to be wound up for a scrap. If she'd started shouting that 'Votes for Women' stuff we'd soon have livened up. It was difficult when she was so reasonable – and funny.

'Don't you wish you was a man?' Ginger Tate shouted before she could start.

'Don't you wish you were?' she shot back.

Then things became uncomfortable when she got to the nub of it.

16

'Have you forgotten the men who came back maimed from the South African War? Or who didn't come back at all…'

The crowd shifted uneasily. Around here everyone knew of the six men from Nordham who were killed on one day on Spion Kop.

'Do you really want to send your brothers and sons to a similar fate without at least a decent effort to stop it?'

We were a bit quiet now. I was beginning to feel ashamed of my eagerness to see others killed for a cause no one cared for. Somebody tried the mouse trick in a last attempt to throw them.

'Eh, watch out, there's a mouse!' he shouted.

A chorus of agreement followed. Once it might have caused ladies to panic. Now, the speaker just waited for the noise to die. 'That's not a mouse,' she said, pointing into the audience. 'It's a man.' Since her finger seemed to light on Jigger Dawley, of whom it wasn't a bad description, she even got a bit of a laugh.

If it hadn't been for Curly, the ladies might well have got away with it.

Robbo and his mate Dobbins were casting black looks our way. Their intended target for the night had obviously disappointed and they seemed to be planning for another. It appeared to me to be a signal to depart. Curly – he'd have made a good general in what was to come – couldn't resist leaving without some provocation. He threw a cabbage.

Maybe it slipped, as he claimed afterwards. Or maybe his throwing was as feeble as his mind. I'm sure he meant it for the Topham lot. However, instead of sailing over the heads of the crowd it skewed across and just missed one of the ladies standing behind the speaker, who was in the act of saying:

'Aren't you ashamed of yourselves?'

The flying cabbage looked like a reply. A guffaw rose from the crowd and before it stopped several other bits of fruit and veg followed. Two of the ladies were hit. There was uproar. The speaker's tone hardened.

'Is this what you want?'

'Yes!!!' chorused some of the most well-oiled. They didn't shut her up. In fact it roused her more.

'To be led to the slaughter by a mindless mob? To bring misery on your families. You wallow in your ignorance. But, mark my words, you'll regret your foolishness when you're drowning in rivers of blood. When you've betrayed your wives' and children's future.'

That did get us going. The crowd turned nasty.

'Who's the betrayers?' someone called out. 'You.'

'Traitors!' came the cry.

We all began to chant. More missiles rained down. We surged forward. I saw the ladies run for the car and scramble in. Men banged on the sides. They'll be trapped in there, I said to myself, they'll need to start it up and then realised that one of them must have slipped away and done that. Perhaps they were used to making swift departures. At any rate, before most of us reached there the car lurched forward and bumped off down the High Street. A clod of earth bounced off the back.

I was relieved in a way because it meant the car avoided a battering. Even if we didn't. Fights broke out in the melee and the Topham lot cornered us. Luckily some of the older men broke it up before we suffered too much damage, though Curly had a nasty black eye. I made myself scarce until it had quietened down and sat on a tree stump in the woods to collect my thoughts.

What the lady had said made sense – it makes much more now – but I couldn't stop thinking: how were we supposed to react if we were attacked ourselves? It was like the Topham lot. What else could we do but fight back? Yes, run away – the memory of that didn't cheer me up. Nor did the thought that there wouldn't be any older men to break it up and restore order.

The whole thing was a hopeless puzzle. I wished that there'd been an opportunity to have these questions out but the way the mood had changed meant there was no hope of getting reasoned answers that might have helped me – or anyone else – understand.

On my way back home raised voices – men's – carried across the Square to where I slipped into the shadows. I wondered if there was still fighting and couldn't resist edging closer to see. The argument was men coming out of *The Bull*. So had there been a difference of views in there, too? I strained to hear.

'He's crippled fool, that's all,' one voice slurred.

'And a bully with piles,' added another and several men laughed. But that brought an angry retort from somebody I couldn't see.

'He's built up their fleet, though, why d'you think he's doing that, for a joke?'

'It's a bloom'nmin cheek,' the first men replied.

'"Mad dog of Europe" the *Daily Express* called him yesterday,' his supporter chortled.

'Exactly, and if there was a mad dog over there…' – I slunk back into the shadows in case he was pointing my way – 'would you be laughing at it?'

'I'm just saying, don't get het up about him, if it comes to it, we'll sort him out and no messing. He backed off soon enough over that place in Africa he wanted, didn't he? I could blow him over like a feather.'

'You won't get the chance, will you? It's his army you'll be blowing bubbles at.'

I realised then that it wasn't Curly they were arguing over, it was the German Kaiser. I wondered why the conversation had turned onto him. Had the women's peace talk all been dismissed out of hand?

I wasn't to know how fast events had started to move. They even spilled over into the vicar's sermon the following day.

When he announced that his subject was 'Fight the good fight' I didn't take much notice. We were always being exhorted to something of that sort. 'Onward Christian Soldiers' and the like. Maybe he'd heard of our efforts against the Topham lads and felt we needed some pluck instilling in us. It was when he said 'This war will be a moral test. It is the judgment of God upon us' that I sat up and paid attention. '*This* war…' Had God dropped him a hint, I wondered. My excitement came back. So there was going to be one, after all? Did he know when it would start? Could he help me get in?

But most of it went over my head. 'War is a kind of purification,' he said, 'in which we can conquer the sloth and hypocrisy that prosperity has led us into.'

I hadn't noticed much prosperity in our house, or sloth since my mum became ill. And purification sounded too much like being forced to wash behind your ears in cold water. So when he concluded with 'If duty calls, do not resist the call, do not be deaf to the summons: it is God's offer of redemption' I was only conscious that for some of us there would be no call. Missing out on purification or redemption I could bear; being deprived of the chance to be in a proper army was what hurt.

On the way out I hoped I might ask the vicar to put in a word for me when this war started so I wouldn't miss out on the purification – since he sounded so keen on it – but he was too busy inquiring about my mum and commiserating; not that he'd got as far as actually visiting her. And before we moved off, a voice behind said 'You're right about that, Vicar, humanity has become rotten. It stinks.'

I turned round quickly. It was the voice I'd caught outside *The Bull* the night before, the angry one objecting to the view of the Kaiser as a buffoon. I didn't recognise the chap, which was strange because I knew almost everyone around here, but he was imposing: tall and strapping, he looked like a soldier, with a serious, weather-beaten face.

The vicar obviously didn't know him either but gave him that ingratiating smile he used for the toffs and started to thank him for his agreement. The stranger cut him off.

'If you think it'll be purged by rifle and artillery fire, you're talking poppycock.'

The vicar took a step back and his throat reddened. I had to shuffle out of the way as the man strode past me and down the path to the lych gate. I'd never heard anyone speak to the vicar like that. Here was more confusion. So was war purification or was that poppycock?

'Did you hear what he said?' I said to my dad.

'Just look to the little ones,' he growled as he swept off to fetch the Wolseley for Lady Hester. I blundered out of the churchyard in a daze.

I suspected that chap might have gone on with his tirade at *The Bull* but Sunday morning meant cutlery cleaning. When I'd wiped the brick dust off my fingers I hoped to go down there to listen. No such luck.

'Too much mooning about, that's what you're doing these days, lad,' my dad said when I asked if I could go out for a bit after he'd passed the knives, forks and spoons as fit. 'Chop that wood out the back before you think of dozing around.'

The wood felt my fury and it came back later that day when Tom told me that there had indeed been more arguments down at *The Bull*.

'But who was the stranger?' I asked to try to hide my sense of disappointment.

'George Robards,' he said. 'The carter, Mickle Robards' son. We wouldn't know him. He's been in South Africa. Stayed on there after the fighting and done well for himself. In the mining.'

'How does that make him an expert on telling the vicar he was talking poppycock?'

'That's what the argument was about at *The Bull*.'

'I wasn't there, was I? How should I know?'

'Harold Winscombe told him he was a disgrace, insulting the vicar like that.'

Harold Winscombe was the blacksmith and a churchwarden.

'George wouldn't back down. He said he knew it was poppycock because he'd seen what things were really like in the field. "Purged and ennobled by slaughter?" he sneered. "I can tell you, the stink and the mess in those trenches on top of Spion Kop when we finally got to clear them up wouldn't have you talking of purification. And you know how else we purged that slaughter? By our own massacre when we caught up with them and then by shutting their women and children up in those concentration camps when the rest gave us the slip.'

'Did that shut Harold up?'

'Yes, but Leonard Jones piped up saying it'd be different next time and that set off George again.'

'How?'

'"More poppycock", he said. Everyone jeered at this but he wouldn't be defeated. "Just wait and see," he retorted. "Every time what they tell you is that you're the finest fighting force in the world. You march off to put the world to rights. And every time you get a slap that stops you in your tracks. Have you forgotten how the Boer gave

21

us pause? Colenso, Tugela River and the one I just mentioned. Oh, we put him down in the end but it was a bloody job. Your German might not be half the sharpshooter *he* was but there's a damn sight more numbers to the German Army than your Boers had." Someone, I don't recall who, poo-pooed this and George threw his arms up in the air. "Be cautious what you hope for," he said and walked out.'

'Was that the end of it, then?' I asked, disappointed at the anti-climax but also half-pleased that I hadn't missed a big bust-up.

'Not entirely.'

My disappointment surged back.

'Why?'

'They all laughed and drank toasts to what they thought was the triumph of good sense then, when things had calmed down a bit, Alf Blunt said "He always was a thinking man, George, what if he has a point?" There was some scoffing at this, though they became shamefaced at the reception they'd given George's claims. Various voices agreed that the South African business had started as a mess – and had taken three years to put right. It got quite mournful until Billy Potts chimed up with "Look, first, the South Africa was our business so it had to be done. We're not going to get lumbered with any foreigners' fights, are we? And if they get uppity, what will we sort them out with – the Fleet!" This brought a bout of cheering but I had to leave then.'

It did feel as if there was a kind of hysteria in the air. Things seemed to be gathering pace. Russia had declared war on Austria, we heard. Rumours had it that the Germans were mobilising. We were mobilising on Salisbury Plain, it was claimed. But we always did at this time of year, for practice, somebody countered. And, although I didn't know of it at the time, the stock exchange was frantic.

There was a wild desire to *do* something. That was my feeling. If it had to be war then let it come. The sooner the better. What drove me mad was the uncertainty. Yet alongside was the irritation that if it did come, I was too young to enlist, to be involved.

Bank Holiday Monday should have provided respite. The Fair, as usual. Normally I'd have been in a fever of excitement about this, unable to settle between the steam roundabout with its horses and motor-cars, the coconut shies, the dart- and ring-throwing and the shooting stalls. This time I felt flat. Until the arrival of the racing car. The famous Singer Ten two-seater.

No one had told me it was coming. Or maybe I was too preoccupied with other things. But there it was, the winner of the Brooklands 100 lap stock car race for cars up to four cylinders. At 57.49 mph average speed. I was awe-struck. If my dad had seen me he would have complained I was mooning about. Unfortunately all you could do *was* look. How I itched to have a chance to try its three-speed gearbox that was said to be so light. I couldn't even manage to speak to the driver as so many of the local worthies monopolised him.

In the end I mooched off to the shooting stall. That added to my frustration since I scored no bulls at all. The more I tried the worse I got. I must have been too tense but it only made me more fretful.

Then Tom came running up waving a newspaper.

'You seen this?'

'No,' I muttered, pretending to check the alignment of the barrel. How would I see a newspaper until everyone else had finished with it?

'It says Germany's declared war on Russia. And France. And invaded Luxembourg.'

'So what?' I grouched.

'It means it's getting closer.'

'They won't come here,' I said. 'And anyway, if they do, we won't be allowed to do anything.'

'They've sent an ultimatum to Belgium.'

'Says who?'

'It's in here.'

'An ultimatum about what? They've got no gripe with Belgium, have they?'

'It says the Germans want to go through Belgium to meet the French. To stop the French invading them.'

'Seems a bit daft to me. Invading somebody to stop them invading you. It's all getting too silly for words.'

'Yes, but listen to this. It also says that if Belgium refuses the Germans' ultimatum and marches into Belgium, then we're bound to step in and help the Belgians.'

I did take notice at this.

'Bound to help?'

'We signed a treaty, guaranteeing Belgian neutrality.'

'Phew. That does put a different complexion on it.'

Mr James' claim that he'd be out hunting by September came back into my mind. So he must have known about this treaty. But, I wondered, if he'd known, hadn't other people, higher up, and if so, why hadn't they done anything to stop it?

Tom went off to show the paper to the rest of our gang. I sloped back to look at the Singer. What a waste it would be if war came and interfered with the next Brooklands season. I had had a thought of persuading my dad to let me go over there next year but if there was a war on that could be another hope dashed. Too young to fight and yet not able to enjoy the things I wanted to do. This war idea was beginning to creep all over my nerves.

The afternoon soon deteriorated. Halfway through I got lumbered with the little ones because my dad said he had to drive over to town on some errand for Lady Hester. I begged him to let me go but he claimed it was too important. So I had to trail round with Cissy, Wilf and Eddy, trying not to ruin their excitement of the Fair with my sulks.

The steam roundabout did bring me out of myself a bit. I had to sit on the horse with Cissy because she was too small to be allowed on by herself. I tried to persuade her that a car would be safer but she wouldn't listen. As we started to plunge up and down my heart was in my mouth in case she panicked and wanted to climb off while it was moving. I needn't have worried. She whooped with delight the faster we went and I found myself sharing her joy.

By the time all was finished I'd left the slough of despond behind. The little ones were worn out and we trudged home heavy-footed, although gabbling about what they'd done kept the two lads going. Cissy I had to carry on my shoulders. We were all looking forward to a nice cup of tea and some bread and jam.

When we arrived at the cottage the tea things were laid out ready but the sight of my dad's face told me something was wrong. He looked pale and I glanced involuntarily at the stairs. He said nothing. I packed the kids off to wash their hands out the back.

'Dad? What is it?' I asked.

'We're mobilising.'

For a moment I didn't take it in. 'How d'you mean?'

'Official announcement. Four o'clock. That's what Lady Hester sent me into town to catch. Read out. From the Town Hall steps.'

My heart thumped. 'So it's war?'

'As good as. One of the officers there said we're asking Germany for assurances they won't violate Belgium's neutrality but he didn't think they'd take kindly to being told. And if they invade Belgium...'

'We'll declare war on them?'

'Don't see how we can't.'

Nor could I but it seemed a let-down after all the noise there'd been leading up to it. I'd imagined a crusade. What should have felt exciting sounded more like slipping bit by bit into something you really weren't that keen on.

But next day the mood was different – like nothing I'd ever seen. My dad took me into town in the Model T and left me to fill it up with petrol. I had to queue for what felt like hours and then was limited to three gallons. On top of everything Millkins almost refused to accept Lady Hester's credit. He demanded cash. Only when he realised I had none and angry customers were mounting up behind me did he relent. I was so embarrassed pushing out past them, as though it was my fault. My dad grumbled when he came back because the doors of the County and Metropolitan Bank were still closed, with a crowd hanging about outside.

There appeared to be panic and queues everywhere. Two women were fighting over a side of bacon outside Higsons butchers, each tugging at it, red-faced and shouting. Another woman came out of Ditchburn's Grocers staggering under large jars of what looked like pickled onions. I was also puzzled to see that the bank hadn't opened. No one had said it was still Bank Holiday.

Fearful of driving off the road from being dazed by this mayhem, I expect, my dad stopped the car and shouted to a chap who was stood reading *The Daily News*, 'Are we at war?'

'Not yet,' he called. 'May be later today. Belgium has said no to the German demand. Everyone's waiting to hear what the Germans are going to do now. It says here that in Berlin they can't understand why we're so bothered about a scrap of paper when all they're doing is protecting their own interests.'

'While it's us has to suffer,' my dad said. It didn't make much sense to me. Everyone's reaction suggested they thought war was a glum inevitability. Nobody seemed to want it. We drove back and I had a deal to do to explain to my dad why I'd not been able to persuade Millikens to give the Model T a full tank. The near refusal of credit drove him furious.

'It's all breaking down,' he said. 'If this goes on, we'll be needing all your spare coppers just to eat.'

Everything was becoming more and more senseless. When we arrived back I asked 'If there's a war coming, why do we need another bank holiday?'

'Go and polish the car,' was the only reply.

I nearly retorted that if war came, having clean cars wouldn't matter but decided the leathering he'd give me in his present mood for answering back wasn't worth it. Anyway, polishing the car at least made more sense than everything else going on.

However, I couldn't concentrate even on that. Too many thoughts skittered about in my head. What was war like? How long would it last? Would we be short of food and petrol, as the people in town seemed to fear? Now it approached it didn't look as alluring as it had a few weeks ago. What had those peace meeting women said: 'You'll regret it when you're drowning in rivers of blood.' I shuddered. A scrap with the Topham lot had spilled blood. Could war be worse than that? It sounded as if it might be. But I had a sense nobody was bothered about that now.

Three

If I thought the scenes on Tuesday were wild, they were nothing to the atmosphere the next day, once news of the declaration of war spread. How people's mood could change.

My dad sent me to town on the pony with firm instructions not to come back without a supply of oil cans. When I arrived the centre was too choked to move. The County Yeomanry were marching through, on their way to defend the coast, someone said. All I could do was stop and watch.

How I envied those lads their moment of glory. The crowds were packed all along the High Street, cheering, shouting and singing. People waved handkerchieves and threw sweets and cigarettes, and even flowers. Some of the youngest boys, who couldn't have been much older than me, I reckoned, looked embarrassed by the whole thing, especially when women tried to kiss them. I began to feel better out of it when I saw that.

As they passed *The Rose and Crown* a group of drinkers standing in the doorway raised their glasses and jeered. 'Here's a mug to you mugs,' one shouted. I was horrified and glanced around to see if anyone would put a stop to it but no one bothered, they were all too busy with the excitement.

Nor were there any oil cans available. Priority had to be given to the military. I trailed home in a dark mood. Excluded from the important movements afoot and likely to be faced with complaints about my incompetence from my dad, my future seemed overshadowed already by a gloom at odds with the euphoria bursting out all around.

Including from Carstairs.

'You're on your own now, son,' he said when I went over to see him. 'I've joined up. Always get in first, that's my motto. The way to take your pick.'

He'd certainly done that. I stared open-mouthed as he told me. Colonel Lumsden was taking him as his driver.

'In the army. And driving a car…?'

'For King and Country,' he winked. 'Don't worry, you can manage yourself now, son.'

That thought was little consolation. When I realised that the one person who encouraged me to drive was leaving, my gloom increased. It felt like a bereavement.

The month of August went on in the same way for me. I mooched about, unable to settle to anything, waiting for news but nothing seemed to happen. The bank re-opened after a few days and life returned to a sort of normality, though shops put out their flags and women especially busied themselves making comforts for the troops. Yet it all felt like a damp squib, this war.

I was busied enough on the harvest. With many of the farmhands having been called away we were very short-handed and had to pitch in with a will to finish the job. As if that wasn't bad enough we were losing horses as well because the requisitioning officers came round with their lists pointing out the ones that were to be taken. Old Matty Cunliffe nearly got himself arrested for the struggle he put up to stop them taking his two best shires. It was a funny spectacle but we shared his anger.

In the absence of any action on our part in this war, anger was the emotion that tended to grow. I hardly noticed it as unusual at the time since my daily mood was one of resentment at my own situation. The Belgian refugee stories that began to circulate fed a lot of the general ire.

The newspapers were full of 'The Agony of Belgium', as the headlines had it. The tales did sound horrifying and people worried what would happen if the Germans came here. Masses of women and children, including young babies, were said to have been shot as the German horde swept on through Belgium. It passed belief but the stories had come from escapees from villages like Andenne, which had been burned to the ground and hundreds of its citizens shot.

If these accounts irked me the more from our own inability to help and my own exclusion from driving, the sight of even women being more involved than me twisted the knife in me further.

'Can I bandage your arm?' Butters asked, stopping me outside the motor house. I liked to look in on the cars on my way home each night to make sure they hadn't been requisitioned.

'It ain't hurt,' I grunted, not in the mood for distractions.

'It's a practice, you'd be helping the war effort.'

That was a red rag to a bull. 'Helping the war effort? I've been slaving all day getting the harvest in. Isn't that enough for the war effort? Can't you find a soldier to practise on?'

'I'm attending Lady Hester's First Aid Home Nursing Classes and I want to shine. If I'm no good, I'll not be allowed to continue. Please?'

Butters was one of the housemaids, a few years older than me. She was a keen sort and I knew she'd take it hard if she was stopped from going. That was an emotion I could understand.

'Righty ho, but can you make it quick, I'm whacked at the moment.'

She was a dab hand at it, I had to admit, and I expressed surprise that she'd worried they'd drop her out.

'There's so many fine ladies there, you never know. Not that they're much use but they don't half put on airs and go round advising everyone how to do it. You feel really small. And if you speak up, you're more than likely to get a telling off for talking out of turn. Mary was stood down last week for just that. I think they'd prefer there were none of us girls there so they could carry on their own chatter.'

'At least you're doing something.'

'You could, too, if you tried.'

'Ouch,' I said as she pulled the bandage too tight, 'what am I supposed to be able to do – join up? Chance 'd be a fine thing. I'm only fourteen.'

'Are you? You don't look it. Why don't you give it a try?'

'My dad wouldn't let me.'

'Then don't tell him.'

'I'd only be laughed out of the recruiting office.'

She tied the last knot in the sling and made me stand up.

'There. You're wounded already,' she laughed. 'That's a fine excuse for not doing your bit.'

'I'm not making excuses,' I protested. 'That's the way it is.'

She started to untie the bandage – roughly.

'Lord, that's all I ever hear all day at the Home Nursing – why these high-and-mighties can't actually do any of the dirty work, and there's no real blood flowing yet, is there? It's us servants that'll cop it when the time comes, you mark my words.'

'Lucky you,' I muttered and found myself being shaken by the arm – not the 'wounded' one.

'Stop your chuntering. If they turn you down, fine. At least you can say you tried. And if this goes on for another four years, you'll have had practice, won't you?'

'Will it go on for four years?'

'Most of the high-ups at the Home Nursing say fourteen days. So you better hurry up, hadn't you?'

With that she swept off. Then she stopped and looked round. 'Thank you for letting me practise,' she said.

'You want to what?' my dad shouted when I raised the subject. 'You go near that recruiting office in the village and I'll tan your hide you won't sit down for a week. You'll make me a laughing stock. You hear?'

I nodded. Failed at the first hurdle. That wasn't the only obstacle. Lol Daly at the village recruiting centre knew I was under age. He'd probably guess at how my dad would take it, too, if he let me through.

Did this count as an attempt, I wondered? I suspected not. What else could I do?

'Go to the one in town,' Tom said.

'How will that help?'

'Less chance anyone'll know us.'

I still wasn't sure. I hummed and hawed.

'Look, Harry, If you really want to do your bit...'

That settled it. At least if I failed to get in, word might not come back to my dad that I'd defied him.

30

The sight outside the recruiting office almost made me give up on the spot. The street was packed with men of all ages, standing, sitting on the pavement, leaning against the wall. It seemed hopeless. Then we bumped into Curly.

'I'm in,' he announced, beaming all over his face. My own face must have shown my incredulity because he added, 'I'm eighteen, why shouldn't I be in?'

I remembered our flight from the Topham lot and tried to mutter congratulations. Curly waved his warrant, as if we still didn't believe him. 'I have to report on Thursday to the depot.'

'How on earth did you even get inside there?' Tom asked, pointing at the doorway half obscured by the crowd.

'Come on, I'll show you.'

Curly did go up in my estimation from then on. Somehow he managed to smuggle us inside, waving his warrant and calling 'Make way there' in his most official voice. Perhaps he was general material after all.

Anyway, we did find ourselves in a longish queue for the reception desk in the main hall. Beyond, the place was divided up by screens and men passed in and out as we waited, some looking cock-a-hoop, some downcast. I could share the feelings of the latter.

It was all very slow. Only one man, a white-haired corporal, was behind the desk and he took an age to weigh up each man who stood before him. As we got close I could hear the sighs and grunts that followed every answer given.

'No hurry, there's only a war on,' Tom whispered to me while the corporal shook his head sadly at a little man who was so obviously undersized he shouldn't have been allowed in the door.

'It'll be over before we get there,' I muttered back. The undersized man was still receiving his explanation.

'Get where? The war – or the desk?' Tom said.

Just before our turn came the men at the desk changed over. A grey-haired sergeant took the place. I groaned. I might have fancied my chances pulling the wool over the old corporal's eyes but this sergeant looked a tough nut. Tom pushed me forward before I realised what he'd done.

I felt the sergeant's steely eyes probing me and quailed.

'Age?' he barked.

'E-eighteen. S-sir.'

'Since when?'

'Er... what do you me...'

'Your birthday, lad. When was it?'

It had been in January.

'You were eighteen last January?'

'Yes, sir.'

'Know what, so was I.'

I stared at him, my mind a blank. I could feel tears well up in my eyes. He must have seen them because his tone softened.

'Listen, son, if you're eighteen I'm a monkey's uncle. You done well to want to do your bit but come back when you're older, eh – and not tomorrow, neither. Dismiss.'

I stumbled out and was surprised to see Tom beside me.

'Did he reject you as well?' I said.

'No fear, I took one look at how he saw through you and chickened out. Still, it was worth a go.'

I wasn't too sure. If the sergeant could pick me out so easily, my hopes of ever getting in before I was eighteen appeared remote indeed. The reflection did nothing to ease my despondency. I was definitely going to miss all the fun.

The month dragged by in a dreary succession of days. The reports of German atrocities continued but no news came through of where our troops were. The newspapers said nothing. Everyone assumed that the Army was holding its own – at least – and the Germans were taking out their frustration on the poor Belgian civilians.

As for us, some took their frustration out on any shopkeeper with a German name. Steiner's the butchers was ransacked one night after the papers carried stories of an outrage in Dinant. The Steiner's son, Bert, had been in my class at school and he was no more German than I was. But people were het up and it took little to set them off.

The only other source of excitement, though again it passed me by, came from the increase in the number of weddings. As the flood of men joining up swelled so did their desire to marry before they went away. Even the Wolesley was loaned out to help, although I never benefited from being able to drive it.

Matters only came to a head on the night of Lady Hester's Ball, held to mark the departure for France of Mr James. I remember it was the last Saturday in August and the atmosphere had become even more febrile in the past few days. First was the shock of the fall of Namur, the second of the Belgians' massive fortresses to collapse, following that of Liege a week earlier. And news of the burning of Louvain had just come in. None of this squared with the assumption that victory was assured, of course. I wondered what Mr James was going to find when he went over but as usual no one had a clue where our chaps were or what they were doing. 'Showing their colours,' was a remark I heard outside *The Bull*. It caused the men to burst into laughter but I couldn't see why.

My role at the Ball was, of course, as dogsbody and – once it began – an invisible one at that. The day was very hot and I lost count of the number of heavy tubs containing rose trees that I sweated to lug into the ballroom. Then there came the sweeping after some fancy arranger-fellow from London had swathed all these bamboo palms with red, white and blue coloured ribbons. You should have seen the mess he left behind.

My clearing-up job carried on apace when things started. Stationed in the service corridor I had loaded on to me the empty bottles, full ashtrays and used glasses that the footmen gathered on their rounds. Too high and mighty they were – too busy, they claimed – to carry them down to the kitchen: that was my pleasure.

Of course, from where I stood I caught glimpses of the junketing and heard all the music. It wasn't just waltzes but the new-fangled stuff like the turkey-trot. I'd have liked to see more of the band but I'd been strictly forbidden to show myself. It certainly sounded jolly. Until Butters dropped a glass bowl.

I heard the crash as I came back up the stairs from the kitchen with a tray of clean glasses. Mine almost went flying, too, twice, as Hemmings the footman flew past me on the way down and then shoved me aside on his way up, clutching a broom and dustpan. Not that he used it himself.

When I arrived at the scene Butters was on her knees brushing the bits into the pan. I could see her shoulders shaking so I guessed she was crying. Before I could offer to help Lady Hester appeared through the curtain and glared at Butters.

'Oh, no, not again,' she said. 'Butters by name, butterfingers by nature. This really won't do. If you can't match up, you are going to have to go back to the kitchen.'

'Sorry, ma'am,' Butters snivelled.

Lady Hester glared in my direction and I shrank into the wall, almost tipping my load over again, but she didn't speak to me.

'Once it's cleared up, leave all this to the others. Do you hear?'

'Yes, ma'am,' Butters muttered without looking up. When the curtain closed she let her head drop to rest on the floor. I went towards her but the curtain twitched and Lady Hester re-appeared, her servant-blasting manner in full swing.

'When you've finished that, go and find Helena and tell her I want her here. At once. Do you think you might be able to manage that?'

Then she was gone again. I was puzzled because I assumed that Lady Helena would have been in there taking part in the dancing.

'She doesn't seem to be enjoying it much,' I said, nodding at the curtain.

Butters clambered to her feet.

'She's not the only one.'

'Here, let me have that,' I said, taking the dustpan from her. 'You better search for Lady Hell.'

'I hardly know where to start.'

Butters gave a despairing sigh. We both knew that giving Helena the summons from mama was likely to provoke her famous temper. If getting on the wrong side of Mr James could bring you a tongue lashing, upsetting Helena felt more like a roasting. She took after her mother in that.

'Don't you have a clue?' I asked.

34

'I wish I didn't,' she replied.

That threw me so I tried to be helpful.

'Want me to give you a hand?'

Butters seemed doubtful, which confused me further but before she could refuse the offer Hemmings swept through the curtain.

'You still here?' he muttered with a nod behind him. 'She's on the warpath and if she comes back...'

'Right.'

Butters dashed off and I thought it wise to make myself scarce, too. I realised I was still holding the dustpan so scampered down the stairs to dispose of the glass in the bins.

'Has anyone seen Lady Hell?' I asked as I passed through the kitchen.

'It's Lady Helena to you,' Cook almost spat at me. The two scullery maids raised their eyebrows at each other and giggled. Why, I didn't know, because they all called her the same.

Outside I stopped to catch my breath in the cold air. My head was whirling with the heat and shouting and I stood letting my thoughts cool down. In the silence I heard whispering and a giggle, followed by a gasp.

Oh, God, will no one leave me in peace, I said to myself and tipped the glass with a crash into the bin. I glared in the direction of the noise and stomped back inside. It sounded as if the racket I'd made had given them a shock. Who it was playing games I couldn't think.

Cook thrust another tray of glasses on me the instant I appeared in the kitchen. Only when I began to climb the stairs did my puzzlement come to the fore. I couldn't for the life of me work out who was missing. One of the temporary staff hired for the evening? None of the regulars would risk the sack for sloping off on such an important occasion.

Again my musings were interrupted. Raised voices stopped me from rounding the corner to the ballroom service door. Mr James's: 'Oh, don't be such a wet fish, mother.'

And Lady Hester's: 'James, I wish you wouldn't...'

A far different tone to that she'd used on Butters. One that stood no chance against Mr James.

'For heaven's sake, mother,' he stormed. 'Why won't you see? If we don't get out there now, it'll all be over.'

'I can't believe that.'

'Believe what you like. The word's all round the mess.'

'If you want my opinion...'

'I don't'

'You sound more like your father every day.'

'At least he was allowed to go off to war.'

'I didn't have much say in the matter.'

'Then don't expect any now.'

'I wish you'd take the time to think.'

'When the regiment's set to leave? Unthinkable. Anyway, we'll be back in a flash.'

'South Africa was going to be over in a flash, too. It was three years before...'

'We're only going across the Channel...'

'And they didn't all come back...'

'Oh God, don't turn on the tears, mother, because it won't wash.'

'Nothing will, will it?' she sighed and must have fled back into the ballroom because it went quiet. Then a woman's footsteps approached, hurrying. I peeped round the corner, hoping to see Lady Helena. It was Butters. Her face told me the search had been fruitless.

'Have you been everywhere?' I asked.

Butters glared at me. 'How could I? Are you mad?'

'Is there anywhere you've not looked that might..?' I offered but my attempt at help received a curt reply.

'The bedrooms...'

I was astounded. Why had she missed Lady Helena's bedroom? To me it sounded like an obvious place to go and rest.

'Do you want me..?' I began.

'No. No..,' Butters sighed, her anger draining away. 'Don't you bother. After all, I only have to knock...'

That seemed obvious, too. I must have frowned because Butters snapped 'Never mind' and turned to leave. Then I remembered the noises outside.

'She wouldn't have gone outside, would she?'

Butters turned back to me. 'What?'

I explained the noises I'd heard. Far from being grateful Butters pushed past me muttering 'Idiot boy, why didn't you say?' and flew down the stairs.

I resumed my drudgery. The relentless gaiety of the ball failed to lift my sprits. My mind pondered on that contrast in Lady Hester's manner. If she'd treated people the other way round, I could have warmed to her. As it was... I saw Butters washing up in the kitchen several times but she either glared at me or turned away. Though I supposed she must have found Lady Helena, I didn't dare ask. By midnight I felt limp and there were still hours to go.

Until the interruption. I was sorting glasses by the service doorway when a loud shout cut through the sway of a waltz. The music broke off in mid-stride and spluttered out as the different players stopped. Cries of alarm and puzzled calls came from the dancers. My own shock was such that I disregarded orders and pulled aside the curtain to see what it was.

The ballroom floor was a confusion of couples. Their heads were turned to a hussar in full dress uniform who stood in the doorway. He waved a paper.

'The British Expeditionary Force has engaged the enemy at Mons, near the Belgian-French border.'

Well, this *was* news. It threw the room into a ferment. So it wasn't going to fizzle out before Mr James and his mates got over there? Lucky them. My own deflation increased the confusion I'd felt all night. It wasn't only the feeling of missing out again. I doubt if any of us knew exactly where Mons was but I couldn't help feeling disquiet. If the massive Belgian fortresses of Liege and Namur had fallen, didn't that suggest we might be on the end of some stiff opposition, too? Had we thrown the Germans back I'm sure that would have been in the forefront of the news that'd come.

However, none of my gloom filtered into the ballroom. After the buzz of conversation died down there was a hushed conference between Mr James and his fellow officers, culminating in an announcement to his mother – who looked more put out than ever – and the band. One more dance and then they must fly. 'The nation calls!'

Lady Hester wilted from this and edged to take cover as the dancers launched into a furious Gay Gordons that wound up into a frenzy. I could at least share her feeling of being pushed aside. We servants looked on as stunned as the older people round the sides, marvelling at and yet horrified by its raucous energy that bordered on violence. No one seemed to bother that we'd forgotten our place. It was as if, now that war was real, anything was allowed. I can't say I appreciated the gift at the time. I felt more left out than ever.

At least we got to our beds a little earlier than expected. When we'd cleared sufficiently for us to leave the rest till morning I bumped into Butters on the stairs.

'Did you find Lady Helena?' I asked.

'What do you think?'

'Where was she?'

She stared at me then closed her eyes and shook her head. Something occurred to me. 'That wasn't her outside that I..?'

Butters didn't turn round. I nearly called after her but decided I'd only receive more scorn. Though for what, I hadn't a clue.

My curiosity let this go. Especially when the whereabouts of the BEF demanded investigation. Before climbing into bed I searched by flickering candle-light on the maps of Belgium I'd cut from newspapers. No sign of Mons. But if it was 'near the border', that was funny because then it ought to be behind the two fortresses – of Liege and Namur – that had already fallen. So were they cut off? Would Mr James and his friends be charging off into a catastrophe? That didn't bear thinking about and within minutes I'd collapsed into sleep.

Like most people, the effort required to weigh up coolly what was happening was too much for me. An omission we all had cause to regret.

Four

With Mr James gone the place lost its spark. Or maybe it was just me. Curly had gone off to war, as had most of the able-bodied men, though there wasn't much sign that they'd found it. Kids and cripples were the only ones left. My mum sickened and I got barked at for moping or not doing enough to help. Which made me sulk more because I was at it harder than ever. We brought the harvest in earlier than usual by working on Sundays, which caused a high old stink from the vicar and bible-bashers.

You had to be seen to be doing something useful. Collecting, sowing and planting every extra bit of ground you had – you can guess who was put to that job – or making comforts for the troops. If running around looking busy would have won us the war, it should easily have been over by now.

Except that it wasn't. All that exhilaration at the Ball with the news from Mons burst like a balloon a few days later. It was the next day, actually, in *The Times* – a special Sunday edition – but the copy took time to come down to us. What a shock. We were falling back. In disorder. With fearful losses. Yes, we'd 'engaged the enemy' but we were in full retreat. And this news was a week old. Where were we now?

After all the jolly stuff we'd been fed about our boys marching forward to free 'gallant little Belgium' this was a blow to take the wind out of your sails. Yet if you thought about it, it was all of a piece with the news we had been getting for weeks. The Germans had been advancing steadily. Nothing appeared able to stop them. Why had we built up this dream that it would be a cinch?

It drove me into a darker gloom. And earned me a pummelling from my dad.

'What's up with you? Drooping about like Mabel's mare,' – I'd dug half the kitchen garden that day – 'with a face as long as a...'

'Why should I laugh?' I cut in. 'We're going to lose the war, aren't we?'

'If wet-legs like you had anything to do with it, yes,' he said, punching my shoulder.

'You read it out yourself,' I retorted, for the first time in my life on the point of hitting him back. If I had, I could have flattened him, I know that.

'Pah. It's early days. You have to learn to take the bad with the good.'

Except I couldn't see any good. Here especially. I nearly threw that in but luckily he went on before I could. 'We took a beating in South Africa at first. 'Course, you wouldn't know any of that, would you? Then we turned it round. Once Bobs arrived and put a bit of spirit into 'em.'

'So where's "Bobs" now?'

'He'll be somewhere about, don't you worry. He'll be doing his bit.'

'Lucky him.'

'You cheeky young sod. You want to do your bit, too.'

'I'm too young, aren't I?'

'Not for hoeing them beds in the long arbour.'

'I did them last week.'

He raised his fist and I stalked out slamming the door behind me. I heard it open and something was shouted after me but I didn't try to catch it.

Jabbing at the dry clods in the long arbour soon cooled my fury but didn't lift my depression. He'd reminded me how useless I was. How could this job possibly make any contribution to the war effort? If we cut down the arbour and ploughed up the whole area then it might help but I'm sure for the family that would be a sacrifice too far. At least they'd sent their son off to fight.

My mind tried to imagine a retreat. 'In disorder' the newspaper had said. I couldn't connect the Yeomanry I'd watched marching through the town with retreat. Did they march backwards? Then I remembered our 'retreat' from the Topham lot. The fear. The frantic running and falling and crashing into trees. It wouldn't be like that, surely? Our retreat stopped when the Topham lot gave up. The Germans wouldn't stop, though, would they? They'd keep coming. So where would it end?

When "Bobs" turned up and put some spirit in them? That claim of my dad's increased my gloom. Yes, I knew about Lord Roberts beating the Boers but he must be an old man now. He wouldn't be over there with the troops. It was General French. And Haig. After Haig's escapade with the Wolseley I had no confidence in him.

I was deep in these reflections when I realised voices were approaching and slipped back into the rhododendrons out of sight. I didn't want to see anyone. Especially Lady Helena. Butters told me she was after me for being a peeping tom. I protested that I was no such thing. That wouldn't stop Lady Hell wringing my neck, Butters laughed.

'When was I a peeping tom?' I almost cried.

Butters looked puzzled at this. 'Outside, at the Ball.'

'I didn't see Lady Hell outside.'

'But you told me…'

'I didn't see anyone, it was dark, I just heard… noises.'

'She saw you looking.'

'Well, I didn't see her. I was emptying the pieces of the bowl you smashed,' – that reminder didn't go down well, either – 'I glanced towards the noise then I tipped the broken glass in the bin and went in. How was I to know who it was.'

'What sort of noises did you hear?'

'I don't know. Whispering, giggles. Then it sounded as if someone was in pain. A moan.'

Butters burst out laughing at this. She refused to tell me why. 'If she does catch up with you, I'd just say you heard voices,' was all she'd offer.

The voices I'd heard in the arbour came nearer. With relief I sensed that neither was Lady Hell. They stopped a few feet away from where I stood. With horror I realised that it was Lady Hester. And her husband. If they'd come out here to talk it could only have been to be out of earshot of any servants. And I was eavesdropping three yards away. I held my breath. I'd like to say that I tried not to listen. But all sorts of rumours spread among the servants and the chance to hear what Sir Brydon was up to was too much for me, especially after the mysterious comments Carstairs had always made about him. It was his voice I heard first. He didn't sound pleased. 'You must surely have known how that would make me look.'

'Why should I?' Lady Hester said. Her voice was taut, which surprised me. I wondered what had put some bite into her. 'You hadn't told me you'd been seconded to the War Office. But then you haven't been near for a month, have you? People are beginning to notice.'

'Don't they know there's a war on?'

Lady Hester gave a bitter laugh at this. 'Yes, I forgot. How convenient.'

This sharpness wouldn't have been unusual to a servant. But to her husband? I couldn't have dragged myself away even if I'd been able to. And my puzzlement deepened.

'I don't want you turning up there again,' he said.

'I can assure you, it's an experience I'm unlikely to want to repeat.'

'Serves you right.'

'Quite. I should have known better.'

It didn't sound as if she meant it and it made no sense to me. What was Lady Hester being blamed for? It sounded as if she'd been to the War Office but why that was such a problem I couldn't fathom. Sir Brydon's answer didn't enlighten me that much.

'As if we haven't enough to do, without women swanning in and trying to interfere.'

'I was hoping to help.'

This time Sir Brydon laughed. 'Help? Good God.'

His sneering, like James's, might have been expected to make her shrivel but this time she responded in kind.

'I know. How stupid of me. When you men are managing the War so well. I suppose I'm lucky Sir Claud didn't have me shot. You know what he did say?'

'"My dear lady, why don't you go home and sit still".'

42

This did sound as though it shocked her.

'He told you?'

'No, the story is all round the club.'

Rather than beating her down further this information seemed to rally her. 'At least I've provided some amusement at such a difficult time,' she retorted. 'While you're all under so much strain.'

'Frankly, if some silly woman had come to me, wanting to interfere when the situation is on a knife edge, I'd have been a damn sight more blunt.'

Wanting to interfere? From what she'd said to James about the War I couldn't imagine Lady Hester wishing to have anything to do with fighting. I heard a sharp intake of breath and waited for an explanation, while startled by the 'knife-edge' remark. He knew things were bad, did he?

And Lady Hester took me unawares once more. Her defiance seemed to dissolve. All she managed to get out was: 'Then I'll know not to trouble you.'

There was a pause. I hoped that was the finish and they'd go back to the house but Sir Brydon cleared his throat. 'There is something else.'

'Another offence I've given to the war effort?'

'I want a divorce.'

'I see,' Lady Hester said after a while. I could almost see her gritted teeth this time but she sounded less surprised than I was. Sir Brydon went on in the same unconcerned tone. 'I'll make all the necessary arrangements. The usual things. You'll not be inconvenienced...'

Now, however, I could tell she was struggling to maintain an even tone. For the first time I felt some sympathy for her.

'How considerate of you,' she said.

'As long as you make no difficulties...'

'To cause you embarrassment at your club?'

'This is not easy for me.'

'How do you think it will be for me?'

'There's no need to take that manner.'

'What manner would you prefer me to take?'

It sounded as if her spirit was reviving. Sir Brydon didn't like that. 'You can be impossible,' he sniffed.

She seemed to take heart from his discomfort. 'Or should I "go home and sit still"?' she said.

'You will be permitted to remain here, yes...'

'Until it is inconvenient? Who is she, by the way?'

'There's no need for...'

'She's not pregnant?'

'That's none of your...'

'Oh, God, Brydon, you are a fool...'

'That's got nothing to do with it.'

'Are you going to tell the children?'

'Tell them what?'

'That their inheritance is under threat.'

'They'll understand.'

'That *would* be a surprise. They take after you.'

'I might have known you'd respond in this way.'

'How am I supposed to respond? Oh, yes, to "sit still", not cause a fuss, quietly accept the role of the wronged wife...'

I was beginning to enjoy Sir Brydon's spluttering.

'I've told you, you'll be provided for,' he said.

'I'm so grateful.'

There was another silence. My heart was so thumping I was struggling to take in shallow breaths and not give away my position. I was desperate now for them to leave. Sir Brydon, too, by the sound of it.

'So that's settled, then. I'll instruct Jeavons to start the process and...'

'Tell Helena. I assume you won't send James a telegram at the Front.'

'I'll let them know in due course.'

'You'll tell Helena now.'

'I...'

'Now, do you hear?'

'Very well, er...'

I heard his feet crunch on the gravel. He started to walk off.

'Oh, and another thing, Brydon,' Lady Hester called.

'Yes?'

'I *do* intend to do something. I'm not going to stay here and "sit still" as your arrogant little Sir Claud requested. There's a war on, as you pointed out. And that's far too important to be taking up one's time with trivialities. Even if I am merely a woman.'

I didn't move for a while after they left. It wasn't just the news, though that was stunning enough. It was the turn-around. Although I'd heard it for myself I could hardly believe it. The dutiful wife standing up for herself. More than that, as I understood more fully later, going to the War Office – that's what his first complaint was all about – and demanding to be involved in the war effort. She hadn't succeeded but the degree of resolve that had taken her there sent her up further in my estimation.

So that's how we came to be at Victoria Station awaiting the arrival of the afternoon troop train. I was trying not to let my excitement show. I still couldn't get over the fact I'd been allowed to come. It had been touch and go. I'd nearly finished loading the boxes of apples in the boot when Hemmings came down with a couple of small cases of what I later found to be cigarettes and chocolate. I asked him if they were to go in the boot, too.

'Not on your nelly, son, these are for her ladyship's hands only.'

'You're not going along?'

'You must be bloody joking. Women dishing out apples to the wounded? You might as well give them white feathers.'

That worried me. Not the white feathers bit, though I was surprised he hadn't been given one himself as he was perfectly fit to volunteer. No, it was the concern who was going to lift the boxes out at Victoria. My dad's back wasn't up to it and as for the ladies... The problem was soon solved.

Hemmings offered his cases to Lady Hester who indicated the boot. I kept a straight face as he thrust them on me.

'Tell her I got taken bad,' he hissed at me. Then he'd gone before I could blink. Lady Hester was fussing about Helena, who hadn't arrived, and looking at her watch.

'What has happened to the girl? Hemm...'

She swung round as if expecting to see him and stared at me as though it was my fault I wasn't him.

'I...I... Mr Hemmings said he w-was taken bad,' I managed to stutter, going red.

She turned up her nose at me as if I'd cursed or something. '"Bad..?"' She swung round on my dad. 'Is this your boy, Butler? He'll have to come instead.'

My dad was about to protest but Butters dashed up to say that Lady Helena wouldn't come, either. Lady Hester went red, too, and seemed to swell up. She glanced from the car to us, no doubt weighing whether to send one of us to fetch Lady Hell – a thankless task, she must know herself – or take to the car. The car won. My regard for her rose again.

'There's no time for more delay,' she said. 'Get in, Butters. And you, too, boy.'

I was in the back like a shot. A proper ride in the Wolseley. To London. And to see wounded troops. I was in Christmas already and it was barely September.

'You just sit quiet and no messing,' my dad hissed at me as he pretended to check the door. I put on my grave face but grinned at Butters when he bent to start her up. No messing? I wasn't going to miss this chance for all the tea in China.

I could tell my dad was furious with my being there because of the way he used the horn every time we passed a farm cart, even if it wasn't blocking the way. Why he was in a mood, I didn't know. Maybe he'd forgotten that if I hadn't come, he'd have had to ruin his back lifting the boxes of apples out of the boot. I pondered Hemmings' comment about apples and white feathers. If I was wounded, would I want an apple? I had no idea. I suspected it was the women aspect that offended him. Or maybe the thought of seeing the wounded. For me, that was enthralling.

London was a wonder. No building seemed to lack an Allied flag and Lord Kitchener's posters with 'Britons: Join Your Country's Army' were everywhere, on hoardings and most of the taxi-cabs we passed. They were still asking for a hundred thousand men though we knew that Kitchener now demanded half a million. In all the excitement I forgot that I couldn't be one of them.

When we arrived at Victoria I was thrown into another wonderland – of khaki. The station was heaving with troops. Not the wounded, we'd arrived too early for the afternoon leave train; these were men waiting to go. There were lines of them, with their packs and rifles, standing smoking Woodbines. Crowds of them at the canteens queuing for tea. Officers striding about looking important. They all looked in their element and ordinarily I'd have felt miffed to be excluded.

But I had no time to worry about this. There were crowds outside as well, women seeing their men off, lots of tearful partings and onlookers just come to gawp. None of it improved my dad's temper since he took I don't know how long to edge his way close to the 'Gateway to the Continent' as Butters said they called the entrance.

'Platform Seven,' Lady Hester said after she'd forced some military policemen to accept our passage through.

'I better stay with the car, ma'am,' my dad announced when he'd opened the boot. 'With this lot,' – he indicated the swirling mass of people, with little ragmuffins careering around under everyone's feet – 'you never know what we'd lose.'

Surveying the hungry eyes watching us, I had to agree but it was typical of him to avoid the heavy jobs. I was horrified to find Butters lifting a box and following me behind Lady Hester.

'What are you doing?' I said. 'You don't have to, I can manage.'

'They're not that heavy,' she grinned. 'One good turn…'

I gave up trying to protest and staggered on, delighted to see we'd been given an escort and were able to push through the crowds of troops. It was like being with the Yeomanry on their march through the town.

While we were carrying in the last load, on the adjacent platform one of the troop trains whistled to signal its departure. All hell broke loose. Hobnailed boots clattered as the last few men raced along the platform and jumped on, doors banged, windows crashed down and hundreds of heads poked out and arms waved. A hiss of steam drowned out the shouts and yells for a moment before it was blotted out itself by the rumbling roar of the engine as it gathered itself and ground forward.

When it had disappeared from view a dejection settled on the crowds of women left behind. The smiles had gone and you could see tears instead. They trailed off now through the big stone archway. That sight made me forget all the glory and excitement for a bit and wonder what those lads going away in the train had before them. It wasn't hard to guess. The news from across the Channel had continued to be vague but it didn't improve.

I got more solid evidence when the afternoon leave train pulled in. Plenty of others had joined us by then, ladies in finery, also with gifts, flowers and the like, and women with more hopeful faces – those who knew their men were coming home safe, I presumed.

Now, however, I felt that people thought we were in the way. Officials pushed us and our boxes back, telling us not to obstruct the platform, and I caught some contemptuous glances. What were we doing wrong? I understood now a bit more of the reception Lady Hester had got from the War Office after she'd gone up to offer her help – the incident I'd overheard in the long arbour when Sir Brydon was laying into her. Weren't we even allowed to do our bit here? I had my answers when the train arrived.

First off were the officers, then the rest of the walking wounded. My initial reaction to seeing them was shock. Because no one was **un**wounded. On a leave train I'd expected men just coming home on leave. But this was a hospital train. The faces of the waiting crowds showed I wasn't alone in my assumption and as the stretchers began to be unloaded those of people whose men still hadn't come off took on a grimmer aspect.

Lady Hester bid me bring a box and stepped out to greet the tide. Most men simply ignored her proffered apples. One or two snorted. A few, who didn't appear to have anyone waiting to meet them, took an apple. There was even an occasional muttered thanks. The men's appearance didn't reduce the initial shock. It wasn't only the bandages, often grubby and blood-stained. Uniforms were torn and dusty, caps missing or pushed to the back of the head. But it was the eyes that disturbed me most. There was no sight in them. It wasn't fear, I think. They stared through you as if you weren't there. As though they were somewhere else.

After the first wave had passed Butters came to join us with the cases of cigarettes and chocolate. Offered a choice, men grabbed them rather than an apple.

'If you want to do summat useful, get off and chuck *them* at the Hun,' a soldier with a bandage across one eye laughed at me as I held up an apple.

'I'm too young,' I said.

'Are you? How young?'

'Sixteen.'

'Aye, well, not long to wait, eh? It'll be still going, don't worry. And we'll need anything we've got to throw at 'em, the way things are.'

'You're never sixteen,' Butters hissed at me when he'd gone. 'I thought you told me you were…'

'Shhh,' I whispered and stuck the box out in front of me to block a staring-eyed man whose unsteady gait threatened to knock into Lady Hester.

'Thank you, Butler,' she said, which cheered me up because I didn't think she'd noticed my presence until then. Next thing, I had to intervene with a chap who was making remarks to Butters. I was beginning to enjoy myself.

'Come on, darlin',' he was saying and grabbing for her shoulder rather than cigarettes. 'What don't a returning hero deserve?'

Lady Hester moved towards him but he waved his other hand at her and she flinched. I jammed the box into his upper arm. He fell back – I'd not realised how hard I'd shoved. In a flash he was coming for me.

'What you on at, eh?'

'She's my sister,' I said, holding the box in front of me as a shield. He threw a punch but hit the box.

'Ouch, you little frigger, you done it now.'

He circled while I thrust the box out in defiance. I could smell the drink on his breath. Apples bobbed out of the box and he stood on one, losing his balance. The next minute two military policemen had him by the arms and were dragging him away, his abuse ringing in my ears.

I felt myself shepherded back by Butters. I could feel myself shaking. She was shaking, too.

'Well done, young man,' Lady Hester said.

I'd not had time to realise what I was doing but being called "young man" brought me to my senses. The stream of men had finished and we'd been moved back to where the stretcher cases were being lined up to wait for a space on an ambulance.

Lady Hester gestured us to follow as she made her way between the rows, placing an apple alongside men who were immobile or asleep. No one seemed to have the strength to protest. Then I noticed a man – a private, by the look of him – glaring at us from the next row. It was clear that he'd lost a leg.

'They don't want your apples,' he called. Lady Hester ignored him but he continued. 'What use is an apple to us?'

Lady Hester stopped and frowned across at him. The lower orders speaking out of turn was something she had no time for. And the apples were this year's crop. But she surprised me by reverting to her timid self, sounding apologetic. 'They're only some small comforts.'

'Too little. And too late for most of 'em. Can't you see that?'

'I'm sorry. I had no idea…'

'Course you don't. Want to know what it's like? Coming round with a crow sitting on your chest, waiting for you to go?'

'Er, I don't think…' Lady Hester began, indicating Butters and me – the boy again, I guessed, though I was desperate to hear him. Lady Hester moved on. He didn't stop. 'What it was really like?' he called after us. 'We'd kill 'em and kill 'em and still they came on. There was no end to 'em. Like lice, they were. And always pulling back, we was. Giving ground and thirst and no sleep for four days.'

This did make Lady Hester pause. She motioned Butters to give him cigarettes. He snatched them with a laugh.

'It's not comforts here we need, lady, it's real help over there. Why don't you get over there? And not with some lousy apples, neither. It's only hard graft that'll be some use.'

'Indeed?' Lady Hester said. I could see she was touched by this but he seemed to feel he was being ignored.

'Indeed, yeah. Get your hands dirty. Do some good. What's really wanted is medical help. See this?' He pointed to where his leg was missing. 'If they'd got me out a couple of days earlier, they'd have saved that, that's what the doc told me. It's over there people could do some good, if they really meant to. Not just coming in your glad rags to make yourself feel good.'

Lady Hester nodded absent-mindedly and then trailed off, back to the car. It looked as though our contribution was over. We drifted after her, unsure whether to leave behind the bits we still had. Butters held on to hers. I tipped the last of the apples out before a group of raggety kids outside the station. They fell on them like a pack of hounds on a fox.

My dad must have seen me because he gave me a filthy look that told me I was in for a leathering when we got home. We set off back in silence. My head whirled with all the shocks and thrills it had had, trying to take them all in and make sense of it. I guessed the others felt the same. The punishment to come I put out of mind.

Anyway, that would be worth it. The legless man filled my thoughts. I could see a crow sitting on my chest but the rest of it I couldn't grasp. Lying out waiting for rescue with your leg smashed? It had occurred to me that if they were pulling back continually he was lucky not to have been left behind but I kept my mouth shut. The surprising thing he said was that it sounded like an orderly retreat, not the disorder the newspapers had talked about. But then I recalled the huge number of casualties and decided it must have been a mess.

When we returned Lady Hester thanked me and Butters, which was nice. What's more, she told my dad how I'd stepped in and protected Butters. He had to swallow hard to hear that but it took his mind off the leathering. Then he had another shock.

'I'm going to obtain an ambulance, Butler,' she said. We all just stared at her, non-plussed, not understanding what she was on about. When she clarified what she meant, non-plussed wasn't the word.

'Next time, we're going to do some proper good,' she said. 'We're going to France, to help the wounded there.'

If my heart had leapt up to hear that, it soon sank again.

'France. How can I go to France?' my dad muttered as he drove the Wolseley round to the motor house. 'Not with your mother in her condition. And driving an ambulance – well!'

'I'll go instead, if you like,' I chirped up.

'No, you bloody well won't.'

'Lady Hester said I did all right at the station.'

'Listen, son, a station ain't a battlefield. And a battlefield ain't no place for a fourteen year-old kid. Don't even mention it again.' He had a way of putting a damper on anything, my dad did. I was tempted to ask what he knew of battlefields but decided it wasn't wise.

So when the ambulance arrived, I wasn't in the mood to take much notice, even of the fact that not many other people did, either. At first I assumed it was a delivery lorry. I'd been sweeping the drive when it pulled up outside the front steps and I almost shouted to the driver to take it round the back. Before I could Lady Hester appeared at the door, followed by another woman I didn't recognise, who had a young girl in tow. I waited to hear the tirade of abuse but had a shock.

The sound of Lady Hester's excited chatter made me look up. You'd have thought she'd taken delivery of a 42 horse-power Daimler with pneumatic tyres for all the capering about. I mean, it was a Model-T with the lorry frame so extended it looked about tip back. All the same, I edged closer, as much to see what they were going to unload. By the time the driver had unrolled the flaps I'd moved so I could catch the inside. Then I realised. Apart from two racks of three stretchers on each side, it was empty.

Now I understood. This over-long, unbalanced Model-T was their ambulance. I nearly burst out laughing. What would the wounded man at Victoria have had to say about it? 'Now you've got something to deliver your b-apples in'? I'd have been embarrassed to be seen in it in town, never mind near a battlefield.

I was about to drift away when something Lady Hester said made me stop.

'No, Butler will drive this, I'll drive the car.'

I don't know which stunned me more, the idea of Lady Hester frightening the cavalry with her driving or getting my dad over to France. Either way the scheme sounded more daft by the minute. But her comment did make me regard the ambulance in a new light. I reckoned I could handle it all right. Carstairs had let me have a few goes on the family's Model-T when my dad was out of the way. He said I took to it like a duck to water. This one might be a bit trickier, with the weight and the balance. But probably no different to steering a farm cart overloaded with hay. My fingers started to itch for a chance to try it out.

The women's gabble again cut short my day-dreaming.

'Oh, Butler will see to all that,' Lady Hester said, quite frostily, as if the other woman was raising objections. 'He maintains all the cars.'

That's what you think, I said to myself, realising what they were going on about. Since Carstairs had joined up I'd taken over that role. My dad could manage a few basic jobs but beyond that… And anyway, he wasn't going to go, was he? Though how could he get out of it?

Then I realised the other woman was trying the same thing. She indicated the child. 'Hester, it's not that easy…'

Lady Hester was having none of it. The excitement of her new toy seemed to have fired her determination. 'I can arrange for her to be looked after,' she said.

'It's not only that,' the other woman replied. She was younger than Lady Hester, mid-thirties, I'd guess now, and dressed like a man, a tweed suit and short hair. More like one of those suffragist ladies. 'You know I can't support this war. It's what I split from the WSPU over…'

'Very wise, too. Those appalling Pankhurst women…'

'With whom I shared a common cause,' the other lady interjected, but with a smile. She didn't appear put out by Lady Hester's servant-blasting mode. That's when I was reminded of the women at the peace rally. No wonder she didn't share Lady Hester's zeal for doing her bit. It was only an ambulance, though, not as if she was being asked to fight. That's what made me feel she was searching for excuses.

I expected from the mood Lady Hester was in that things could turn ugly but she seemed to crumble in the face of the other's self-assurance. She looked down, as she had when Sir Brydon brought up the subject of divorce. For a moment she said nothing then sighed. 'The truth is, Magda, you're my last hope.'

'How flattering,' the woman, Magda, laughed. 'So everyone else had too much sense?'

'No, they were too scared.'

'Scared?'

'All talk but when it came to it…'

'As I said, it's not that easy…'

'I've never claimed it will be.'

Lady Hester was much more measured now. Her plan, it became clear, hadn't simply been a fad. She'd given it plenty of thought. This seemed to carry more weight with Magda than the earlier appeal to her patriotism. Then I heard something that did astound me.

'I need someone unflappable, able to stand up for herself,' Lady Hester was saying. 'What I mean is, there's Helena…'

Helena was going, too? I wondered how she'd agreed.

'… and though Butters is a sensible girl…'

Butters? Did Butters realise she'd been conscripted? This whole affair was becoming comical the more I heard. Magda sounded amused, if puzzled, too. 'So you need someone who's not sensible, and not young?'

Lady Hester didn't appreciate this humour. 'I need someone who knows what it is to stand up for women,' she said.

'By going to war?' Magda retorted, still with a smile.

Again, resistance made Lady Hester ease off. I thought it was a bit much, her climbing on her high horse about standing up for women. It was rumoured that she'd once threatened to horse-whip a serving girl who'd asked for time off to attend a suffrage meeting. Now, she must have realised bluster wouldn't get her anywhere.

'We're going to *the* war to help the victims, the wounded…'

'Who've volunteered to fight…'

'… and to clear up the mess left by men.'

The little girl tugged at her mother's sleeve then and Magda bent down to listen to her. Then they went inside. I never did learn what finally convinced her to agree.

Only the knowledge that I'd been eavesdropping again and needed to stay inconspicuous stopped me dashing off at once to inform Butters about her fortune. I'd have said 'good fortune' but the reminder that I was missing out dampened my mood. Besides, I still couldn't imagine any of it actually happening.

I'd not allowed for Lady Hester's powers of persuasion, that seemed to grow with the acquisition of the Model-T. It was more a case of brow-beating, I suspect. Butters accepted it as if she had no choice. Which she didn't, of course. My dad puzzled me. To Lady Hester he was all 'Yes, ma'am', 'no ma'am' but at home he muttered darkly to himself and when my mum panicked and had a relapse he said nothing would come of it, he was only going along with the idea to avoid queering his pitch with Lady Hester.

Yet here we were at Dover and he still hadn't told Lady Hester he wanted to be out of it. All the way down – I was in the Model-T, the car, that is, with Hemmings driving, we'd been brought to help with the loading – I worried about the rumpus that would occur when he announced it. They'd be stuck, with only the one driver, because I knew Hemmings had no intention of going: he was having the shakes at the thought of being so close to the army machine, as if they might drag him in.

For me, Dover was even better than Victoria. Here, all was action, constant streams of traffic and a great noise of loading the ships. We were directed to a quayside almost before I'd realised we'd arrived, joining a queue of vehicles waiting to be hoisted up into the hold of the SS *Beaumaris Castle*. She didn't look too much like a castle, if I'm honest, since the rust was peeling off her sides and the superstructure didn't strike me as very fitting for somebody of Lady Hester's status.

Though it soon became clear that Lady Hester's rank counted for nothing in this world. We waited I don't know how long while she argued with some port official before he gave in and waved us forward.

At that point all became panic as Butters and I had the ladies' portmanteaus thrust upon us with orders to take them up the gangway. Once the vehicles were stowed there'd be no way of getting to them before France.

Of course, there was a stream of stuff going up the gangway, too, and it was a long one, with no chance of stopping for a rest in the crush of stevedores and troops boarding. So only when I was on deck and out of the main flow did it hit me that Hemmings had taken no part in this. Peering down I could see that the Model-T car was out of the queue and facing back towards land: Hemmings was supposed to drive me home in it when everything was loaded. Of him I could make out no trace. My dad must be manoeuvring the ambulance towards the hoists.

An army officer with a clipboard shouted at us to move and in answer to Butters' plea barked orders at us to carry the cases down below. The directions just swam in my head but Butters seemed to understand and I stumbled after her down a series of steep and slippery ladders, the pong of salty sweat everywhere. We reached a grimy corridor with a string of grubby doors that had once been white. My mind kept protesting that Lady Hester wouldn't accept this. Surely she should be up in one of the deck cabins? I still couldn't switch my thoughts into this new world.

'Thirty-two and thirty-three, he said,' Butters muttered, pushing open a door that let on to a cramped room with two metal bunks and a porthole. I'd seen larger stalls in stables. And cleaner. Lady Hester definitely would have something to say about this, even if she was only going to be in here for a few hours. If I was that officer I'd make myself scarce before she found out.

I let drop the three cases I'd been struggling with.

'Which ones go where?' I asked but Butters looked as stunned as I felt. 'Lil?'

'If there are only two cabins and two bunks in each...'

'My dad'll have to stay on deck,' I laughed. I think I'd have preferred that anyway to this prison cell.

'No,' she said, in some distress, 'how can I share with one of the ladies?'

She had a point. 'Go and ask that officer,' I suggested.

Her furious stare had me quail as much as the officer's had her. Then she seemed to shrink with the horror of it.

'Would you like me to go?' I blurted out without realising what I'd said. Her pathetic look of gratitude made it impossible for me to withdraw the offer.

'I'll see what I can do,' I mumbled, hoping he'd gone off somewhere else.

I'm not sure what I hoped to achieve. When I finally reached the deck, after losing my way several times in the maze of corridors below, the place was so crowded with troops – rough-looking Highlanders in kilts, most of them – that I could see no sign of the officer. I did, however, catch a glimpse of the three ladies being guided through the crush by a merchant navy officer and was in two minds whether to give up the search and rush down to warn Butters they were coming.

The ship's hooter drowned out these thoughts. I fought my way to the rail to see if the officer was on the quayside. The gangway was now clear. Of the man there was no sign. A voice in my ear boomed:

'Ach, it's too late for regrets now, sonny.'

I gawped round. One of the Scots soldiers was eyeing me with scorn. I pulled away from the rail.

'No, I…' I began and pushed my way through the crowd. The gangplank had gone. A sailor was dragging the chain across the gap. I turned back in bewilderment. How had I not noticed the ship preparing to leave? But that wasn't what was making my heart thump so wildly. As I'd swung away from the Scot my eye had caught something that only now registered. The Model-T was moving, towards the exit from the quay. And there were two men sitting in it. The one on the passenger side was my dad.

Five

'Damn him! Damn him! The infernal coward! I'll have him whipped and flung onto the streets, into a cell for this. Damn and blast the man! All men. Damn and blast them!'

I shrank from Lady Hester's fury. I could never have imagined the language. It was bad enough being associated with its targets.

Breaking the news she lacked a driver hadn't been my choice. I'd flitted about on deck once we'd sailed, trying to keep out of sight of any officers and away from ribbing from troops who couldn't help notice my age and the absence of uniform.

'Which regimental uniform are ye?' and 'If they're sending oot the boys, they mighta dressed 'em first' were only two of the taunts I hid from. I'd decided my best course was to find a ship's officer and confess the truth, hoping they'd send me back with it when the ship turned round. That's when Butters stumbled on me.

'Harry?'

I peered out from behind the lifeboat I'd been using as a hiding place. Butters' frown met me. She held a lump of bread.

'What are you…? Where's your dad, this bread's for…'

I came out from my hide and told her what I'd seen.

'You'd better have this, then.'

I hadn't realised how hungry I was and wolfed down the bread while Butters sighed.

'Hey, Jimmy, would you look at that. I thought they told us it was the uniform would get the girls.'

I glanced up. I didn't recognise the Scot or know if he'd been one of those who'd scoffed at me. Now he was grinning and gave me a wink as he went off. I felt myself going red but it was also pleasing to be regarded favourably for a change.

'You'll have to tell Lady Hester,' Butters said.

'Me?' I gasped. 'You mean she doesn't know?'

'She thought he was up here.'

'But why me?'

'He's *your* father.'

This stumped me. At least, because he hadn't boarded and found me here, I'd been spared a leathering, I reflected. On balance, that would have been preferable to this lashing from lady Hester's tongue. The tirade hadn't eased.

'When I've finished with him, he'll wish he'd been a Belgian peasant put up against a wall and shot.'

I couldn't disagree with that sentiment and gave a weak smile to Magda, who seemed to be on the verge of bursting out laughing. Lady Hester must have thought my smile was impudence.

'And turn all his brood out onto the streets,' she fumed. 'It's ingratitude on top of everything else. Do you know what gratitude is, my lad?'

'Yes, ma'am,' I whispered, wishing she'd return to timidity.

'You didn't get it from your father, then, did you?'

'No, ma'am.'

'The fool has wrecked my whole mission, do you realise that?'

'Yes, ma'am.'

I was on the verge of tears but she didn't let up.

'Did you know about this?'

'No ma'am. Not at all.'

'Humph.'

'Er, excuse me, ma'am,' Butters said. 'Mr Carstairs did show me how the Model-T worked once…'

I gaped at her, open-mouthed. Had Carstairs betrayed me by teaching all and sundry? Lady Hester's astonishment was more unalloyed than mine.

'Don't be stupid, girl, this is no time for games. Even if Mr Carstairs had shown you how it works, we're not talking about a mere car. Handling an ambulance is quite another matter.'

Listen to the expert talking, I thought and saw Lady Hester's efforts with the Wolseley on the Downs little more than two months earlier.

Since when I doubted if she'd driven it twice before today. A heavy silence followed.

'We may have to face facts, Hester and pause in Ostend until we can send for a new driver,' the woman, Magda, said.

'Or give up the whole thing while we still can, mama.' This was Helena, who didn't sound too disappointed at that prospect.

'Maybe the army will lend us a man until a replacement arrives,' her mother said.

'And where will he come from?' Lady Helena retorted. 'Look how many of us you managed to gather in the first place – and those by force. What chance is there of anyone else being browbeaten into it, from a distance.'

'I'm not giving up now,' Lady Hester snapped.

'I may be able to persuade someone from the Movement,' Magda, put in. 'Some of them can drive. You don't need to depend on a man.'

I felt them glance at me and my gorge rose but I kept quiet. I was thinking of those ladies at the peace rally. Their driver would fit the bill.

'Thank you, Magda,' Lady Hester said. 'It's not as simple as that. What if one of the vehicles has a breakdown? Who knows where we could be? Without someone who could get it going we could be stranded – and putting all your lives in danger.'

'What did I tell you, mama?' Lady Helena chipped in. I noticed that Butters, too, was looking more cheerful at the likelihood of a cancellation. Obviously Carstairs' teaching hadn't made a deep impression. One of his bits of advice, about how handling a car was like handling a woman, came into my mind. But this situation called for firmness, not the shilly-shallying about that was taking over. Having got over feeling let down at not being able to do my bit, I was now seeing my dreams of their adventure being quashed. Damn my dad. And them.

'Sadly, you may be right, Helena,' she said. 'If the worm, Butler, had a use it was for his maintaining the health of the vehicles.'

Without meaning to, I snorted.

'Think this is all an amusement, do you, my lad?' Lady Hester snapped at me.

'No, ma'am,' I replied, looking her in the face for the first time. Amusement wasn't the word for it.

'So you think it funny that I refer to your father as a worm?'

'No, ma'am, but…'

'But?'

'He didn't look after the engines of the cars, ma'am.'

'What?'

'That's what Mr Carstairs came over for.' I glanced at Butters and thought I saw her face flush.

'Your father didn't know how to maintain the cars?'

'No, ma'am.'

Lady Hester's shoulders sagged.

'I think that seals it, mama,' Lady Helena said. She seemed to be grow more upright. Her mother turned away. Something in her aspect of defeat and the idea of Helena getting her way stung me. And a reckless thought struck me, too.

'But I do…' I blurted out.

I felt eyes glaring at me. Lady Hester glanced round, her frown deeper. Now it had all gone to pieces I didn't care if I gave offence. It wasn't my fault.

'…Know how to maintain the cars, ma'am. Carstairs taught me. I used to do all the regular stuff. For my dad.'

'Absurd. You little…'

'Ma'am, I believe he did,' Butters put in. 'Mr Carstairs told me, once. He said he was a "natural" with engines and things.'

'I suppose Mr Carstairs taught you to drive, as well?' Lady Helena sniffed at me.

'Yes, ma'am.'

'He let you drive the Wolseley?' Lady Hester snapped.

'Oh, no, ma'am, he showed me how to service the Wolseley but I only drove the Model-T. To test it.'

'Hmm.'

'Mama, he's merely a child. You can't…'

'How old did you say you were?' Lady Hester demanded.

'S-seventeen.'

Helena snorted now. I glanced at Butters but she was staring at the

61

floor. Lady Hester glared at me. I could feel the disappointment starting to drain back into me.

'That ambulance is heavier than the car,' Lady Hester said.

'No heavier than a hay waggon, ma'am.'

'Mama!'

'Would you say he looks eighteen, Magda, Butters?'

Magda smiled. 'I never judge by appearances.'

Lady Hester turned her glare on Butters, who, still looking down, muttered 'I couldn't say, ma'am, I'm sure.' A wave of gratitude to her swept over me.

'You're clutching at straws, mama,' Lady Helena grumbled.

'Butters, take the la… the young man next door and prepare the cases for disembarkation. Magda, would you like a turn up on deck for some fresh air?'

And we were out. Not that the grilling stopped.

'You're never seventeen,' Butters stated when we were next door. 'I'm sure you told me fourteen. How old are you?'

'Old enough.'

'You used to play with my little brother Jem and he's only thirteen.'

'I'm older than him.'

'Aye, not by much.'

'And I can handle that Ford better than my dad, anyway.'

'So you reckon.'

'You said Carstairs thought I was a natural.'

'Tell you anything, he would.'

'What he told me about cars was always right.'

'Lucky you.'

She bit her lip. I remembered Helena's earlier accusation to her mother and realised that my bravado had now led Butters into something she hadn't volunteered for.

'I'm sorry,' I said.

'No, you're not,' she shot back at me. 'You just want to be tearing about playing soldiers like all the rest.'

'I don't,' I lied. 'Anyway, you should have stood up to Lady Hester, if you were that bothered.'

'I was going to,' she said, 'until we went to Victoria. I wanted to do something. And my brother, Frank, went and joined up.'

'There you are, then,' I retorted. 'You're in the same boat as me.'

'How?'

'Both of us are having to work to do our bit.'

She grunted and began to gather the cases. I could hardly believe what I'd pulled off. Would it lead to a leathering when I got home? My dad wouldn't be in a position to lord it over me after what he'd done. I began to feel pleased with myself. Until Butters put me in my place.

'You make sure you don't give yourself away when we get off this boat.'

'What do you mean?'

'Acting like a boy.'

'Me? You've got a cheek…'

'Hiding behind a lifeboat isn't what a grown-up man would do.'

'My dad's grown up and look what he did.'

'It'll be proper soldiers you'll need to convince when we're with the army.'

I recalled the recruiting sergeant's comments when I'd tried to enlist and my resolve wilted. I tried to sound jaunty.

'So will you, don't forget. A bunch of women. They don't like women getting in the way.'

'I'd be careful what you say about women, Harry. You know there's a jailbird amongst us?'

I blinked and went through the list. There could only be one possibility, but even so…

'Not you…?'

Butters laughed. 'No. Lady Magdalena Somerton.'

'Lady Magda? I don't believe you.'

'Six months for assaulting a policeman. Bow Street Magistrates.'

'But why?'

'He called her a silly little woman.'

'For doing what?'

'Chaining herself to the railings in Downing Street.'

Now I did fully understand. 'Ah, she's one of them…'

Butters raised her hand to stop me.

'Don't even think it. You may need to act big in front of other men but if you try it in present company, you might not live to join them. Remember your place.'

That was good advice. Butters rubbed some dust in my face to roughen it up and, loaded with cases, I followed the ladies down the gangway at Ostend without attracting unwelcome attention. The disembarking troops were too busy to notice us. I shared their eagerness but we were kept back until everyone else had got off. Then kept waiting even longer while Lady Hester tried to find somebody who might take us seriously.

'You wanna go where?' the guard at the gates from the quay laughed at Lady Hester's request for directions to the Front. 'Not a chance, lady.'

'What do you think this ambulance is for?'

The sentry looked us up and down. The red crosses now emblazoned on the sides of both car and ambulance didn't appear to alter his stance.

'Sorry. I can't let you past this point without a chitty.'

'A chitty?'

'Saying where you're going and that you got permission.'

'I don't need permission.'

'Now that's where you're wrong, Miss…'

'Your Ladyship to you.'

'Suit yourself. But without permission…'

'And from whom do I obtain this "permission"?'

The sentry jerked his head towards a low building to our right. 'If you could back up and park over there so you're not blocking this road. Your Ladyship.'

Oh, God, I thought, does she know how to reverse? What embarrassment this was going to be. She knew how to think, I'll give her that. My eyes widened to see her get out of the car.

'When you've parked the ambulance, move my car back, too,

would you, Butler,' she said and stalked towards the low building.

'Flipping heck,' I muttered to Butters. 'She don't half land you in it, doesn't she?'

'You've really never driven the Wolseley?'

I was too busy hoping I could engage reverse gear sweetly in the Ford to answer but it flowed as smooth as milk.

'Not once,' I said after I'd parked up and we both got down.

'Oh, dear. What will you do? Aren't all cars different?'

'Carstairs said they're like women,' I threw off and was surprised to see Butters flinch. 'He let me sit in the driver's seat once and pointed things out to me,' I added to hide my awkwardness as much as hers. 'I'm trying to remember.'

'And can you?'

'Not yet. Will you go and talk to that bloke to distract him?'

When I took my seat it all came back. I could hear Carstairs telling me. 'Push and slide. Makes the old "T" feel like backing up a fully-loaded knacker's cart.'

I glanced at the women half-masking the sentry and took a deep breath. If I crashed the gear, he'd hear it. Butters' 'Tell you anything, he would,' of Carstairs crossed my mind. He'd never let *me* down. I frowned away the thought, concentrated and prayed.

He didn't let me down this time, either. In fact, the gear engaged so easily I nearly shot back too fast.

I was on the point of sauntering over to join the ladies when I noticed how much I was shaking. To ease my breathing down I lifted the bonnet and pretended to check the engine before risking walking across. There was no sign of Lady Hester.

'Got a problem with the big motor, chum?' the sentry asked.

'The Wolseley?' Why did I have to show off? 'No, just checking. We'll need petrol, though, before carrying on.'

The sentry laughed. 'Petrol? You'll be lucky. Everything's requisitioned here, chum. Still, if you got enough to turn 'em round and line 'em up to be re-loaded on board, you'll be OK.'

My spirits sank. I turned away hoping to see Lady Hester had re-appeared. Pretending looked like becoming a way of life.

'Fag, chum?'

I said 'no' before realising this might be another revelation of my age. I had tried them, once, without success. He gave me a strange look but Lady Magda butted in. I thought she'd gone with Lady Hester.

'I will, thanks,' she said. 'We don't encourage the drivers to. They need both hands on the wheel.'

The sentry chortled. 'That so? Once you got a few wounded in the back you'll be at 'em all the time, son, so will they, mark my words.'

At length Lady Hester returned. Seething.

'Obstinate, narrow-minded and tied up in red tape,' she said as she reached us, glaring at the sentry.

'Oh, men?' Magda laughed. I looked away.

'Here's your "chitty,"' I heard her say. She waved it at the soldier before sweeping us to the vehicles.

'But you beat them into submission, mama?' Lady Helena asked. She sounded more resigned after the tongue-lashing I guessed she'd received on the boat.

'Not a bit of it. We're not wanted.'

'What does that mean?'

I sensed some hope creep back in that question.

'It means, as far as the British Army Expeditionary Force is concerned, that there is no place for us. Against Army regulations. We're in the way. They'd be obliged if we would go home.'

'And sit still?' Magda said. If that was a joke, it didn't go down well.

'But what's the "chitty", mama?' Helena asked. 'I thought you...'

'Oh, we're directed to the Station Hotel to spend the night. Or until space can be found on a returning ship. It's most inconvenient for them as they have to prioritise space for the wounded. And if we remain here we risk obstructing the quay.'

'We'll have a decent bed, anyway,' Helena said. Her mother gave her a filthy look but said nothing. I shared Lady Hester's disappointment. To have made it this far and then be rejected. It was bad enough for me even though I'd never expected to be here.

The sentry insisted on scanning the chitty before lifting the barrier at the gate. As I followed the Wolseley out he laughed and called to me, 'Enjoy your posh hotel, chum – it got bombed last night.'

I perked up on hearing that. I'd see something of the war before being sent back. And the strange town was exciting, too, if terrifying, driving on the wrong side of the road and all. Luckily, we crawled along because the place was choked with military vehicles and troops, though there was no panic or disorder. Belgian people seemed glad to see us and cheered us as we passed. If only they'd known we weren't coming to their aid any more.

The Station Hotel was huge, like a palace to my eyes, and here Lady Hester's position meant something. The ladies were given rooms almost like the bedrooms back at the House. Even the servants' quarters, where Butters and I were put up, were better than anything I'd slept in. I was worried that we'd be in the way but Magda told Butters there were spare rooms because many of the staff had gone off to fight.

Lucky them, I thought, but we did get to see the hole made by the bomb the night before. Fortunately it had landed in the garden at the back, though a number of windows had been shattered by the blast. Compared to what we saw later it was a piddling little thing but at the time I was impressed. I had a sneaking hope the aeroplane would return and drop another one that night.

No such luck. Not only that, all lights were switched off at eight-thirty so it was early to bed. I tried to lie awake listening but after the turmoil of the day I soon fell asleep.

Butters shook me awake before dawn.

'Get up, we're going to Antwerp.'

'Uh?'

'We're going to help the Belgians. Offer to work with their Red Cross.'

My head was still fuzzy. I hadn't a clue where Antwerp was. Weren't we supposed to have come to France?

'I thought we'd been told to go home?' I asked.

'That was only the Army. Lady Hester says we can do what we want. It's not their country.'

I didn't protest. Lady Hester had got her dander up over this war

67

lark and her new spirit was infectious. I was game for whatever she decided as long as we saw some action. There was one problem.

'No petrol?' Lady Hester squawked when I broke the news. 'There must be petrol, with all the transport here.'

'The sentry said it was all controlled by the Army, ma'am,' Butler volunteered.

'*They* won't give us any,' Magda said. 'Especially when they know what we're up to.'

Lady Hester turned on me. 'Didn't Butl... your father load up some extra cans before we left?'

I shook my head. Guess whose job it would have been to fill those. Nothing had been said to me. We were stuck.

Helena gave me a look of gratitude but I took no pleasure in relaying the bad news. Especially since the blame seemed to be mine.

'Oh, this is impossible,' Lady Hester said. 'Infuriating. Is every man around going to stand in our way?'

'Mama, perhaps...' Helena began but her mother brushed her aside.

'No, they're not,' she fumed and stormed out.

'Someone's in for it,' Magda said. '"What larks, Pip."'

I frowned, thinking she'd forgotten my name but Helena sighed and gave me another cause for irritation. 'I wish she'd calm down and see sense. I mean, look at us. A handful of women and a boy. What do we think we can achieve? By the time we see a German it'll all be over. I hope. She'll get nowhere throwing her weight about.'

But she did. Bruges. The hotel had told Lady Hester she might be able to obtain petrol freely in Bruges, which was on our way to Antwerp. That perked her up again. She swanned around more like a kid than me at the prospect. And, as I said, her example lifted my spirits, too. In truth, they didn't need much lifting. This was already an adventure beyond my wildest longings. The things I'd have to tell Curly and co when I got back home.

But the journey was a nightmare. Not just because it was my first time driving the ambulance at any speed but because of the road, the surface of which made driving torture. Its cobbles sloped down from the centre and the edge was mud-covered before falling into a water-filled ditch. If I lost control and skidded, the unbalanced ambulance would be over and sinking in no time. I'd never struggled so much, even with a sparky horse on a trap, to keep a vehicle straight.

As though that wasn't bad enough Lady Hester gave the Wolseley its head. I knew why and that was the main source of my torment: she'd asked me if I thought we had enough petrol to make Bruges – about twenty miles, she guessed – and I said yes. I didn't add 'perhaps' and the more I pondered on it, the more I decided it would be touch and go. Otherwise, we faced being stranded in the middle of nowhere. I remembered my boast about how I could maintain the engines. I'd forgotten I couldn't make them run on air. The only consolation in all this was that there was no time for other worries.

Fortunately the road was dead straight for miles, along an endless avenue of poplars and for some reason the traffic was light. Occasional groups of people straggled towards us, laden with bundles, but they shrank onto the mud as the cars screeched past.

'Refugees,' Butters said. I hadn't realised. I wondered why. The news – Lady Hester had bought a foreign paper in Ostend and been able to read it – suggested the Germans had been held up and further over, in France, had been pushed back from the Marne to the Aisne, wherever they were.

'Carstairs told me that you use more petrol driving fast,' I said as the road cleared and the Wolseley picked up speed. The drive to Dover and her sense of mission must have given her confidence. Or maybe like me she felt more at ease in a car.

'Why don't you tell her ladyship, then?' Butters retorted.

I bit my lip for using his name. I could see I'd have to suffer alone. What caused Butters' attitude to Carstairs I couldn't imagine.

Being held up at sentry posts didn't ease my anxiety. Keeping the engine running drained the petrol and cutting it only meant a surge on starting up. And there was another problem. I had no passport. At the first post this led to endless wrangling in a language I couldn't understand before Lady Hester got her way. After that I was told to wave the chitty in the hope whoever stopped us couldn't read English. It worked a treat.

We limped into Bruges, Lady Hester nearly overturning a milk cart drawn by a dog, and were directed to a petrol supply. At last I could breathe freely.

But not for long. We'd just crossed over the canal on the way out of the town towards Ghent when I saw the sentry at the next barrier shaking his head at Lady Hester. I got down with the chitty and went up to the car, feeling like joining in with the shouting that seemed to do the trick. I'd had enough of all these obstacles put in our way when all we wanted was to help. And see some action, as well, of course though I didn't admit that to myself at the time.

Lady Hester was waving the passports. 'Nous allons vers Antwerpen,' she shouted. The Belgians generally understood French but this one kept shaking his head. Then he pointed up the road ahead. In the far distance there was a dust cloud above the trees. My heart thumped. Germans? Here already? I wasn't that ready to see action.

That shut up Lady Hester. She gestured in sign language and French, I think, to know what it signified.

'Antwerpen finis,' the man said and then gabbled. All I caught was the word 'Deutsch.' I glanced again at the cloud. It seemed to be blowing this way at some speed. But frantic pointing and repetition of 'Deutsch?' from the ladies only brought more shaking of the head from the sentry.

'Oh, they're refugees,' Magda said. 'Fleeing.' And to the guard 'Belge?' For once he nodded. Again the relief was short-lived. From the dust it looked as if half the population of Belgium was in flight. Even if we wanted to go on, the road ahead would be impassable.

A staff car screeched up to the barrier from that direction, followed quickly by others. Barked orders had the sentry raise the barrier and leave it up. Several Red Cross lorries raced past. I glimpsed wounded men piled up in the back.

'We have to turn back, mama,' Lady Helena said.

'We can't turn here, your Ladyship...' I began.

'Stop calling me "your ladyship",' she snapped. 'Why not?'

70

'There's not space and with the vehicles coming fast...'

I couldn't remember when we'd passed a crossroads since the canal and didn't relish the idea of reversing on this surface. A sign-language conversation went on with the sentry, which made no headway. If we went on and got caught up in the advancing crowd... And where were the Germans?

A Red Cross ambulance stopped and provided the answer. The driver was American and so I was able to follow what he had to say. The Germans were miles away, still around Antwerp, which *had* fallen, but the people, mindful of the tales of atrocities they'd been fed for weeks, were in no mind to take the risk. They were clogging up all the roads and making an orderly retreat by the army impossible. He'd been based in Ghent but they'd pulled out. It had taken him two hours to make it this far. Now he had to go, his wounded were dying fast in the back.

'What should we do?' Lady Hester asked, sounding deflated. 'We just want to help. We have ambulance space. Should we go on and try...'

'Wasting your time, lady. And energy. You'll get nowhere up there. Or be cut off.'

'Then where..?'

He shrugged, found his gear and drove off. The ladies looked at each other in despair.

'The first thing to do, ma'am, is turn round,' Butters said. 'If we don't, we will be caught in the flood.'

This jerked them into life.

'In Ostend, there was an English nurse in the kitchen,' Butters added. 'She said they were making for somewhere called "Furnes", I think it was. Inland from Ostend. A convent hospital. She expected to be busy there. Maybe we could...'

'Let's see how far we can make, first, Butters. There's clearly a need up ahead.'

We went on. The crowd loomed closer. From time to time a staff car would struggle out of the mass and hurtle towards us, as if desperate to escape. I'd been working out if I could swing the ambulance round but the road was far too narrow. Now the gap to the refugees had

71

reduced, the chances of being hit by one of these escaping cars was also too great.

So we were swallowed by the flood. Once in it, I realised how slow-moving it was. We could only crawl but the people passing us did little more. Many dragged or pushed hand barrows, a few had horse-drawn carts, these piled high with all sorts and topped by women and children. Everyone was laden, some just with ornaments that couldn't have been of any practical use. Most looked as if they'd just grabbed whatever came to hand first and stumbled out into the flood. An old woman trudged beside a small cart pulled by an injured dog, its leg bleeding. In the cart were two babies, like everyone else, mute.

That was the strange thing. The American had described panic but I could see none. People shuffled along without complaint under a low, featureless sky that seemed to have dropped its greyness into them. They trudged in a dream, faces set and eyes sightless, with no apparent expectation that this journey would ever end. It was also almost silent, the main sound being a kind of muffled dragging noise that rose from the mass. With the stench. *That* did have a kick. What a pong.

Lady Hester's hope to go on, it became apparent at once, was futile. The crowd thickened all the time. If we didn't turn round, we'd come to a halt. I was starting to feel faint, from the smell and the strain of going so slowly. Then an ambulance heading our way nearly hit the Wolseley. I caught angry words. As it passed me the driver pointed back the way he'd come and made a circular gesture. Somewhere to turn, I prayed he meant.

It was a junction of sorts on the right. Enough to turn into and back out of. Until I remembered that Lady Hester couldn't reverse. Past tense. Every challenge now seemed to bring the best out of Lady Hester. This time I heard a crash and grinding and after first starting forward the Wolseley bumped backwards and onto the road. People, who'd seemed asleep, darted out of the way with surprising speed.

'Now you'll have to manage this one properly,' Butters laughed.

'Get down and make sure nobody is run over,' I snapped, knowing I'd be able to see little as I swung the long body back.

What happened was the reverse of what I expected. It was us who were over-run. The realisation we were going in their direction galvanised the comatose into life and they were climbing all over the back even as I was reversing out onto the main road. A young woman thrust a baby up into Butters' arms and scrambled into the cab beside us.

'What do I do?' Butters asked. I shrugged. Ahead, a couple of men stood on the running boards of the Wolseley. If Lady Hester wasn't throwing them off, I wasn't either.

We crawled at last out of the mass and were able to pick up speed. I hoped Lady Hester's passengers were holding on tight. Our lady jabbered away but I hadn't a clue about what. Until she saw the belfry beyond the canal and I recognised the word 'Brugge'.

In the main square we stopped and Lady Hester tried to persuade our passengers to descend. Some did but others clamoured for 'Oostende'. The thought of returning there and risking being enshipped again startled me but Lady Hester appeared to give in.

'They'll show us the road to Furnes,' Butters said when she clambered back in. 'And Lady Hester thinks if we've got refugees on board, we're more likely to be allowed through any checkpoints.'

This proved to be the case. My nerves were still on edge as we crept through Ostend but the journey was uneventful. Though again disappointment followed. It turned out that Furnes wasn't far inland but further down the coast from Ostend. And further from the Front, I guessed. Further from seeing any action.

At least I did see British cavalry. They were clogging the roads now but a more resplendent sight than refugees. I wondered if Mr James's lot were with them though Lady Hester's attempts to find out only brought suspicion that we were spies. And when they were convinced we weren't my own attempt to learn what they were doing brought me no consolation: 'being buggered about from arsehole to breakfast time,' the trooper said then noticed Butters beside me and added 'Sorry, miss, military term.'

The result of all these delays was that dusk was falling by the time we crawled into Furnes and finally persuaded our passengers to alight. Again I had to re-adjust my thinking. I'd assumed that because Furnes was south of Ostend it must be farther away from the Front. But the Grande Place, Town Hall and all, was smashed and full of armoured cars, bicycles and sentries. Only later could I put it together and understand that the German advance curved round and was coming from the east as well as the north now. From where a rumble of guns also came.

I was famished by this time so stopping to eat cheese and thick rye bread gave some relief, even if it made me realise how tired I was. Then it became clear that this convent we'd heard about wasn't in Furnes but outside the town. Lady Hester insisted that we set out for it at once. For me and, I suspect for the others, the allure of being near the Front was losing some of its shine.

'Mama, wouldn't it make more sense to arrive in daylight – go back to Ostend and have a good night's rest first?' Helena asked.

'And find ourselves marched onto a ship? If we arrive by night, there's less chance of some busybody being there to turn us away. I've had quite enough of being turned this way and that for one day.'

No one could argue with that. So we arrived at the convent at night. On later reflection, being turned away might have had its advantages.

Six

Until now, all Belgium's roads had been straight and flat. But in the gathering darkness we wound round a low hill. Several vehicles shot past us going down. At the top the road narrowed even more and turned sharply to the right through a gate set in high walls. I was surprised that Lady Hester swung into it without a hitch. Carstairs would have called her a natural, too.

My day-dreaming had to stop. The Model-T's headlights picked out the midden in the centre of what looked like a large farmyard, with stables to the right. Seated in a little pool of candlelight outside them was an old man, reading. Then the frontage of an imposing facade came round. We ground to a stop behind a battered lorry parked in front of the entrance steps.

A nurse with a clipboard ran down these steps to the Wolseley. I glimpsed two nuns with those high white collars dash to the back of the ambulance. Next minute there was angry shouting and they hurried to the nurse, with a glance at us that seemed as confused as I was. Not wanted again, I guessed and let out a deep sigh.

'Oh, we're going,' Butters said.

The battered lorry, which I now saw was an ambulance, moved off. The Wolseley pulled away. Waving and pointing arms from the nuns indicated that I was to follow them.

'Not wanted again,' I groaned. 'Where to now?'

'At least somebody might know where,' Butters laughed.

I was too busy peering through the dark to join her. And startled at the foot of the hill when we turned left, away from the town towards where the rumble of guns had come from. And where, now, streaks of light shot across the sky. This looked an odd way to be going home, or for somewhere to spend the night.

The road was straight, anyway. After a short while the lead

ambulance stopped and switched off its lights. The Wolseley did the same so I doused mine, too. A figure ran back to us.

'We're going to collect wounded,' Magda shouted up to me. 'There's been a big enemy attack. We have to keep our lights off. Just follow and do as you're told.'

'I'm not a child,' I almost snapped back but the thought that we were actually going into action stunned me. I think I just grunted then wondered how we'd manage to drive without lights – on these slippery, narrow roads.

I also noticed, since the engine was idling, how much deeper the booming roll of the guns had become, punctuated by louder shocks. The palms of my hands felt damp.

I needn't have worried about the dark. Our road was elevated above a flat plain with several villages dotted over it. The two ahead to our right and left were already burning. Flames stood up like torches. Periodically a building would take a hit and a sharp flare of fire stab into the air. Visibility for driving wasn't a problem though you had to screw up your eyes hard in case there was anything dark in the road. From a distance the sight was also exhilarating and I began to perk up. It was like being at a firework display beyond your wildest dreams.

'I hope the poor souls in those houses had left,' Butters said, breaking up my daydream. That side of it I hadn't thought about.

The vehicles ahead suddenly braked and I only just pulled up before crashing into the back of the Wolseley. The engine cut. My ears were deafened by the roar of the artillery. In the distance, from both sides, lines of flashes showed how hard each army was going at it. My heart thumped as I picked up another sound: the screech of shells above my head. A dull thud and flash of flame not far off in a field made me realise not all were going over. Good God, were they even firing at us?

There wasn't much leisure to dwell on this.

'Butler… lend a hand up ahead?' Lady Hester's voice came through the thunder.

I climbed down and slithered to the Wolseley, wondering if it had broken down. Typical, before we'd seen anything close up. Me and my pathetic dreams. She pointed past the lead ambulance. A dark shape bulged on the road surface.

'Horse. Needs moving out of the way,' I guessed were her words and made my way to where a man holding a rope was hesitating. I'd seen a dead horse before and took heart. If we looped the rope round the neck, we ought to be able to pull the animal aside sufficiently to pass. My fears were unfounded.

Then I saw that there wasn't a neck. I turned away and knelt over.

'All right, Butler?' Lady Hester called.

'Yes,' I shouted above the din, ashamed that I'd acted like a child. That bloody cheese! Then I saw the other driver looked equally shaken.

'Round the legs,' I said and my indicating galvanised him into action. The horse's flanks felt slimy and only as we tightened the knot did I glimpse the red on my hands. A glance beyond the corpse made me retch again. I understood why the man had looked pale. There were three others and their riders down the side of the road. But the remains were smaller than this one.

The need for action saved me. We lugged and tugged to no effect. Then there was a loud sucking sound. I ducked, thinking it was a shell and found myself on my knees in the mud, being pulled towards the edge of the road. I let go the rope. With a plop the horse disappeared from sight into the ditch. I bent my head, gasping, the foul stink from the filth threatening my stomach and the drumming in my ears beating under the roll of the guns.

My arm was being shaken. The driver helped me up and thrust a small metal flask on me, gesturing to me to drink. I took a swig and choked into a coughing fit. My throat burned. Spluttering, I offered the flask back. How many times had I given myself away here? But he beamed with what looked like approval then gesticulated at the hole in the road. I gathered my wits as he gabbled and pointed, understanding that he was indicating to me to steer round it.

'Shell hole, keep left, follow him,' I managed to splutter to Lady Hester and staggered to the ambulance.

'Butler,' I heard her call but just waved her away with my arm.

'Good Lord,' Butters said when I climbed up beside her. 'You look a fright.'

I felt like one. The brandy – I think that's what it was – mixed with the taste of sick made me want to throw up again. Butters pressed a canteen of water on me and, smelling first to see it wasn't more firewater, I drank the cooling liquid.

'Your hands. You need to wipe…'

'No t-time,' I said, 'we're moving.'

I was also shaking. And cold. I'd have taken the driver's flask again if he'd been here. But I forced myself to concentrate to edge past the crater. It was a relief not having to see the details. Butters did, to her obvious shock. 'There were more of them,' she said. 'Heavens, Harry, that must have been awful for you?'

I grunted, relieved she hadn't noticed my weakness. Now I'd seen that I'd be better the next time, I told myself, then remembered that it had only been a horse. I'd not had a close-up of the dead men. This is what you were so desperate to see, I thought, and there's no turning back now.

If anything the noise increased. Butters went quiet. I wondered of she was thinking what I was, that if a shell had landed on the road back there, one could easily land on us. And do the same… I forced the idea away. Get on with the job, I made myself say. Stop thinking.

It was easier said than done. Those sights and smells swelled up to fill my mind. I wished Butters would have kept talking, to cover the awful pictures in my head.

Just when I'd decided my nerves were going to snap, we pulled up by a group of cottages beside the road. One was on fire and the rest smashed, as far as I could tell. Bricks, chunks of plaster and bits of wood were strewn across the road. There was a table tilted on three legs and half a dresser, thrown out of a wrecked house.

A Belgian officer guided our vehicles to the shelter of a still-standing wall. Some shelter, only the front wall of this row of cottages now stood. I was about to climb down when he gestured to us to stay put. There was a patter of metal across the back of the van and the road then we were waved to cross into a building that still had its roof. I hadn't a clue what all that was about.

Inside, huddled against one wall under the exposed roof beams, crouched a line of soldiers. Not British. Whether they were Belgian or French, I couldn't tell.

The officer pointed to his ears and seemed to mime rain. I gathered later that we had to listen for shells that were coming close and that the pattering we'd shrunk from had been shrapnel bullets. In the inferno of noise, how you were supposed to tell which ones were destined for you, I couldn't imagine. I soon learned.

The officer was shaking his head in disbelief and I saw why in the state of our crew. The ladies were deathly pale. Magda seemed to be trying to pull herself together though Lady Helena was eyeing the soldiers. The driver produced his flask, which brought a flush back into cheeks. I took it more carefully this time and appreciated the glow.

'Les blesses?' the driver asked. The officer bid us follow. Outside. Reluctant to lose the inner warmth, I handed back the flask and complied. Outside, the night wasn't cool – the heat from the burning building ensured that. We entered the one cottage that appeared undamaged.

It was another sight to catch your breath, if more orderly than that on the road. The wounded – blesses – sat or lay against the walls of the downstairs room, which had been cleared of furniture. That explained the stuff in the road. Several men moaned and a couple lay still. A hatless soldier glanced up at us from kneeling wiping blood from a comrade's eyes. I looked away.

'We'll need the stretchers,' Lady Hester said, decisive again. 'Butler...'

I was already in the doorway, Butters behind me.

'Careful,' she hissed in my ear and I looked up, for all the use it would have been. We dashed across to the ambulance. Magda followed. A sudden rattle of machine gun fire close by made me jump until I realised it was one of ours. Ours! I was in it, but there was no time to savour the thought. Or inclination. With two stretchers each grasped in both arms we staggered back to the cottage.

Loading was a struggle. The officer went out and came back with two of his unwounded men. They helped Butters and me lift or roll the bad cases onto stretchers and hump them into the slings in the ambulance. Cries of agony as we jolted them didn't ease our nerves, never mind theirs.

I noticed how the other driver filled four of his stretchers with walking wounded. There was room for everyone but as we struggled to fix the heavily-laden stretchers into our ambulance I noted the tricks of his experience. However, the muscle-bursting effort did mean you were too busy to look or think.

Lady Hester and Magda helped a couple of walking wounded to the Wolseley. I was surprised to see Lady Helena absorbed in comforting one serious case. She accompanied him and stayed in the back of our ambulance holding his hand.

It was time to go. The hiss and scream of a shell had me instinctively ducking by the cab. It exploded just past the cottages and soil spattered down over us. I was learning a bit, anyway.

Of course, we had to turn round – something else to remember for next time – which meant extra jolting for the wounded. I let the other two go first and then edged about. Jolting over some bricks brought a shriek from the back but there was nothing I could do.

'Drive slowly,' Lady Helena called. The other two had set off at a fine lick and I was damned if I was going to be left behind. I shouted 'Right' and took no notice, keeping my eyes straining for the place where the crater was. The first two had slowed for it so I was able to catch them up and kept in touch the remainder of the way back. My arms ached as I pulled the Model-T round the tight bend and into the courtyard at last. We'd made it.

I must have expected our job to be nearly over now. That was just one of many misconceptions. The whole place was in chaos. Three other ambulances were ahead of us and a stream of wounded were carried or made their way inside. It was clear we had to help with them before our own lot could be unloaded.

Although I ached all over and could feel myself quivering, somehow I was no longer tired. My ears rang still from the noise but that dulled my hearing so the screams of the wounded sounded less piercing, which was some relief. I took a walking wounded man on my shoulder and led him towards the entrance. After three steps he groaned and had to stop. His weight crushed me. We set off and did two more steps. He kept apologising, I think – he might have been cursing me, for all I know – but little by little we made it up the steps.

Where the next shock met me. If I'd thought outside was chaos, inside was bedlam. I'm not sure what hit me first, the noise, the smell or the sight. What must have been the entrance hall was now packed with casualties – lying, standing, slumped, still, rocking, writhing. A low, rolling moan came in waves from the mass, quieter than the roll of the guns but with an anguish that tore at my heart. While I gagged on the warm, dank stink.

My wounded man went limp and I battled to drag him to a space, stumbling over bodies. Sudden shrieks cut into me though I soon realised they weren't occasioned by my clumsiness, they rose out of the pit of horror as if with a mind of their own.

In the gloom I bumped into a nun with a huge white collar that startled me and she guided me to a side wall where a space had appeared. We lay the man down. She bent to him and I staggered back towards the doors, to flee the thick, rancid miasma that seemed to fill the room.

Outside I gasped in the cold air, my breath coming in sharp gulps, all my energy drained, hardly aware any more of the stream of injury passing me.

'Oo's is this one? Ooever's it is, shift it,' made me blink awake and peer at the line of ambulances, now stretching back round the courtyard. My brain struggled to make sense of the sight. Then the instruction clicked. I should have moved the ambulance to clear the way to the entrance. As I heaved myself up, Butters came towards me.

'Harry, are you all right?'

'Gotta shift ambulance,' I mumbled and felt her arm holding me up, guiding my faltering steps. Next moment I was at the wheel, gaping at a red-faced man whose mouth appeared to be bawling at me and his arm pointing.

When I opened my eyes, there was a dull light. My whole body ached and I didn't feel I could move. Something heavy covered me. It stank of sweat and cigarette smoke. I must have let out a groan because I heard an echo, my name and sensed movement next to me. I blinked and realised where I was. I'd been asleep hunched in the driver's seat. I frowned to my left. Butters was stirring under a blanket, her face a white mask of concern.

'Harry?' she asked. 'You awake?'

If I was, nobody had told my body, which seemed to have locked during the night. I could only groan as I tried to sit up. The night? I blinked and saw the grey walls of the courtyard ahead and to my right. Meaning filtered down to me. I'd parked the ambulance, had I? I must have fallen asleep as I did. Someone had draped an army greatcoat over me. Butters? I nodded what I hoped was reassurance at her. 'What time is it?'

She shrugged. 'Breakfast time.'

I remembered the cheese from yesterday and the nausea welled up. When it subsided, my stomach felt hollow. I was starving. But how were we to eat here? And where were the others?

'We'll have to find where the kitchens are,' Butters said, unrolling herself from her blanket. I found that my legs would work and swung myself to the ground, blundering to the back of the ambulance to meet her.

'We could have slept in there,' I said.

She laughed. 'You dropped where you were. Anyway, you might not be so keen to sleep inside if you look too closely.'

I shivered. Memories of the dark swarmed back and I glanced round the courtyard to push them away. Several ambulances were parked around us. The Wolseley was over the other side. A man in shirtsleeves heaved a bucket of water into the back of one of the ambulances. That made me shudder again at what Butters had said. For the first time I realised that I'd done what I'd dreamed about for the past two months: seen action.

I jammed my eyes shut. The clamour made me open them, fast. My heart pounded. We were in the middle of it now. For the first time, too, no one had turned us away. I was stuck. And too stunned to feel anything, let alone regret.

'Come on,' Butters said and led me to the steps. I think I faltered because she grabbed my arm. I took a deep breath.

The scene was calmer and more ordered. And the noises less frenetic, more a low hum. We hurried through. The smell of antiseptic dominated now but I glimpsed rows of still, covered figures on the floor.

Butters swept me down a long dark corridor, its gloom only broken by a couple of candles guttering low on window ledges. At the far end gleamed a light. And I caught the sound of laughter. From several people. I stopped.

It just didn't seem to fit. How could you laugh? Here? It was as much as I could do to stop gibbering if I let my mind dwell on any one of twenty – fifty – sights and sounds I'd come across in the last twelve hours. Laughter felt even more obscene.

Butters tugged my arm and we lurched into what I saw was the convent kitchen.

'And then I said to him,' the broad Scottish accent paused for a moment as the piercing blue eyes of the speaker flicked up at us from the table where he sat. He was grey-haired and wore a blood-stained once-white coat. 'I can do lots of things,' he went on, 'but sewing two halves of a body back together when you're not sure if they're the same chap, isn't one of them.'

The group sitting round the large, bare refectory table burst into more laughter. With horror I saw they included Lady Hester and Magda, consorting with nurses and men in these dirty and bloody shirtsleeves.

'You two, where've you been hiding?' Magda called, waving us across to join them. I hesitated and felt Butters do the same. Before we could protest a tall, angular man holding bloody hands in front of him gestured us forward and we had no choice but comply. Dumbly I watched him go to the big sink and rinse the blood off his arms.

'Tea, tea, tea, come on,' he said, drying his hands on what looked like a tea towel. 'Is there any bacon left?'

A thin, dark-haired foreign-looking lady jumped up with a grin and went over to the range. I sat down, keeping Butters between me and Lady Magda. The tall man threw himself on the bench beside me – and offered me his hand. It was still wet. 'Dickie Craxton,' he said.

'H-harry B-butler,' I stuttered, unable to look him in the eye. He reached across me and offered his hand to Butters, too.

'You come in with last night's butcher's bag?' he went on, smiling. I couldn't speak.

'Something of a baptism of fire,' Lady Hester said, to my relief. 'We only arrived from England yesterday morning. That's our young expert ambulance driver you've just met.'

I'm sure I went bright red. I could feel tears welling up in my eyes. Mr Craxton – Doctor, I should say – put his arm round my shoulders. 'Welcome to the madhouse. May you bring us luck, though unless you're the Kaiser's grandson, I suspect it'll only be bodies.'

'N-n-no...' I began, terrified at being thought of as a German, until I saw him wink at me. Two plates of bacon and fried potatoes were thrust in front of us and spoons clattered on the table. He handed me one. 'Sorry, all the knives and forks have to be kept for operating. Needs must,' and scooped up a spoonful. Confused and grateful to avoid speech, I followed his lead.

The sweet aroma of the bacon was delirium. I lost myself in it, aware now of the depth of my hunger, while the hum of conversation flowed over me. My head hummed. 'Remember your manners,' my mum's voice admonished me. I glanced up, guiltily, but none of the dozen or so people at the table seemed to take any notice. Both my neighbours were eating with equal gusto. Welcome to the madhouse, Dickie had said. It was certainly that.

Bowls of porridge appeared in front of us and tin mugs of sweet tea. The Scotsman had stopped telling jokes and sat back, eyes closed, smoking. He looked sad. Above and behind him on the walls were paintings, I saw, of the Virgin Mary holding the infant Christ and other religious figures. They all looked sad, too, and I didn't wonder why. It was all too easy here to be weighed down by what was happening. And if the conversation ceased, you could catch moans or cries from the nearby ward. I began to wish the Scots doctor would come out with another funny story to lift the gloom.

Instead I had a slap on my back. From Dr Craxton.

'Now we have to sing for our supper,' he said, getting up from the bench. I did likewise, bewildered and fearful of being shown up if there was singing. My voice was still prone to come out with strange sounds at times. But he was striding to the sink, from which steam now rose. 'War and washing up wait for no man,' he added and plunged his hands into the hot depths – where minutes earlier he'd rinsed away blood that must have come from the operating theatre.

Warm cloths were handed round and we all set to, to dry the pots and pans the doctor washed. Butters tried to stop the ladies from joining in but it seemed here that there were no boundaries. Doctors telling jokes and washing up. Ladies sitting down to eat with us servants. I wasn't sure if I was appalled or intoxicated. The exhaustion of the night and stiffness of sleep had lifted in the warmth and vigour of the kitchen. I began to feel ready to face more horror and madness, whatever it might turn out to be.

Seven

A mistake. It occurred to me that, once we'd finished the washing up, I'd need to check the motors – and clean them out – before we found out what we were to do next. A curt voice broke into my musing.

'Hey, you lads, give us an 'and to shift some a this lot outside.'

I glanced round. The Scottish doctor grinned and held his tea towel out to Butters. Dr Craxton was drying his hands and the only other man besides me, a short, wiry chap who seemed to be a driver, also responded to the call. I decided it must include me and, wondering if the convent's furniture was to be disposed of to make more space for the wounded, I trailed after them.

Until then I hadn't realised how big the convent was. We passed several large rooms off to the side of the corridor and I saw they were now wards, crammed in with beds close together. Nuns with those high-necked collars and other nurses flitted in and out, often laden with piles of bandage or lint. Occasional cries of pain came from opened doors. Further on we had to make our way between stretchers laid on the corridor floor. I wondered again if we were to empty another room for this host we'd brought in last night. But it was a different space we were clearing.

My first thought, when I followed Dr Craxton into the gloomy, high-ceilinged room, was that it *was* empty. And it was – of furniture. As my eyes became accustomed to the dark and glanced down, I saw. Dead bodies.

'OK, this lot, if you would.'

I wrenched my gaze away from a jumbled pile of bodies to see the row of white sheets on the floor to the right. Even in the gloom I'd seen that not all the bodies in that tangle were complete. I forced my teeth to stop chattering and focussed on the wrapped-up bodies.

'Head or feet?' the Scottish doctor asked the little man. I didn't hear the reply.

'I'll take the shoulders,' Dr Craxton said to me. I glimpsed a look of concern on his face, nodded and bent to take what I assumed to be the legs of the figure in the sheet. And nearly passed out. I could feel only one leg.

'All right?' the doctor asked.

'Um, yes,' I gulped. 'There's only one…'

'Ah,' Craxton said. 'Here, you take this end. I'll feel for…' I never did find out what he was feeling for, something to hold on to, I suppose because the Scottish doctor butted in. 'That's the damnation of it, you amputate and still they die. I had three of them last night. It's beyond a joke, Dickie.'

We shuffled out, my inexperience in leading and the awkward shape not helping progress. I turned to go down the long corridor to the entrance hall.

'No, this way,' Dr Craxton said, indicating the kitchen door. I stared at him.

'Nothing to do with the morale of those in the hall,' he added. 'Won't be the first they've seen. Just difficult to pick your way through the stretchers on the floor.'

The kitchen was empty now, except for a large red-faced woman who was scraping turnips. We edged our way round the table and out down the service corridor.

Into an argument. Two young boys, about my age or younger but much smaller, waited with a low cart. They started jabbering in a language I didn't understand. It sounded like a complaint. Dr Craxton motioned to me to put our bundle on their cart and then jabbered back at them, pointing to the main entrance and shaking his head. They shook their heads in reply and trundled off towards a gate in the wall. Across the yard I noticed Butters carrying a bucket towards the ambulance.

'We've pinched their job,' the doctor said as we made our way inside.

'I'm quite happy to give it back.'

'They can't get the cart inside today and as you can see they're not really big enough to lift. But they're worried that if they don't work the nuns will send them away.'

'Aren't they a bit young to be doing this?' I asked, feeling a fraud then kicking myself in case the doctor thought I was, too.

'Aren't we all?' was his reply. 'Apart from wanting to help, I thought this might be useful experience for me. Though for what, I now wonder every day. I'm not sure I could face Smithfield Market after this.'

I mumbled as if I understood and followed him to collect our next burden. We made several journeys from the mortuary then had to remove some corpses from the hall. I started to become used to handling the dead. At least they kept still and quiet. Dr Craxton suddenly looked weary.

'Why are you doctors having to do this work?' I asked.

'Who else is there? We all pitch in at whatever needs doing.'

'When do you sleep?'

He laughed. 'While I'm operating. No...' he added quickly. My face must have expressed shock. 'I'll go and put my head down in a bit. Before we start on the routine cases. It's good to get some exercise in between.'

'Were you a doctor in England, before..?'

It came out before I realised how much of a child's question it was. But instead of laughing at me he looked worried. 'Does it show?'

'What do you mean?' I frowned. He seemed to relax.

'I was barely out of medical school. Doctor McLean offered the chance to anybody in our class and I was the only one mad enough to grab it. Does that sound stupid?'

'No, no,' I gushed, amazed that my opinion was sought and knowing I was in no position to judge. 'Not at all.'

'So what's your excuse for being here?'

'I, er... Well...' I groped for an answer, not sure what to admit. That made him laugh.

'You wanted a chance to see some blood and guts?'

I began to protest but he only laughed more.

'Why deny it? It's the response of all the youth of England. Fortunately for Kitchener. Who doesn't tell them how many of them will end up like those in here.'

He didn't push me further. We finished the job in silence. He sat on the front steps and sighed. I glanced from the Wolseley to the ambulance and was about to tell him I had to go when he looked up. 'Why didn't you become one of Kitchener's boys? You don't seem likely to have failed as unfit.'

I glanced both ways to see if I'd be overheard and gulped. 'I wasn't old enough.'

He looked me up and down. 'Good God.'

I looked at the ground, my face feeling red, regretting being lured into honesty and waiting to be grilled about my age and told I should go home now.

'It doesn't show,' he said.

I looked up sharply. 'No? I thought...'

'Kitchener's loss,' he retorted. 'Anyway, you're better off here – at least they usually aren't intending to aim at us. Have you got long to wait?'

'Wait?'

'Until you are old enough for the mincer.'

'Er, no, well, that is...'

I was thinking better of total honesty.

'Butler!'

Lady Hester's cry let me escape, with hasty apologies. I'd nearly said yes and stopped myself from being honest just in time. I decided later that that probably would have seen me being sent home, no matter what age I looked. Dr Craxton was a good sort but I shouldn't compromise his professional integrity by expecting him to keep too much of a secret. From now on the safest course was to admit to seventeen. Until I decided I wanted to be sent home.

I hurried over to Lady Hester, worried that my absence had caused offence. She did startle me, by her fierceness. 'Have you seen my daughter?'

'Er, no, Lady Hes...'

'Oh, that girl. I should have known it was a mistake to bring her.'

The night's experiences didn't seem to have distracted Lady Hester. I remembered the wounded man from last night. 'Have you tried the wards? She may be…'

'Ah, no.' She swung round. 'Butters!'

Butters came over, holding the bucket. I noticed pale red stains on her wet hands.

'Butters, go and look in the wards and see if you can find Helena. Tell her I want her.'

'Yes, ma'am.' She held up the bucket. 'Shall I..?'

'No, er, Butler will finish that.'

I was handed the bucket. Butters raised her eyebrows at me and went off. I made to go.

'No, give me that,' Lady Hester said, taking the handle. 'I need you to check the engines. The Wolseley misfired once or twice last night.'

I thought that was unlikely but seized the opportunity to give the cars a check-over. They both looked a mess. I could have cried. The mud and dirt was one thing. But no amount of polishing would get rid of the pock marks from the shrapnel and the front fender of the Wolseley was bent. God knows what Lady Hester had bulldozed to do that.

I shook my head and decided all that mattered was that the cars worked. Both the engines were fine, including the timing on the Wolseley, though I thought it best not to let on to Lady Hester.

'I've adjusted the timing a little, Lady Hester,' I said when I came back to the ambulance.

'Thank you, Butler, I knew it wasn't quite right.' She frowned at me and held up a bloodstained cloth. 'I'm not making much impression here, I'm afraid.'

I remembered Carstairs' expression 'It's no use fanning it with your hat' but decided against offering it to her ladyship. I was still in a state of shock from seeing her working.

'A slow job with a cloth,' she said. 'If you could find a brush…'

At that point Butters re-appeared followed by a grim-faced Lady Helena. I saw that her cheeks were wet.

'Don't start, mother,' she snapped as soon as Lady Hester turned to her. 'I've just spent the night comforting a dying man. I can't take any more just now.'

Butters drew me away so their argument went on out of earshot and changed the subject. 'How are you bearing up, Harry?'

'Oh, all right, I suppose. Last night wasn't what I expected. By a long chalk.'

'You can say that again. Do you think now we've done our bit, we can go home?'

'I wouldn't count on it. Lady Hester didn't mention anything like that.'

We looked across to the two of them. Lady Hester thrust the cloth into her daughter's hand and stomped off with the bucket. Helena pulled a face at the cloth and then shook her head at the stains on her dress.

'If we are staying on this kind of work, we'll need more sensible clothes,' Butters said.

'What do you mean?'

'You don't see soldiers parading round in skirts, do you? They're not the most practical…'

'What about the Scots?'

'You'd have us wear kilts? At the knee. Lady Hester would have apoplexy. Though I'm not sure about Helena.'

'Was she really comforting a dying man?'

'Among others. Though I have to say they did seem quite happy to have her in there cheering them up.'

'Are we really much use here?'

'Listen to Mr Impatience. Didn't you like carrying out bodies? Someone has to do it.'

'Yes, but…'

'You wanted to be a hero? Who filled your head with such fancy ideas?' Her face clouded. 'Oh, as if I didn't know.'

I knew as well. 'Why are you so down on Mr Carstairs?'

'None of your business.'

'He taught me a lot about cars.'

'That's because you're not a wom… Oh, never mind.'

I was going to ask why she hadn't learned about cars but we were interrupted. A thick-set young officer in a foreign uniform said something that neither of us understood.

'Ah, English?' he smiled, his accent quite faint. 'My name is Brokelen. Lieutenant Brokelen.' He bowed to Butters, who blushed. 'My role is to organise the journeys of the ambulances from here. Last night you went to Ouistkirchen, I believe?'

His English was very good. I could see Butters was as nonplussed as I was.

'Er, I don't know, sir. We… followed the car until we came to a place, village, where…'

'It was hot.' He smiled again and she blushed more. 'That was very brave of you.'

'We didn't know what to expect,' I said, not knowing where to look either.

'And now you do?'

'I beg your pardon, sir?' Butters asked.

'There's no need to call me "sir",' he replied, still with the smile. 'You aren't in the Belgian army.'

'No, t-thank…' she managed to stutter.

I laughed to myself, knowing that wasn't the reason for her courtesy. The world had turned upside down, even when there weren't shells dropping, and it was no wonder we were all of a tither.

The lieutenant didn't appear amused by our confusion but he did become hesitant. 'Tonight, we need to send ambulances into Dixmude…'

I could see Butters also gaping at him. He must have taken our ignorance – Dixmude might have been near Eastbourne for all I knew – for reluctance because he became apologetic. 'Ah, I understand. That is not a problem. The other English ambulance has had to be withdrawn from so close to the Front Line…'

'No, no, it's not that,' I butted in. 'It's just, well…' I looked at Butters for support but she was looking down. '… we don't know where Dixmude is…' I'm sure I went red at the admission. '…and, besides…'

'Butters! Butler!' Lady Hester called. I turned to see her coming towards us. I gave the lieutenant a sheepish smile but Butters spoke before I could.

'I'm only my lady's maid, sir. You'll have to ask Lady Hester...'

His face was a picture. Of disappointment, I thought.

Dixmude was further along the straight road than the village of last night. As we waited for nightfall, I began to regret my enthusiasm to the lieutenant. If I'd only had my wits about me, we could have been out of this. Though at the same time I felt guilty for those thoughts. Everyone here was so friendly and so busy doing such good work. But it didn't look so good for their health. And out on that flat road, lit up by the dozens of fires, there was no shelter anywhere.

Still, you mug, I told myself, who was the one who landed you into this? Try and act like a grown-up. That only took my thoughts back to my dad. Is that how a grown-up should act? Then I had a momentary panic. What would he be thinking now? Would he have guessed where I was? Told my mum? Would he report me? Demand that I be brought back? I imagined the embarrassment if that happened in front of my new friends.

No, grin and bear it, I ordered myself. You'd only be moping about at home if you hadn't come. And there are lots worse off than you. Those Belgian infantrymen huddled in the barns near the Front Line, for one. How would they feel if, when they were wounded, there was no one to bring them back here to give them a chance of life?

So my head went round in a whirl. I even wondered where Curly was. Training somewhere in England, I expected and felt smug at the thought. He may have joined up before me but I'd made it out here first. I pondered on where our own army was. A place called the Aisne, somebody had said. Things had settled down. Like here, I wondered? Some 'settling'. Without my maps from home I hadn't a clue where anywhere was. Beyond the road to Dixmude.

Yet it was strange that we were working for the Belgian Army and unwanted by our own. Did they really not need us? That wasn't what the wounded man at Victoria had said. I decided it came back to the women. I recalled Sir Brydon's conversation with Lady Hester that I'd overheard in the arbour. 'Go home, dear lady and sit still.'

So we were left to help 'poor little Belgium'. I perked up at that. All the newspapers had been talking about 'poor little Belgium' for weeks but we'd actually come out to do something. We had nothing to be ashamed of.

A big German attack was expected on Dixmude tonight, people reckoned. Everyone's nerves were on edge. I tried to imagine what could be bigger than last night but couldn't. Or rather, I could and preferred not to linger on the idea. "Very hot", the lieutenant had said of yesterday. Would his English run to a more extreme expression for this one?

It was a relief to spend the afternoon lugging mattresses into a new ward that was being set up for the expected casualties. They came from the asylum in the town, so the rumour was. Who knows what had become of the inmates. Their bedding was nothing to write home about. Still, farmyard smells had never bothered me and I reflected that the stains on the mattresses were nothing to what they'd receive before the night was out.

Then there were the sausages. The thin, dark-haired, foreign-looking lady I'd noticed at breakfast turned out to be Italian and was in charge of provisions. She was a wizard. Although the old hands complained they were always eating bully beef and other army rations, she seemed able to find all kinds of sumptuous stuff in the surrounding countryside, war-devastated though it was. And the cook did wonders with it. Maybe it was just my boyish hunger that made anything appetising but I can still catch the sound and smell of those sausages sizzling in the huge frying pans.

Some hours after darkness fell, we were on our way.

The bombardment was lighter than the previous night and some effort had been made to plug the shell holes in the road so we ran into Dixmude for the first time not long after ten. I was behind the Wolseley, in a convoy of Belgian ambulances at first.

However, when we reached the cottages we were stopped by a

Belgian officer, who seemed to object to the ladies' going on. Too dangerous, apparently. Lady Hester lost her rag with him but to no effect. Then Lieutenant Brokelen arrived on a lorry carrying Belgian troops and he persuaded the officer to let us go on. But I had to lead, the car, with the lieutenant in as well, following so that if things became too risky he could order it to turn round and go back.

If I'd felt more comfortable in the convoy, being alone and leading didn't ease my nerves. The sight of the town gave me another jolt. The place had been devastated. I drove down a deserted street in which the buildings on either side were reduced to roofless shells. You could tell this from the fires still blazing in many of them.

The booming of artillery began again. Ahead of us a wall fell inwards into the ruins of its house. On a corner a shop just collapsed like a house of cards. I glimpsed shadowy figures flitting in and out of the ruins but had no time to bother about who they might be. I had to concentrate to steer round the debris, fearful that losing a tyre or wheel here could be disastrous. As it was the journey was too bumpy for my liking – and we were still empty.

Thanks to Lieutenant Brokelen's directions, passed on to me by Butters who leaned out of the cab to see where he pointed, we made it into the town square. It was a broad, cobbled expanse and once must have been imposing. Now it was a wreck. On one side all the buildings had gone and on the others none was untouched. Bright orange flames rose high in the sky from several. The centre was a mass of rubble, some of it covering abandoned vehicles, including, I noted with dismay, an ambulance.

We pulled up in front of a grand building that had once been fronted by columns. Only the two over the entrance still stood upright. As I stopped a pillar straight ahead slowly toppled down in slow motion. A shell bursting across the Square and the clattering of shrapnel bullets on the cobbles cut my musing on that.

We scurried up the steps of what I later learned was the Town Hall to the shelter of the standing columns, where a Belgian officer waited. 'Shelter', I saw at once, wasn't the right word. Among the piles of fallen stone were dark shapes that could only be bodies. Staring at me were the blue eyes of a young soldier, propped against one of the columns. I started forward to help him but Butters hand held me back.

'He's dead, Harry,' she said.

I gaped round, taking in other figures, flinching as more shells dropped on the Square.

'Blesses, ou sont-ils?' Lady Hester asked – the lingo was becoming familiar already – and I came awake, remembering why we were here. And anxious to get out.

The officer pointed down some steps to the side. The tradesmen's entrance. It led to a dark hole, with a faint light inside, by which you could make out huddled figures. Our wounded.

The thought of going into the cellar, even if it did offer some shelter from the bombardment, didn't appeal but the officer had his men bring up the casualties. Butters and I ran down for stretchers and after much staggering and help from the unwounded Belgians we had three of them loaded. I noticed the car already had its complement of two walking wounded, slumped beside Lady Helena.

Brokelen was shouting 'Go, you must go now!' and the Wolseley swung round and screeched off. A flurry of shrapnel bullets like a volley of marbles sprayed across the space it left. 'Mind my tyres,' flashed through my mind as I ducked into the Model-T's cab.

'Wait, Harry,' Butters called, 'there's two more,' and I saw them being carried down the steps. We strapped them to stretchers and heaved those into the racks. With an almighty roar the roof of the building next door fell in and a shower of sparks shot upwards. Butters was shouting something at me but I couldn't hear a thing and shook my head. She seemed to indicate we should go so I leapt to the wheel, as always praying the Ford would start, which it always did, and careered off out of the mayhem.

Our wounded remained quiet, which was a marvel, until I wondered if they were dead. The flames behind us appeared higher than ever and I thought of the Belgian soldiers left behind in that inferno. Out in the countryside the noise of the cannonade from both sides rose to a crescendo. In addition, Belgian machine guns – mitrailleuses, they were called – broke out in a terrifying rattle that made my hair stand on end.

At the cottages we took on four more casualties, two wedged in beside me while Butters stayed in the back to look after a stretcher case we had to lie on the floor. He cried out continuously though one of the ones with me sounded glad to be out of it. 'Ca y est,' he kept saying to me, 'Ca y est.' I didn't know what he meant.

It was the same old chaos when we got back. An argument broke out at the ambulance in front of us because all the men in it were dead. We couldn't unload so I went to see. The row wasn't about who was to blame so much as what to do with the bodies. The nuns just seemed to want the ambulance to move on and let us in but the driver demanded that his passengers be unloaded first. I looked round for Lieutenant Brokelen to sort things out but he must have been inside. Or with the Wolseley because there was no sign of it.

Next thing I knew one of the nuns had my arm and was pushing me and the driver to take a body over to the corner of the courtyard. We looked at each other. He muttered something I didn't understand. Then we pulled out a stretcher and blundered off with it.

In the corner was a pile of what looked like hay. I was letting the stretcher down when it was tipped over and the body slid off: onto, I realised with horror, a couple of others in the straw. Then I was following him back and the rest went the same way, if anything with less ceremony.

His job done, the driver ran back and jumped into his cab. I gasped to get my breath back then remembered the point of that nightmare had been so I could drive closer to the entrance. But I saw that the back of the Model-T was now almost empty. Except for the man who'd been put on the floor at the cottages.

'He died on the way,' Butters said, her face drained. 'Can you help move him? I'm not sure where.'

I closed my eyes.

After we'd finished that – it was slower because, although Butters was tough, he was a heavy weight and I think we both felt the need to show more respect – I looked round for instructions as to where to go next. Again I was puzzled because no one appeared in charge.

'Brokelen?' I asked one of the nuns. She shook her head but gestured as though he might be inside.

'Want me to come with you?' Butters said.

I was too busy choking on the gust of wet, gangrenous chloroformed stink I'd walked into to answer so she followed me through the heaving hall down the corridor. All of the candles had blown out here. We blundered into figures – nurses, nuns, casualties? I could hardly tell – asked passing shapes who didn't reply and peered into wards in a fruitless quest.

We stopped outside a closed door. I hesitated. It wasn't the mortuary but I couldn't recall having been to it before. I was about to suggest going back when the door swung open and light flooded out. I squinted. The Scots doctor's face, flecked with blood, stared through me. He wore an apron smeared with thick red and darker stains. The rubber gloves on his hands ran with blood. His eyes focused.

'In here,' he rapped. 'Clear the table, we have to get on.'

I stepped in, the light still blinding me and nearly slid over on the slippery floor. It was the operating room. I took in the back of Dr Craxton, I presumed, bent over a trestle table at the rear and nurses, their own once-white gowns stained and filthy. On the table in front of me was a bloodied lump.

'Damn, damn, damn, why don't they check properly?' the Scots doctor cursed while I gaped at the sight. Beside me Butters retched. The thought of touching the thing paralysed me. Somehow the other dead had seemed inert. This one looked almost still living. A sudden terror shook me and I nearly was sick. Was it still alive?

'Is he still al…?' I managed to gasp. The doctor looked at me as if I was mad.

'Of course he's not. A double amputation without seeing the stomach wound, what do you think? But if you don't shift him, it'll be someone else's turn to be too late.'

'Is there a stretch…?' Butters began.

'Oh, for God's sake!' the Scot shouted, bundling me to take the head and throwing himself at the bloody trunk. In one movement we swung the corpse off the table and at the wall, where it lay crumpled.

Hardly had it gone when a nurse swilled the surface from a bucket then cleared the water with a sweep of a brush.

I slithered to the door, Butters backing out before me. I glimpsed Dr Craxton glance round and his tired face give a thin smile. As we left the Scot kicked open another door to the side and bawled 'Next!

In the corridor I leaned against the wall, gasping for breath. I felt Butters' hand on my shoulder. I remembered why we'd come down here.

'Where can he be?' I asked. 'He ought to be here somewhere.'

'I thought he left Dixmude in the car?' Butters said.

'No,' I replied. 'When?'

'In the Square.'

'The car left full, the ladies and two walking wounded, in the back with Helena. He wasn't in it.'

'But you shook your head.'

'What?'

'I shouted to you, when we were about to leave, was the Lieutenant still inside?'

'I didn't hear you,' I said. 'I thought you were asking me if there were any more to take.'

We stared at each other. If Lieutenant Brokelen hadn't been in the car, he must be in Dixmude. I'd left him behind. What kind of a useless kid was I?

Eight

'No, Butler, I absolutely forbid it.'

Lady Hester stood with hands on her hips, blocking the way. She seemed to have grown taller. The Wolseley had returned from the cottages with another three casualties, the last for the night.

They knew nothing of the Lieutenant. When we'd helped their wounded inside I asked each of the ladies if they'd seen him. Helena looked distraught at the news he was still in Dixmude and supported my request to take the car back to see.

'You've never driven it,' Lady Hester said.

Well, I had reversed it without a hitch but this wasn't the best time to boast.

'And in the dark is no time to start. Besides, the battle there was reaching a climax. The Belgian officer said their prospects were grim.'

'Then isn't it more important to try?'

'Perhaps in the morning. If things...'

'Tomorrow will be too late,' I shouted. Lady Hester flinched and I knew I'd gone too far.

'Butler, you'll do as you're told. You are under my protection.'

'But, ma'am...' I began.

'No more. It's been a long day. If we're going to be of use, we all need to rest.'

That reminder made me feel drained. Lady Magda patted my shoulder as she left and said 'She's right. Sorry.'

I shrugged at Butters. 'Heartless B.'

'Mind your language. She's right.'

'But...'

'What good would charging about in the dark do? You know how difficult it would be going back now.'

'But leaving him, after all...'

'Grow up, Harry…'

'Grow up!'

'Yes. It's no use if you rush off and get yourself killed just to ease your conscience…'

'I wouldn't get myself killed.'

'Oh, don't be stupid.'

'I'm stupid as well, now, am I?'

Butters gave a deep sigh. 'Let's stop all this. I'm tired, too. We'll achieve nothing by arguing.'

I wasn't in the mood to stop but her next words did leave me stunned.

'Though where are we supposed to sleep?'

Somehow, in the rush of the day, arranging sleeping quarters had slipped both our minds. I nodded at the ambulance. Butters shuddered.

'Not again. It stinks worse today.'

'Doesn't everywhere?' I said. I was ready to drop.

'The kitchen.'

'We can't sleep in the kitchen.'

'Why not? It's warm and the floor's not covered in blood.'

The first part was right. The rest I couldn't vouch for. Anyway, the warmth was enough for me.

When the clatter of pans woke me it was almost light. Butters was stirring on one of the benches. I must have gone out as soon as I slumped down against the wall and been deaf to anything. It amuses me to think how untroubled my sleep was then. After I came back closing my eyes often unleashed all sorts of horror.

'Why are you sleeping here? Want to be first in the queue?'

I blinked. It was Magda, not the cook, who'd set the pans on the range. Her reaction to the answer made me smile, even as I was wincing at the stiffness in my back.

'You mean, we forgot all about you?'

It was the way she made it seem strange that was so amusing. What did she think had changed, just because we were out here? She banged the pots about and I winced at the noise this time.

'We'll have to see about this,' she said.

I grunted and stumbled outside for a wash, since she blocked the way to the sink. I half-expected to find a body in the horse trough but although the surface looked greasy the pump worked and I felt better for sloshing the cold water over me. It was a clear, cool morning, with only the occasional crump of a shell in the distance. The blue sky had a grey haze beneath it that I realised must be smoke rather than cloud. Then I remembered Lieutenant Brokelen. I rushed back inside.

His absence had registered. Butters and I were cross-examined by the Scottish doctor – McLean, I remembered his name was – and a decision taken to send a car to find if he was in Dixmude. I was chafing to be off, until it became clear they were sending one of the Belgian chauffeurs.

'But we..,' I looked to Butters for support, 'know where he was last seen.'

'It was the Town Hall, Harry.' Dr Craxton gave me a smile of reassurance. My anger began to flare. Too young again, was I?

'I can do it.'

'Of course, but Gilbert's little car will be faster.'

'Stuff and nonsense!'

'Butler,' Lady Hester snapped.

I bowed my head and nodded. Once, if Lady Hester spoke, you'd jump to it because of who she was. Here, her voice took on an authority of its own. During breakfast I ate with my eyes down, saying nothing. Gilbert left.

'You'll want to see your quarters,' Magda's voice broke into my seething. 'Where are your things?'

I looked up. 'What things. Your Ladysh…'

She brushed this aside. 'You brought some clothes?'

I shook my head. 'I wasn't…'

'Of course, you weren't meant to be here,' Lady Hester said. I squirmed, looking down again, hoping the accidental nature of my joining wouldn't come out.

'We'll have to find you some spare clothes,' Lady Hester went on.

'There's no need,' I muttered. What did she think we did at home? I could feel my face burning. I stumbled to my feet. 'Where do we go?' I asked.

Butters must have noticed my embarrassment because she ushered me to the door. My eyes were fixed on the ground.

'Harry?'

I had to stop and turn round at Dr Craxton's call.

'Ran away to join up, eh? Good man.'

I turned and shot after Butters.

Cleaning out the cars didn't take my mind off the Lieutenant. The dead I'd seen and handled had been bad enough but, apart from his courtesy and kindness, he was the first I'd known who was... missing, I told myself. The smashed heads and bodies I'd seen wouldn't stop pushing themselves forward to block my thoughts and that shower of sparks from the building next to the Town Hall grew to swallow the whole of Dixmude.

I could have done it in half the time, I kept telling myself. Then the blue Peugeot Bebe (I only learned the name afterwards) roared into the courtyard. I threw down my rag and raced over. The passenger seat was empty. My mind also went blank. No Brokelen.

I stared at the car. Its front mudguards were buckled and the canopy torn off yet I couldn't help thinking it must be a new car. What a sacrifice that was, to bring it here.

A crowd surrounded Gilbert but, infuriatingly, the interrogation went on in French. Even worse, I gathered that he'd not been allowed beyond the cottages. Or not wanted to take the Bebe into the inferno, I thought darkly. I'm sure I wouldn't have been keen to, if I'd owned it. The debris-littered roads would have made short work of its slight body. So the uncertainty remained. That was worse than having confirmation he'd been killed.

I stomped back to the Wolseley and scrubbed at the rear seats, which were now filthy. Hadn't any of those stupid women thought to put a sheet over it, I grumbled, though another part of my mind asked how they could commandeer a clean sheet when so many were used up every day in the wards. Never stopped them before if they needed something, my complaint raged on.

'Butler. Your chance to try out the Wolseley.'

I started. Lady Hester and Helena stood beside the car. I gaped at her.

'In daylight. Always useful to have you know how to… In case of emergency.'

I muttered thanks, scrambled out and went to start her up. Helena climbed in the back.

'Oh, those seats are still we…'

'Don't worry, we're prepared.'

Helena held up a white sheet but sat down without spreading it and I saw what she meant. Both she and her mother wore thick tweed skirts. She seemed to have noticed I existed, as well, which puzzled me.

I drove carefully out of the gates, missing the gears once to maintain my pretence. 'Where should I..?' I asked.

'Where do you think, Butler?'

I turned and stared at Lady Hester. 'Oh… oh.'

At the foot of the hill I swung the Wolseley left and let her go. Only once had Carstairs allowed me to see him test its full speed and I remembered it well.

'Careful, Butler,' Lady Hester said. 'The road. And you haven't driven it before.'

I slowed down, hoping my red face didn't show.

'Sometimes I wonder,' she called over her shoulder, 'Just how much of what goes on in my household I really do know about.'

'I'm sure you know everything, mama,' Helena said.

I kept quiet, recalling what I'd heard by the dustbins on the night of the Ball. Besides, Lady Hester was right. The road did need watching. If I ran into the ditch, it wouldn't be what others had to say that would constitute my greatest shame.

Arriving at the cottages I realised something else. There was no artillery fire. When we stopped at the checkpoint the silence cast an ominous pall over us. We were refused permission to go on. I kept the engine running while the usual argument began, in French so I couldn't understand the details. Lady Hester got back in and when Helena said 'Well?' she just muttered 'waiting' and said no more.

My attention wandered and I watched an old man pushing a cart approach the barrier. Where he'd emerged from, I couldn't imagine. The barrier lifted for him and he stopped under it to engage the sentry in conversation. There were smiles. How, in this place, they could find anything to smile about, I couldn't think. Then I did.

'Stand clear,' I shouted to the Belgian officer, slipped the gear and shot under the barrier before anyone had time to react. I caught the sound of shouts from behind but only pressed harder on the accelerator. I hoped they wouldn't shoot.

'Well done, Butler,' Lady Hester said.

'I just saw…' I mumbled.

'No, it was good thinking. Are you sure you're only seventeen?'

I concentrated on the driving. As we neared Dixmude I could see that even in daylight the glow of the fires had grown since last night.

'At least the artillery has stopped,' I said, to relieve myself as much as anything.

'You didn't hear what he said?' Lady Hester asked.

'No, I…'

'Of course. They've stopped firing – both sides – because the Front Line is now somewhere in the town. They'd risk shelling their own men. That's why he wouldn't let us through.'

What had I done? You stupid fool, I cursed myself. Always thinking you know what's best. And you don't even know what's going on. I spluttered apologies.

Lady Hester put her hand on my arm. 'I'd have done exactly the same. Don't forget why we're here.'

It was whether we'd get back out that occupied me from then on. We were in the streets. The embers in the shells of houses still seethed, flaring up every time a beam or floor crashed down. Then we passed an enclave of houses that had been untouched. Except the heat had swollen their window frames and the glass lay in broken piles on the road where it had been forced out.

As we turned the corner a hail of shrapnel burst against the wall behind us and I saw ahead that the road was blocked. Then, soldiers. I glanced back, reaching for reverse gear.

'They're Belgians,' Helena called.

I squinted to see. They were grouped round a figure on the ground. I eased the Wolseley forward. We had room for one casualty. My nerves took another shock.

Two old ladies dressed all in black materialised from an alleyway on my left and I had to tug the wheel over sharply to avoid them. The car almost stopped.

'We can't take civilians,' Lady Hester said.

'I don't think we need to,' Helena added. 'They're more interested in searching through the rubble.'

We reached the group and Lady Hester climbed down. She seemed to be asking if we should take their wounded man but their officer shook his head. She pointed up ahead and I caught the word 'Impossible', followed by more head-shaking. My reckless decision to bring us here was looking more futile by the minute. All it needed next was for the Germans to appear.

'Can you turn back, Butler?' Lady Hester said, climbing in once more. I had already engaged reverse gear and edged back, praying the old ladies would keep out of the way.

'We're going back empty?' Helena asked. 'That man...'

'Is dying, the officer said. And the Grande Place is in the hands of the Germans.'

I heard a gasp from the rear seat. 'So Guy...' She pronounced it 'Ghee' but I guessed it must be the Lieutenant.

'We have no way of knowing but there are wounded in a tavern in the street to the right past this corner.'

I followed the directions and was able to turn round in an alley just beyond the tavern. It looked shut but when we pushed open the door the interior was crammed with Belgian troops, many of them asleep. The air was thick with cigarette smoke. Whether anyone was in charge it was impossible to tell. A corporal tended to a man with a leg wound that resembled a piece of raw meat.

I searched for any sign of Lieutenant Brokelen and Helena went round hissing his name into dulled faces. If she got any response, it was negative. He wasn't here.

'Deux blesses,' I heard Lady Hester say. She was winding a bandage round the leg of the wounded man with an expertise that surprised me: I remembered Butters' rude comments about the First Aid course at the House.

The door burst open and cut my daydreaming. A corporal barked harsh orders and the sleepers shot awake and hared out of the door. We were left with the wounded.

Lady Hester answered my bemused frown. 'The Germans have broken through. We should go.'

'But mama, we've not…' Helena began.

'Choose two of the wounded. Quickly.'

She struggled to ease the man with the leg wound off the table. I reached her just before he fell and we dragged him to the car. The sheet hadn't been spread but it was too late for that now.

Back inside Helena pointed to a young man hunched against the wall, his head swathed in a bandage. His eyes stared and there were tears on his face. She indicated to me to help but as she took hold of him he writhed and sounded like he didn't want to be moved.

'It'll take too long,' I said.

We ushered a sergeant with a shattered arm to the car. Helena gave a backward glance, wistful, I thought. There's no time for romantic gestures, I told her in my mind. Butters' "Grow up!" followed it as a rebuke.

I did drive more gingerly on the way out, only partly because of the casualties. What the Belgian officer would have to say about my breaching his barrier was also looming. I needn't have worried.

He seemed quite cheerful. Maybe relieved that we had come back. And the sight of their wounded brought out always roused the gratitude of any Belgian. It was only when I slowed to pass a group of soldiers after clearing the barrier that I realised there was another reason.

'Ghee!'

Helena's scream nearly lifted me out of my seat. I swung round. It *was* him. Standing in the group. I searched for damage. There seemed none.

Helena had the door open and was scrambling out. I glanced with concern at the two wounded but she didn't appear to have trampled on them. She wrapped herself round Brokelen. I looked away and then away again from Lady Hester's expressionless face.

When I looked back Helena was leading him over. He was smiling!

'It is good to see you are safe,' he said.

Lady Hester forced a smile. 'And you.'

'But you took a big risk in going back to Dixmude.'

There was a pause.

'We were looking for you,' I said.

'For me?'

'We left you behind, yesterday,' Lady Hester explained.

'No, no, that was my fault. I went back into the cellar and forgot I'd told you to leave. You were not to blame.'

I breathed a silent sigh of relief, the second in a few minutes.

'But how did you get here?' Helena had found her voice again. 'When we came through earlier we didn't see you.'

'The bombardment became so heavy there was no escape last night. This morning the Germans advanced on the Grande Place. We had to leave the wounded. Only those who could travel got out the back way.'

'So while we were in Dixmude you were driving here?' Lady Hester said.

'Walking,' he replied. 'No vehicles were allowed in.'

You're right, there, I thought and hoped he wouldn't ask the obvious question.

Somehow Dixmude didn't fall. The Belgians re-took most of it and French reinforcements were brought in to strengthen the line. I wondered where our lads were. They didn't seem to be much help here. Further east, Dr Craxton said, they were involved in some heavy scraps, he'd heard. If things eased off here, he hoped to go and join them.

Things didn't ease off for long although they settled into a pattern. A few quieter days would occur while the Germans re-gathered their forces for the next offensive. These gave the surgeons the chance to catch up on the less desperate cases and us to bring a bit of order to the place. We even had a day off.

Since his 'error', as he called it, had led us into danger, Lieutenant Brokelen had looked for a way to repay us. Helena seemed to spend a lot of time suggesting how. When he learned we were to have a day off, he came up with the idea of a visit to the sea.

I wasn't overwhelmed by the proposal. Would they expect me to make sandcastles? I'd have preferred our original choice, which was to drive over to Ostend. My nerves were becoming a bit frayed by the ceaseless streams of wounded so the prospect of seeing the bustle of normal life was attractive. However, when the Lieutenant revealed that he could obtain horses for the ladies to ride on the beach, that sealed it.

At least I got to drive the Wolseley again. Butters had to stay behind as there wasn't room for us all. With the Lieutenant sitting beside me in his uniform I felt like an official chauffeur as we passed villagers at the side of the road to the coast. What would Carstairs think of me now?

It was a grey day and the tide was a long way out. The place was called something des Dunes but the sand dunes only ran a little way to the north of the town, which was hardly more than a short row of buildings behind a sea wall. Some of the buildings had been hotels and now they were crammed with refugees, who didn't appear any more delighted at being by the seaside than I was.

I stopped the car at the end of the 'promenade' nearest the dunes. A man arrived leading four horses, which was a relief to me since I regarded horsepower as beneath my dignity now. When the ladies made a show of concern over who should miss out, I gallantly volunteered to remain with the car, 'to make sure none of those ragamuffins steals anything.'

I regretted my brashness as soon as I said it. The Lieutenant looked dismayed and I remembered that those people were his countrymen who'd lost everything. Besides, who was I to talk? I resembled a scarecrow myself.

Brokelen was very attentive in helping them mount up. Helena seemed to need a lot of assistance. Funny, I remarked to myself, when she won the Gamsworth point-to-point last year she managed a much bigger horse than that with no trouble.

I was glad when at last they set off. I watched them ride out towards the distant line of the sea. Beyond, lines of shipping cluttered the horizon. I could make out the sleeker shapes of warships but there was no firing. It might have been a typical Autumn day on manoeuvres.

Except it wasn't. The sands might look as if they stretched away for ever in front of me. They were nothing compared to the vast expanse behind me for who knows how far that was being churned up into a huge, foul grave for thousands of men. It wasn't supposed to have been like this. When would there be an end to it? I wondered. It was difficult to believe anything could stop the madness that had been unleashed.

Maybe the gloominess of the sky impressed itself on me. And the dull emptiness I gazed out over. The receding figures became ever smaller, ever more insignificant. Endless sands and endless war.

That was it, the endlessness. We'd only been here a few weeks yet it felt like eternity. The war would be over by Christmas, everyone had predicted. Where was Christmas? Beyond some unbridgeable gulf.

And how would it be over? By our winning, of course. Well, no one was winning here. It was a battle of push and tug. The Belgians were hanging on, to their own amazement as well as everyone else's, I expect, but that was all. They might shove the Germans back now and then, like in Dixmude, but we all waited for the Germans to gather enough forces to batter their way through. This part mustn't be a priority for them. We knew it was only a matter of time before it became one. And when that happened, who would be there to help?

Not the British Army, I mused bitterly. The full story of the debacle at Antwerp had filtered through to us during the past weeks. 'We came, we swore, we melted away,' Dr Craxton put it. We laughed but also felt the shame. If we were in no position to win, was it merely a question of time before the Germans did?

What would happen then? I closed my mind to the question. After what I'd experienced already I couldn't see how I could fit in at the old life. What would I want to do? Drive cars. Too young. Work in a car factory, like Carstairs had done. Too young again? Maybe. Learn how to be a mechanic? Yes, I'd like that. But who'd let me? You needed your papers signing and I could rehearse my dad's arguments against without any effort. We couldn't afford it. And the unspoken reason that I had to do what he wasn't fit to. The resentment I felt at his cowardice – I'd accepted that that's what it was – flooded back, even though his running off had presented me with the chance I so craved. That was just my foolishness – childishness, I made myself say then argued that it couldn't be because the whole country had felt the same way. Anyway, whatever the cause, the reality was that I was stuck with it.

The horse figures were a long way away to my right, close beside the dunes. I wished some of the refugee children would come up and talk to me, though I knew that would be pointless because none of us would understand the other. Having time for reflection was certainly no rest.

I pondered checking the car. No need, the previous calmer days had allowed plenty of opportunity for that. Polish it up? Ha, a waste of time here. Thinking about practicalities only came round to the work – and the wounded.

You thought you became accustomed to them, the wounds, the smells, the ways in which a human body could be shredded. Then another would force your stomach into your mouth. But, again, it was the relentlessness that wore you down. The guns carried on pounding, we carried on bringing out the wounded and they carried on dying along the way.

Something had just occurred to me when I became aware of the whirring of an engine. I scanned the sky and saw the speck beyond the dunes. 'Oh, Shuggins,' I said aloud, 'I bet it's a Taube.' I looked round, hoping to see somewhere to hide the car. Nowhere. In the lea of a building? Not unless I wanted a wall to collapse on it. Should I make a run for it? Futile, on the bare landscape I'd be an easy target. Run it into the dunes? We'd never get it out. A lone tree just past the side of the end building gave the only chance.

I fumbled to start her and heard the sound of gunfire. The Taube had swung out over the beach and, I realised with horror, was going for the riders. I slammed the Wolseley across the road and slithered to a stop beneath the tree. Its leaves were already dropping but it would have to do.

I dashed out onto the dunes yelling and waving. What I hoped to achieve, I didn't know. The noise of the plane's engine would drown any squeaks I made and the group of horses was a larger target by far. A bomb dropped on the sands not far behind the group. It threw up a thin cloud of dust. One of the horses reared and its rider slipped off, I couldn't see who. As the plane wheeled for another run someone – it must have been Brokelen – leapt from their horse, gathered up the prostrate figure and scurried into the dunes. The other horses scattered.

This action saved the day. As I ploughed my way through the sand towards them the Taube veered this way and that, pursuing lone figures but wasting bombs on empty space. A loud scream had my heart in my mouth. One of the riderless horses had been caught and thrashed about in a heap. I hared for where the fallen rider had been rushed.

It was Helena, starting to come round, though making a lot of it, if you ask me. Brokelen had leaned her against a bank and was endeavouring to comfort her.

'Keep down,' he said, 'You'll draw them to us.'

I scuttled away to the edge of the dunes and saw that the plane had fixed on one target. The other rider came galloping towards me. Lady Magda jumped off, flinging the reins away so the horse bolted, and shouted in my face.

'Helena, is she alive?'

'I think she'll survive,' I said, 'But come away or we'll make too much of a target.'

She pointed out onto the beach, where Lady Hester was weaving away towards the shoreline. 'He's not interested in us.'

I heard more shots but horse and rider still moved, doubling back and forcing the plane into sudden pitches to turn and follow. A couple more bombs dropped into the sand but detonated with a plop. Yet all it would take was a lucky throw...

Next moment a small cloud burst in the sky. Then another. They were well above the plane but at once it ceased manoeuvring and lurched off inland to the north. I squinted to find the source of the shells. A battery near Ostend? I didn't think we were that close.

Lady Hester cantered up to us. The horse slavered and was shaking. Her hair was disordered and her face red.

'Are you all right, Hester?' Magda asked.

Lady Hester smiled at the absurdity of the question.

'I hoped one of the destroyers out there might have seen the plane. Lucky they did, I'm not sure how long I could have kept up this caper.'

Far better than General Haig, I nearly said but stopped myself. Danger drew something you'd never have guessed at out of Lady Hester. Then her expression darkened.

'Helena, how is..?' she began.

'Coming round, ma'am. Lieutenant Brokelen is…'

'Threw herself off deliberately, did she?'

'No, I… er…'

'Where?'

She was off the horse and striding into the dunes, following my pointing arm.

'Some day off, this has turned out to be.' Magda shook her head then smiled. 'We must do it more often.'

I gazed out at the injured horse that now lay still. As an antidote to thinking, the threat of death certainly had some merits.

What the argument was really about I never did discover. Butters claimed that Lady Hester wanted to remove Helena from Guy's presence. When I asked why she just said 'Nothing you need worry about.' Magda told me afterwards that once the Belgians had stabilized the line they preferred to consolidate the medical services into a more official body. The apparent reason, which Lady Hester stuck to, was the need to move closer to the action so that fewer wounded would die in transit.

I had no difficulty in believing this. The loss of men between Dixmude and Furnes had become a big problem. Whether you drove fast to deliver them quicker, with the greater jolting that involved, or drove slower and more carefully, seemed to make no difference. A

113

casualty station in the village, where they could rest before undergoing further stresses, made sense to me.

However, I hardly noticed that there was an argument. A big German offensive loomed. We made several runs during the next few nights. Everything was being cleared in preparation for the massive casualties expected. There even existed a plan to withdraw us to Ypres if the defences were overwhelmed. So all my senses strained to catch a hint as to when the blow would fall. When we did actually pull out, therefore, it was no surprise to me.

The surprise fell a day earlier. The previous night the German artillery bombardment had intensified. Casualties rose and the risks along the road increased. A Belgian ambulance from Ostend took a direct hit. So when I staggered into the kitchen in the morning the heightened buzz of conversation only confirmed my worst fears. Then I saw that Dr Craxton was smiling.

'Were they held, then?' I asked.

'They will be,' he laughed.

'What do you mean?'

'You'll never guess.'

'I don't want to guess,' I grumbled. Then a bright thought struck me. 'The British haven't come?'

'It's more reliable than that.'

'Stop teasing him, Dick,' Dr McLean said.

'Water,' Magda put in.

I frowned from her to Dr Craxton. Shouldn't good news make me feel cheerful? Dr Craxton pulled a wry face.

'The Belgians opened the sluice gates at Nieuport last night.'

I shrugged my shoulders at him as if to say 'So what?'

'The whole area from their Front Line north to the Yser River has been flooded. It's impassable. There can be no major offensive between Dixmude and the sea now. Or ever.'

I sat down and pretended the news hadn't had any effect. In fact, I was confused rather than relieved. Oh, I was pleased but what had struck me more forcibly was 'What happens to us now?' That wasn't an altogether unpleasant feeling but nor was it delight. If we were finished here, would we go home? Again, my response to that was mixed. Relief, reluctance to face the family but also, since it might come to it, regret at leaving this group of people.

'Doesn't that mean the need for an aid post in the village has gone, mama?' Helena asked. Lady Hester didn't look at her.

'Perhaps.'

Helena glanced towards Lieutenant Brokelen, who also didn't meet her gaze. I was musing on why this could be when Lady Hester carried on. 'In which case we will go to Ypres and offer our services to the British.'

'No!'

Helena's shriek made everyone turn. Except her mother who continued to eat as if she hadn't heard.

'They rejected us once, what makes you think they won't simply turn us away again?' Helena persisted.

'Helena,' the Lieutenant murmured.

'We'll be treated like dirt again,' she said. 'Whereas here…'

Lady Hester glared at her. 'I've written to Douglas Haig to tell him to find us a place.'

I nearly fell off the bench. Haig! Shouldn't he be the last person to address? What had she done, threatened to knock him off the horse this time? What if he recognised the Wolseley? Calm down, you're panicking, I told myself. A cavalryman like him probably wouldn't be able to identify a car if it did run him down. But Helena had a point. I couldn't see the Army changing its mind over us.

'So the matter is final,' Lady Hester said.

I glanced at Butters. She seemed as bemused as I was. Not that we counted, of course. It was more a question of knowing which way to turn. Helena stood up.

'For you, maybe. I'm staying here.'

With that she swept out of the door. Mine wasn't the only mouth left half-open. Had it not been for that public falling-out, I'm sure our departure wouldn't have been so precipitate. And consequently have landed us in a far greater mess.

Nine

Lady Hester had never struck me as the impulsive sort. Not that I was exactly observant. She could be fierce when cornered but I assumed she was used to that. Then I recalled the decision to confront the War Office; and the visit to Victoria. But all sorts of ladies were doing that, I told myself. And buying the ambulance followed on from what the wounded man had accused us of. There was, however, the snap decision to go our own way when the Army rejected her help at Ostend. But then, what else could she do?

As usual my thoughts swung to and fro. What weighed me down rather more this time was still the doubt that things would have changed much with the Army. When I thought of Haig I expected them to be worse. Still, never mind, I comforted myself, if he says no, he says no. We'll find something.

What we did find wasn't a comfort.

The Wolseley led as usual and I assumed Lady Hester knew where she was heading. We passed through a couple of the wrecked villages we'd usually only seen to our right, burning in the night. They did look a sorry sight. In the second we picked up two Belgians with serious leg wounds to take on to Ypres.

I wasn't paying much attention to the route. Part of me listened to Butters rambling on about what our troops – by whom she meant her brother and Mr James – were up to and whether we'd run into them and part puzzled about what I'd overheard before we left.

I'd not intended to eavesdrop. I was helping Butters load up the two ladies' things and went to wait outside their room for her to return because the last trunk needed the two of us to carry it. I almost walked in to the doorway when Lady Hester's voice stopped me.

'You know exactly why I don't, why I *can't*, approve.'

'It isn't what you think.'

This was Helena. It didn't sound like a friendly parting.

'It soon will be if we, you, stay here.'

'Your mind is so twisted.'

'With good reason.'

'Oh, don't tar everyone with your own brush.'

'I won't be spoken to like this.'

'Who says? We're not at home now, mama.'

'I knew it was a mistake to bring you.'

'Force me to come, you mean. If you hadn't always insisted on my doing what you…'

'Don't be absurd.'

'Absurd?' Helena laughed. 'It's plain fact.'

'Lieutenant Brokelen is a married man.'

Was he? That gave me a jolt. And threw a different light on the situation. I could sympathise with anyone under the lash of the unreasonable parent, even Helena but now Lady Hester's attitude seemed more justified. Helena didn't sound cowed by this accusation.

'Aren't you forgetting something, mama?'

'Not likely to, am I?'

'We're at war.'

'What's that got to do with anything?'

It had thrown me, too. I knew the Belgians were our allies and we'd come to help them, but…

My musing was broken by the sound of footsteps. I tried to gesture to Butters not to enter the room but she strode in, shaking her head at me as if she thought I'd gone mad.

'Oh, sorry, ma'am, Lady… Can we take out this last trunk? Harry,' she called to me and I slouched in, no doubt looking shifty had anyone bothered to notice.

We carried the trunk out and I heard no more.

'Makes you wonder if they're all right, doesn't it, after all we've seen here,' Butters was saying, still on about her brother and Mr James. I wondered whether to relate the exchange I'd overheard. Did she know Lieutenant Brokelen was married? She'd probably tell me to mind my own business and that anyway it was behind us now. Helena

117

had stayed at the convent. She'd not come out to wave us off though the Lieutenant had. Lady Hester avoided speaking to him, I noticed.

So we'd pulled to a stop in the deserted hamlet before I realised we were approaching one. Was this Ypres? It couldn't be, could it? Ypres must be bigger. And be full of people. Then I saw it wasn't just the silence that was odd. The buildings were mostly intact.

I'd lost any sense of direction. Although Ypres was straight ahead past Dixmude, so I learned, we couldn't follow that road since the Front Line was too close. We were supposed to be on a roundabout route that would bring us up into Ypres from the seaward side. It had become even more circuitous because the flooding had affected some areas behind the Belgian lines as well. Where we were at present I couldn't tell.

We needed some water for the radiator of the ambulance and I went to look in some of the houses. My puzzlement increased. They were undamaged but empty. There was food on a kitchen table, bread with mould starting to appear and the smell of sour milk. A mouse scurried away on my entry.

Where were the people? These had left in a hurry but why? There were sounds of artillery fire off to our right and to our left. This sector was quiet. Had the inhabitants panicked and fled? The place ought to be too far behind the lines for that.

I found a pump and had nearly finished topping up the radiator when a stifled cry made me slosh the last of the water wide of the hole. I screwed the cap, lowered the bonnet and followed Butters, who was striding towards the sound. Round a corner in a narrow lane Magda, grim-faced for once, comforted Lady Hester, who appeared to be choking. Butters bent to help. I started past, to see the source of the trouble.

'No, Butler, don't...' Lady Hester said.

I stopped and turned to Magda. 'What was it?'

She stared at me, her eyes watering and shook her head. This, and Lady Hester's shaking, should have given me pause.

'Don't..,' Magda began.

I seized a spade leaning against a wall and moved forward, raising it as I reached the back of the house, ready for whoever might come at me beyond it.

They were unlikely to do that. The spade slowly lowered until it touched the ground. I leaned on it, unable to move, wishing I had obeyed her command. My head was spinning. I could feel my stomach beginning to lurch. Now I knew why the place was deserted.

There must have been twenty or thirty bodies. Spread out over a vegetable patch. Men, women – and children, I saw. Pitched at all sorts of angles, with all kinds of injury. One body nearest to me was already swelling. The blood had turned black. Beyond them lay several black and white cattle, stiff and swollen, too.

I heard retching behind me. Butters held her hand to her mouth. 'What happened here?' she whispered.

I'd been asking myself the same question. I'd seen piles of bodies before, tossed together by a shell. But there was no crater. There were no wounds that resembled those from explosives. The answer was starting to form.

'Machine-gunned,' Lady Hester's brittle voice confirmed. Since when did you become an expert? I wanted to say but I'm not sure I could have done even if I'd dared. A bloodstained rag doll lay cut in half, its stuffing dribbling out. The sight locked my eyes onto it. I shut them to stop seeing how its owner had died.

'Should we try to bury them?' Butters' voice echoed in my head.

'Some task,' Magda said.

I opened my eyes and flicked a glance over the bodies as I turned away. Digging a grave for that many was impossible for us.

'We could throw some soil over them,' I offered. I'm not sure whether I meant it for their dignity or just to hide the sight. Magda's shout put a stop to our deliberation.

'Come here. Quickly.'

She was beside the car, pointing up the road the way we'd come. 'Cavalry,' she cried. 'Perhaps they may help us to...'

'Except they're not Belgian,' I said. The lances could have been Belgian but I knew what those distinctive flat top-pieces to the helmets meant. 'They're Uhlans.'

'Germans?' Butters gasped.

'How can they be?' Magda asked.

'I don't know, but I'm sure they are.'

We stared as they trotted steadily towards us. They appeared unbothered by any possible threat. How could they be so complacent this far behind our lines. Unless... A horrid possibility began to form.

'Let's go,' Magda urged. 'Those helmets give me the collywobbles.'

'Too late, we've been seen,' Lady Hester said.

The surge of movement in their column did seem to confirm this. I had no time to ponder the implications. Lady Hester bundled me round the front of the Model-T then pointed at a cottage door I'd left open. 'In there. Hide.'

'But...' I protested.

'Don't argue.'

And I found myself shoved inside. The clatter of the horses' hooves resounded on the cobbles. My eyes darted this way and that, searching for something that might give shelter. I went for the larder but decided if anyone came pillaging, they would find me. At one end of the room an upturned tin bath stood on its side on a low ledge. I crawled behind it and huddled up to make sure it would obscure me. I listened as the hooves rang louder then became sporadic. Guttural voices broke the quiet. They weren't Belgian.

An authoritative voice snapped out what sounded like questions. Oh, heck, I thought, now they're in for it. I was about to crawl out to join the others when I heard someone replying. Lady Hester. So she spoke German, too?

The conversation carried on. The German's tone became milder and I suspected Lady Hester was asking him questions. Did they think we also were Germans? This was a very different-sounding Lady Hester from the one I'd overheard quail in front of her husband.

Then she gave what I guessed was an order, in which the only words I understood were 'Magda' and something like 'verwunden' – German for 'wounded'. I recognised that from some wounded German prisoners we'd brought back from Dixmude when the street fighting was at its heaviest. What was going on? I caught the sound of boots on the cobbles as if someone – more than one man – was moving about and a cry of pain. The Uhlans must have a wounded man with them.

The shuffling went on for a while. I strained to hear but could make little sense of it. At one point Lady Hester cried out what sounded like a warning. I longed to creep out and take a peek but restrained myself.

Then there were more angry cries. More rasped questions. Lady Hester's voice stayed steady but now and again it wavered. The German barked orders, which brought protests from Lady Hester, shouted down roughly. More clattering of boots, more hurried this time, and shouting, followed. Thumps as of someone falling. Had he hit Lady Hester? This almost had me rushing out but there came loud cries of pain. Men's. I understood. In opening the tarpaulin on the back of the ambulance they must have found the wounded Belgians.

An angry exchange followed, the German accusing and Lady Hester protesting, I guessed. At length the German shouted an order and there was more clattering of boots. Cries of pain drowned Lady Hester's protests. The clattering faded slightly. Lady Hester kept up a steady stream of accusation, the way I once heard her addressing a footman who was being sacked for thieving. The German made no response.

Several shots shattered the calm and reverberated in my tin box. Lady Hester gave a furious cry and I caught another scream then sobbing. The sound of boots clattered back and a different German voice – more satisfied – seemed to be reporting. The first German acknowledged this and gave more orders, also in a measured tone. I hoped he wasn't telling the ladies to leave: Butters' fumbling attempt to drive the ambulance might alert them to my absence.

Instead, boots clattered again. A cottage door sounded as if it was kicked in. I went cold. Were they searching for me? How could they know? The door to my hiding place creaked open on its hinges. Footsteps came in. Would it be too tempting to use my tin bath as a target?

I held my breath. The footsteps stopped. There was sniffing. Oh, God, had he smelled me? He coughed, with disgust I thought. The footsteps resumed and a door – the larder door? – was wrenched open. Breaking glass echoed inside my tin. A cork popped and someone sniffed before drinking, it seemed. There was rummaging, things fell or were thrown to smash on the stone flags.

The man must have come out into the room again. He breathed heavily but with satisfaction. Was he now going to search in here? I waited, chest heaving. I'd taken in a deep breath but I couldn't hold it much longer.

'Hans, schnell,' a voice interrupted from the doorway. This led to a grunted exchange. The newcomer withdrew, followed by Hans. I let out my breath slowly. A crash shook my refuge and I had to press my hands against the sides to stop it toppling off the shelf. My eyes stared, my heart pounded. I waited for more. A slight bulge showed in the bottom of the tin bath. The target practice had been with a full jar of something.

The only noise was of horses being mounted and hooves rattling on the cobbles. Then the German who'd done all the ordering barked out more instructions, I presumed at Lady Hester, before, with a shout, urging his horse into action. The troop clattered off, the way they'd come, it seemed. Puzzlement joined my fear.

I stayed hunched and immobile until the hooves had gone. My body shook and my mouth was dry. The voices outside were low. A scuffing noise made me start.

'Harry? Are you in here?'

I let the tin bath topple over and startled Butters. Her face was a deathly pale. I held up a hand to allow her to pull me out of my foetal position. She steadied me while the circulation returned to my legs. Neither of us spoke. I followed her outside.

Lady Hester sat on the running board of the Wolseley with her head in her hands. Magda leaned over the back. For a moment I thought she'd been shot but she stirred and peered at me. 'They didn't find you?'

'He hid in the bath, ma'am,' Butters said.

Lady Hester looked up. Her face was stained with tears. Her glance drew mine along the street. Two bodies, our Belgian wounded, lay sprawled against a wall.

'They shot the wounded men,' Magda muttered. 'To display the nobility of their cause.'

'I heard,' I said.

'And us, as well, no doubt, if it hadn't been for you, Hester,' Magda added.

'How I hated those lessons, Magda. But Frau Henscher was obviously a good teacher.'

'I was praying your accent wouldn't give you away.'

'I was praying he wouldn't address *you*. They were Prussians. I said we were Swiss. Red Cross. It satisfied him. That's the only reason he accepted we'd got Belgians, I think.'

'Isn't it risky to talk now?' I murmured, indicating the ambulance.

Lady Hester gave me a searching look. 'You made out that as well, did you? Don't worry, he's unconscious.'

I nodded. For a few minutes no one spoke. I suppose, like me, they were trying to get their thoughts straight.

'What I couldn't work out,' I said at length. 'Was where we are.'

'Behind the German lines, would you believe?' Magda said.

'I thought we must be, but how?'

Magda arched her eyebrows but said nothing.

'My fault,' Lady Hester sighed. 'I'm sorry, somehow with my stupid certainty that I knew what was best I must have blundered through no man's land.'

'I didn't mean it was your fault, Lady Hes…' I began then realised what I was saying and stopped.

She gave me another of those hard stares and I thought I was going to be put in my place. Instead, she smiled.

'It certainly wasn't your fault. How could it not be mine?'

'What I meant, your Ladyship…'

Now she did cut me off. 'Can we find some other form of address than this? Magda?'

'He can hardly call you Hester.'

'Then I suppose ma'am will have to do. I'm sorry, Butler. No, wait. At least I can call *you* by your Christian name, er…'

'Harry, ma'am,' I offered, thoroughly confused.

'Harry, good. This is the last place for English reserve. You were saying, Harry?'

Was I? I'd forgotten. 'Oh, yes. We've crossed the Front Line, you say, but there was no line. We'd have known. We'd have been turned back on the Belgian side. It was no one's fault.' I realised again it wasn't my place to tell her what was what but I wanted to clarify it in my own head. 'What I was trying to say, La… ma'am, was, what's going on? If there's no Front Line, is this a gap that neither side has realised has opened up. That's not possible.'

'Almost the Uhlan officer's exact words, Harry. That's what they were attempting to establish. He suspected they might have stumbled on a gap. They came here to water the horses before going on to check.'

'Then we need to go back and warn the…'

'That's the way the Uhlans went,' Magda said.

'And we've been ordered to take their casualty to a dressing station further ahead.'

'You're not going to? Ma'am?'

'I'm trying to think *what* to do.'

'I could take the car and go back…'

'Harry…' Butters cautioned.

'We can't just surrender,' I protested.

Lady Hester shook her head. 'No.'

I breathed a sigh of relief. Too soon.

'Not to some forward unit like we've just had the pleasure to meet,' she went on.

I didn't understand. She frowned at me and glanced down the street. 'They only spared us at first because we were women. From some reports, we may have been lucky in that.'

'I don't follow you, either, Hester,' Magda said.

Lady Hester's thinking had left me behind, too. When she explained, I was stunned.

'I think this stage of our war is over,' she said.

I groaned. 'Surely, if we hid the vehicles, waited until nightfall, we could make a dash for it in the dark?'

'It's too dangerous. If we're caught we *will* be shot.'

'I don't care. Ma'am.'

'Well, I do. And you're my responsibility.'

'Better than being a prisoner...'

'Harry, no more, thank you.'

So much for our new mateyness. Put in my place, I stared down at the ground. Lady Hester gave a deep sigh.

'Our best chance is to drive on, fast, passing any checkpoints by claiming our wounded man has to be taken straight to hospital. Then, when we are far enough behind the lines, to surrender ourselves to the highest ranking German we can find.'

No one said anything. Whether it was despair or like me they were thinking about what happened next if this fanciful idea actually worked, I don't know.

'Are we agreed?'

Did it matter if we weren't?

'Will we be held prisoner, ma'am?' Butters asked.

'I will ask that we be repatriated through Holland.'

So, going to tell the Germans what to do now, was she? Her new-found self-confidence must have gone to her head. The Swiss ruse wouldn't last long once they started asking questions. I suppose our best hope was that they'd be glad to get rid of us. Being harangued by Lady Hester wouldn't aid their war effort.

'What alternative have we got?' Magda said.

'We couldn't make for Holland ourselves?' Butters asked. I closed my eyes, shaking my head. I remembered the maps I'd cut out of the newspapers. 'It's too far. And if we were caught driving along behind the German front lines, they'd suspect we were spies.'

'Harry's right,' Lady Hester said.

I congratulated myself on being back in favour. As usual my satisfaction received its immediate come-uppance.

'However, we will need to take some precautions. Harry, you'll have to dress up as a woman.'

'What?' I spluttered. Magda laughed out loud.

'You can't pass for a German if we're stopped,' Lady Hester added. 'And in that case they will take you for a spy.'

I doubted if I could pass for a woman, either, and when they saw through that disguise wouldn't I seem an even more devious spy? But I gave in without a protest. What was the use? I'd be over-ruled anyway. The whole thing was a crazy stunt and this might save me from being shot on sight.

They told me that in Magda's full-length dark green dress and a bonnet of Butters' I'd pass for a woman anywhere. I gritted my teeth through the jokes.

'You have a sweet face, Harry,' Magda laughed.

What could I say to that? I stood there, hoping my grim expression would make them relent. Some hope. Butters joined in with a reservation. 'He didn't ought to be too attractive, ma'am. In case...'

I squirmed. Being shot on sight might be preferable to the indignities this was piling on me.

'Rub some dust on his face,' Magda suggested.

'No.' They stopped and stared at me. 'Soot, from the exhaust pipe would be better. Hide more.'

It would be even more convincing if they all did the same, I thought of adding, but kept my mouth shut. Besides, we were dawdling. If the Uhlans returned...

Lady Hester echoed my fears. 'We should be going.'

'The Belgian wounded, ma'am,' Butters interrupted. 'Shouldn't we..?'

I remembered where the spade was, nearly tripping over myself in the dress. It was an excuse to pull it off, for a while at least.

We had to bury them next to the pile of bodies, where the ground had been tilled and was soft. I found a second spade and the ladies made a show of helping, though only Butters had much idea. The sight, and smell now, from the dead villagers intensified the misery of the work.

'Had those Uhlans killed them, ma'am, the villagers?' I asked at one point when I stopped to rest, the soot running down my cheek with the sweat. I rubbed it all in.

'I don't think so. I didn't dare mention them. They'd obviously done something that whichever Germans came through here didn't like.'

Such as dressing up as a woman, I thought as I struggled back into my disguise. Something else struck me.

'Do I have a name, as a woman?'

'Harriet,' Butters grinned.

It sounded too posh to me but I doubted if the Germans would worry too much about that. When they shot me. The others greeted my new incarnation with similar jollity. Then Lady Hester looked serious.

'Butters?' she asked.

'Yes, ma'am?'

'I don't know *your* Christian name.'

'No, ma'am. It's Lily.'

'Lily. Very well. Lily. Good. I shall call you "Lily" from now on.'

That's all right, then, I thought. We're all ladies together now. Let's jolly well go home and prepare for the Ball. I never was one for dancing.

Ten

So began our journey through occupied Belgium. This wasn't what I'd expected. Mind you, not much had been, so far. Yet I had an uneasy feeling things were going to deteriorate even further before long.

After a while the road ran along an embankment beside a canal and I realised how the gap between the lines might have opened up. On both sides what was I took to be a lake, until I remembered the opening of the sluices. The river must have backed up and the spillage reached a long way inland. We'd passed a similar feature sometime before we reached the village, I vaguely recalled, but I'd taken no notice, assuming we were still in Belgian territory. So as the waters caused the opposing armies to shift, a gap had opened between them? I still thought I should have gone back to alert our side. What were a few horses? The Wolseley would soon have seen them off. As it had once before.

My attention was brought back to the present. Lady Hester's deception met its first test. To my amazement, it passed. We ran into a large body of troops marching towards the gap behind us. They kept to one side of the road and allowed us to pass. Then we came to a checkpoint.

I could feel my pulse quickening as the guard raised his hand. Lady Hester's shouting wafted back to us but the soldier didn't appear rebuffed. My heart thumped to see him order two others our way. I huddled back into my disguise, for the first time glad I wore it.

The two went past me and I heard them at the back. I kept my gaze on the floor. Then they returned. A question barked close to. I nodded, hoping it was the right answer. But the question – or something else – was repeated.

I started. Lady Hester had come up and was jabbering at them. I glanced at Butters. Her face was also looking down. There was a guttural acknowledgement from one of the Germans, who then shouted some instruction. The sound of boots on the pave made me risk a look. They were walking back to the Wolseley. Lady Hester followed and climbed in. Had we survived? It seemed so. The Wolseley set off and I did, too.

How many more times would we have to go through this? The chances of pulling off the trick every time felt remote and a dull resignation began to settle on me. Butters said nothing, either. Other, practical difficulties swarmed over me. At some point we'd need petrol. How would Lady Hester persuade the Germans to part with that? Or maybe she assumed we'd have surrendered before then? That thought hardly cheered me up.

We came to a village that wasn't much damaged and slowed, as if Lady Hester hoped to find a headquarters but then shot away. It occurred to me to ask the villagers to hide us but there were Germans about and I decided it was a silly idea: too dangerous for the Belgians and, for us, too awkward to hide the vehicles. And we still had our casualty in the back.

We drove through a couple more villages without stopping. The concentration of troops and materials grew larger, increasing my sense of imminent detection all the time. We were stopped again but Lady Hester's protestations cut off any investigation. Not long afterwards, on a stretch of road bare of traffic, the Wolseley stopped.

Lady Hester strode back to us and pointed to the left.

'There's a chateau in the trees. We'll go and see if it's a headquarters.'

I could only nod. The end so near hit me hard.

We turned off onto a cobbled driveway between tall poplars. It was an ornate sort of place, with turrets at the corners. I remembered a couple of similar ones from our early days. But the absence of vehicles told me it looked an unlikely site for a headquarters. In fact, there was little sign of life anywhere. Those visions of hiding away surged back. I followed the Wolseley along the drive that curved in front of the broad steps to the entrance.

My hopes of hiding received a smack. A German guard stood at attention beside the double doors. As I eased to a halt one of the doors opened and a young woman, wearing a green dress much bolder than mine, dashed out waving to Lady Hester to move on and round to the back of the chateau. Oh, God, maybe it *is* somebody's headquarters, I thought, and we're off to the tradesmen's entrance. We complied anyway.

The rear of the building was plain, red brick. What surprised me was the crowd of women, also in gaudy dresses of several colours, who surged out of the rear entrance and crowded round the Wolseley. If this was a headquarters, I couldn't for the life of me think what regiment this was. Maybe the Germans hoped to jig their way to victory.

I stopped and sat watching while the commotion went on.

'I'd better go and look at our casualty,' Butters said. 'With luck he might have died.'

'Don't leave me on my own.'

She laughed. 'I don't think you're in any danger from these, Harry.'

I should have told Lady Hester to inform everyone we met that I was deaf mute. I didn't know who the danger would come from but I felt certain it wasn't far away. Butters' cry had me panicking that it was behind us. I swung round as she appeared at the passenger side.

'He has died.'

That did add to my comfort, I'm sure. A spy, in disguise, carrying a dead German around. Who was going to believe we hadn't done him in?

'Are you sure?' I asked. It sounded stupid as I said it.

'I'll go and tell Lady Hester,' she said.

'You don't need to, she's coming this way.'

She had to swat away those women to do so. Closer to, they looked nothing like anyone military. And the jabbering never stopped.

'We have something of a problem here, I'm afraid,' were Lady Hester's opening words.

'So do we, ma'am,' Butters said.

Lady Hester ignored that. The women crowded close in around her. I'd not seen so much powder and bright lipstick since the night of the Ball. But it suddenly struck me that their babbling didn't sound like German. Yet the guard at the front was German…

130

'These women want us to take them with us,' Lady Hester said. She looked very uncomfortable and I could understand why. With them on board how far would the Swiss Red Cross ruse last? Even under blankets those faces would pass for wounded German soldiers less than I could for a woman.

'Do they know who we really are, ma'am?' Butters asked.

'I don't think they care. They just want to get away from here.'

'Looks better than half the places we've seen,' I said.

'Yes, er…' Lady Hester looked flustered.

'Anyway,' I added, 'they won't want to travel with us. In the back. The wounded German has died.'

Lady Hester only seemed to be half-listening. She broke off to remonstrate with the women and whatever she said calmed them down a bit. She turned back to us and went on.

'I don't see how we can refuse them.'

'*How?*' I spluttered. 'They'll give us away as soon as anyone stops us.'

'They think they know where a German headquarters is not far away.'

'Then can't they walk there, ma'am?'

'They're afraid the guard would catch up with them.'

'Well, if they're so worried about that, what's the point of giving themselves up to a lot of Germans up the road?'

'It's, er… delicate. Butters, might I speak to you?'

She drew Butters away and muttered something to her, with sideways glances at me. What a palaver. If we were going to have all this fuss every time we met somebody who wanted helping out, we'd never escape from our own mess.

The women seemed be addressing me but I avoided their eyes and shrugged. No one appeared to call attention to who I was, which did cheer me up. I needed something to.

Butters came back, while Lady Hester returned, her crowd in tow, to the Wolseley. Magda leaned against it, in conversation with an older woman who'd emerged from the chateau.

'What was all that about?' I asked.

131

'Not for your ears, Harry.'

'Eh? Come on, Lil, tell me.'

'Promise not to let on?'

'Cross my heart,' I said. This was worse than Curly's gang.

'It's house of ill-repute.'

'Is that all? What's the fuss about, then?'

'Do you know what a house of ill-repute is?'

'Course I do,' I lied. 'It'll put a curse on us if we don't clear off.'

Butters laughed. 'It's a brothel.'

'Is it?' That didn't enlighten me much. I looked at the red brick again. The front seemed far too dignified for whatever a brothel was. Maybe it was only at the back.

'Those women have been forced to work here.'

'I can think of worse places to work.'

'They're desperate to get away.'

'I can hear that. But if they are desperate… why do they want taking from one lot of Germans and delivering to another?'

'This was an officers' brothel. It's being changed to one for ordinary soldiers.'

I couldn't see what difference it would make. 'If we don't get a move on, the whole German army will be here and no one will care either way,' I said.

'Yes, I don't know why Lady Hester's taking so long to decide.'

I did but something else came to mind. 'We need to dispose of our dead body first.'

'Bury him, you mean?'

'I don't care. Dump him in the shrubbery. His mates didn't give the Belgians much thought. We just have to be shut of him, before…'

As if reading my mind, the sound of engines approaching stopped me.

'Quick,' I gasped, running to the back. I grabbed the two handles of the stretcher and jerked it out. The weight tipped it over and the body slid off, evading my grasp.

'You'd have called me butter-fingers if I'd done that,' Butters laughed. I grunted and we struggled to lift the corpse back on.

'Never mind the stretcher,' I said. 'Get his arms.'

We bumped him onto the ground and dragged him to the thick bushes under the window. With a heave and much shoving we had him out of sight. The engines cut out and I realised there was silence. The women had all stopped jabbering. But it was us rather than the engines that they gaped at. I stumbled back into the cab, panting and wishing that Lady Hester would give the order to go.

She didn't. If she had intended to, she was already too late. The sound of boots hurrying on the gravel grew loud. A German voice barked what sounded like orders in my ear. I looked up to see Magda waving me to come. Was that what the order was? I stumbled out of the cab and let myself be bundled to join the others, hoping my boots wouldn't be noticed. Still looking down I wormed my way behind Lady Hester. A glance showed me half a dozen German soldiers behind a sergeant, presumably the one who'd ordered me to move. With relief I saw they weren't Uhlans.

After much shouting and fruitless protests from Lady Hester we found ourselves forced down into in what must have been a wine cellar. That's what Butters claimed, though it was empty now and covered in dust. A couple of grilles gave faint light from which the low, arched ceiling of dull brick could just about be made out. Making out the clank of the thick wooden door and the rattle of an ancient key was less difficult. Even if our situation wasn't. We were locked in.

'God, Hester, this brings back memories...' Magda's laugh tailed off as Lady Hester glared at her. I couldn't see the funny side, either. Was Magda used to being locked in wine cellars? Then she shuddered.

'As long as there's no force feeding,' she said. All that did was remind me of my hunger. I wouldn't need force feeding, whatever that was.

Lady Hester also shivered and nodded towards the other women. 'They must think we're all part of the same...'

My eyes followed her nod. It wouldn't take much for any German to realise the difference. When they did we'd be for the high jump so maybe she thought being confused with the rest was an advantage. Not that it seemed to give her much comfort. I could tell Butters was agitated, too.

'Why were the Germans so angry, ma'am?' Butters asked in a hushed whisper as Lady Hester gathered us together on one corner.

'These… women's anxiety to escape had been noticed. Our captors were sent to prevent it.'

Which they'd done just in time, thanks to all our bumbling about, I reflected. But I kept quiet.

'What do we do now, ma'am?' Butters asked in a low voice, unusual for her.

'Wait and see.'

Lady Hester seemed cowed as well. I was going to suggest trying the grilles to find out if we could break through them when Magda spoke.

'We have to remember Harry, Hester.'

Oh, good, I thought. Are they going to help me escape?

'What do you mean?'

'When, if, they discover he's not a woman…'

The three of them stared at me.

'Don't worry about me,' I said airily. I couldn't see any of us getting out of this so what did it matter?

'Don't be silly, boy,' Lady Hester snapped.

Shot down again. Huh. So what were they going to do to protect the little boy? I awaited the answer.

'We also have to think how we are going to respond,' Magda said. The concern for me hadn't lasted long. Besides that, she looked too serious for my liking.

'Respond to what?' I asked, since Butters shrank at the suggestion. What else could we do but beg for mercy? Even if, from the evidence of our own eyes, mercy didn't seem to be that abundant in this part of the world.

Magda gave me no answer to that, either. All three were avoiding my eyes. Obviously the 'boy' no longer came into it.

'I shall demand to see the commanding officer,' Lady Hester announced.

'There may not be one,' Magda replied, 'from what the women said about…'

'Yes, yes…' Lady Hester's agitation had grown. I looked at Butters, hoping for some enlightenment. She shook her head, as if I shouldn't bother her with questions. One of the Belgian women approached and began talking rapidly to Lady Hester and Magda, in French, I presumed. I took the opportunity to press Butters.

'I can't work out what they're going on about, Lil.'

'It's probably better you don't know.'

'But I don't like mysteries.'

'I'm surprised your Mr Carstairs didn't enlighten you.'

'Carstairs? What's he got to do with this?'

But the woman went back to her friends and the ladies turned to us again.

'They're going to rush the guards when the door is opened,' Lady Hester said. 'They want us to join in.'

'What, spread out and surround them?' I asked. If anyone in Curly's gang had come up with a plan like that, we'd have groaned and given him the bumps.

'You're the military expert, now, are you, Harry?' At least Lady Hester hadn't called me 'boy' this time.

'No, Lady… ma'am, but look at the doorway. There's only space for one person at a time. One woman can't overpower a guard, can she?'

'It may be better to try,' Magda said.

I gaped at her. She didn't appear to be joking. I was fast revising my view of Curly's one military tactic – running away. Admittedly, in this situation here, that didn't offer much opportunity.

'Do we really want to rile them further?' I countered. Again I was ignored. It was beginning to grow dusk outside. I turned away and studied the door.

'Did you agree, ma'am?' Butters enquired.

'I said we'd follow their lead.'

Someone was turning the key in the lock. With all the chatter no one heard it.

'Watch…' I began when the door flung open and two Germans were inside, rifles lowered at each group of us. I waited for the charge. There was space. No one moved.

The German sergeant who'd barked orders at me strode in and glanced up and down at each group. I was relieved that his gaze didn't linger on me. The women's gaudy dresses seemed more of an attraction.

'Now look here,' Lady Hester said then switched to German. The German snapped something, taking out his pistol. Whether it was what he said or the levelling of his pistol at her that stopped Lady Hester, I couldn't tell. Her mouth hung open and she turned pale. The German pointed to two of the women and barked something to the soldier on his left. The soldier gestured to one of the women, the one in a bright green dress, to come forward. When she hesitated he freed one hand and seized her shoulder. Now, if ever, was the chance to rush him but the others did nothing. The soldier swung her out of the door.

The second woman, also one of the younger ones, in a red dress, obeyed the order without demur. The soldiers backed out of the doorway behind the sergeant, the last man to leave leering as he pulled the door shut.

No one spoke. Magda and Butters looked as pale as Lady Hester. One of the women began to sob.

'I'd be crying if I'd messed up my plan like that,' I said. 'What were they waiting for?'

'Oh, do be quiet,' Lady Hester snapped.

Why should I? 'When he lowered his rifle. If there was the chance to rush, that was i…'

Lady Hester's glare froze my flow. Another woman began to weep. I threw myself down against the wall under a low arch. I couldn't resist a parting shot.

'It's a bit early for the wailing. They shoot you at dawn. Tell them to start then.'

I thought Lady Hester was going to give me both barrels but she swung away. Magda looked at me and forced a smile. She muttered something to Butters. After a while Butters came over and looked down on me. 'You are making a fool of yourself, Harry, with those remarks.'

'If someone would tell me what's going on, I'd know better, then, wouldn't I?'

Butters hesitated. 'They didn't select those two women to be taken away to be shot.'

'Didn't they? Isn't that good n…'

'No, it isn't, Harry.'

I stared at her. 'Oh…' I said as the realisation hit me. I could feel my face burning with shame. 'I see.'

I'm not sure I did, fully. Butters went on, 'And that's what's so… upsetting for all of us.'

I closed my eyes to be able to think. I saw now why Magda had raised the question of what would happen when they realised I wasn't a woman. If they went along with the Germans, they might escape. Except the thought of that horrified them. If I were a woman, would I take that way out? I couldn't imagine it. I looked at the other group of women. They seemed to know what was what and they had wanted to escape.

I couldn't get any of it clear in my head but I had to do something. I sauntered over and slumped down beside the door. Once it opened I'd be hidden by it when someone walked in. If I could seize his rifle… I knew it was stupid so I said nothing to anyone. What if two men enter, like last time, I asked myself? I should have told Butters my plan and stationed her at the other side of the door. Acting together we might manage to surprise them. As it was…

I debated whether to go and ask her. Before I could, the key turned in the lock. Not quietly this time. I pushed myself up. I glimpsed faces turn to the door. It shot open, swinging back on me as I moved forward, halting my momentum. I staggered back.

Two figures stumbled in. The door slammed shut. There were cries. Of fright, relief? I wasn't sure. The two women embraced their friends and the cries sounded like relief. I was too stunned by the failure of my plan to take much notice but Lady Hester went across to them. I suppose it was lucky I did fail. Otherwise I'd have grabbed the woman in the green dress round the neck.

I went to join the other two.

'You weren't going to jump out and save us all, were you, Harry?' Magda asked, the smile back behind her eyes.

I shrugged and threw myself down in my old place.

'I'm grateful,' she added. 'But don't put yourself in danger for us.'

I glanced up. Her smile had gone.

'I don't need to,' I said. 'We're in enough as it is.'

Lady Hester came back.

'That was quick work,' Magda said.

'We may have a stay of execution,' Lady Hester replied.

That's one way of putting it, I thought, frowning. Lady Hester must have seen my puzzlement. 'There seems to have been a Belgian breakthrough. The troops that were due here and most of the guards have been rushed to fill the gap. So, we're being left here…'

Did her voice tail off because she'd realised what I had? That if we'd stayed in the village, we might have been rescued by now? Anyway, a quiet night was in prospect. That appeared to cheer the women up somewhat.

Who was I to argue?

Although I was exhausted I had an unquiet night. From embarrassment, more than anything. The women did their toilet under the archway beside ours. They sounded quite open about it all but we could hear everything. The ladies and Butters seemed upset by it, also. I wondered about asking Lady Hester if we should tell them about me, in case it might calm them down but I couldn't think how to put it. My bones ached and wouldn't let me settle.

Pangs of hunger gnawed at me. There was no water, either. During the night the boom of artillery fire rolled across the silence but sounded distant. The hope of being freed from here by a Belgian advance felt remote.

Magda became more unsettled as the night wore on. Her sighs and fidgeting kept me awake.

'You all right?' I asked at length, though even I could tell she wasn't.

'I thought these days were over.'

'You mean you've done this before?'

My gormless gasp did make her smile. 'I don't expect you've been in prison, have you, Harry?'

'No. But you haven't, have you?'

I'd blurted it out before Butters' comment about one of us being a jailbird flew into my mind. I was really showing my age but she was too preoccupied to laugh this time.

'It seemed such fun as well. Badge of honour. Others were doing much more…'

'Some fun,' I said, seeing as she was shaking.

'At first, it was. There were so many of us in Holloway. Then it became more serious. The hunger strikes…'

She gave a deep sigh and stared into the distance. I caught on, with a bit of a shock, I must say. She'd been one of the suffragists? I should have remembered but my mind was stuck on the first sight I had of her, when the ambulance arrived – and she had a little girl with her. I couldn't square that with being imprisoned. She broke into my confusion.

'I don't suppose you've ever had a feeding tube thrust up your nose and down into your stomach, either, have you?' she asked.

'No fear,' I gulped. The sick feeling only reminded me of the hollowness in my stomach.

Magda shuddered again. 'That's what's coming back,' she said.

I looked round, not catching on to what she meant. They wouldn't need any forcing here.

'It was vicious, inhuman,' she went on. 'It wrecked your health…'

'More than starving?' I asked. I didn't mean it as a joke, it was my hunger talking, but she turned on me – the only time she did.

'You can't imagine it, can you?'

I shook my head, as much with embarrassment as ignorance. I could understand starving. Once more she looked away and was silent for a while. Then she spoke again. 'We were ready to die for the cause, you know that?'

The question didn't seem to require an answer so I said nothing. I recalled the ladies in the village. They hadn't lacked courage. Magda was in a world of her own now.

'Some did, of course. And were then dismissed as suicidal. Emily for one was never that. It was a measure of how far she'd go – we'd go – for the cause.'

I remembered my dad's reaction to that woman dying under the King's horse at the Derby. I wanted to ask what else it could have been. I mean, I would have thought twice about grabbing for the bridle of one lone running horse, let alone jumping into a bunch of them. Magda had moved on.

'You know what beat us in the end?' she said with a grim laugh. 'We'd have gone on, despite the forced feeding,' – though the memory made her shudder again – and the Cat and Mouse Act, and the betrayals…'

I just looked blank. She waved her hand round the cellar. 'The same thing as here…'

I followed her gesture then shrugged at her. What did she mean, women falling asleep?

'Violence,' she said. 'That was the mistake. Oh, compared to here it was a petty thing, but it split us up – and lost us any sympathy we might have gained.'

When I thought back to the village I couldn't recall much sympathy in evidence but she continued as if I wasn't there.

'And then this bloody war. Put the seal on it, that did. The split. And any hope of change. You fight the established order for years and then you become cheer-leaders for their blood lust? It makes as much sense as all this that we're embroiled in.'

All this embroiling did seem to have drained her restlessness. Enough to let me drift off to sleep.

Grey light at the grilles was a long time coming. Day brought no new sounds and the noise of bombardment faded. We were stuck with waiting. And starving. Together with the worry, part hope and part dread, that we might have been forgotten about.

Butters had mentioned my aborted plan to Lady Hester, who grabbed at the idea. Typical, once I'd established how futile it was. She told the women. They became excited, though how much of that was because of the news I was male, I couldn't be sure. It did make them crowd round me all a-twitter. I was poked and cooed at. What they were saying about me I didn't dare guess. I could tell some of it was rude and the one in the red dress made a show of dragging me down the archway.

I tried to resist without giving offence but she became insistent. Fortunately Lady Hester intervened and gave them a lecture. She seemed to be telling them about the plan. They became more serious. Lady Hester indicated where they should stand. The woman in the red dress attached herself to me and winked. She kept whispering in my ear. I was on the point of asking Lady Hester to tell her how old I was until I remembered that too many secrets had already slipped out.

'There's no need to take up positions now,' I said to Lady Hester. 'As long as someone listens for the sound of an approach.'

I gestured to Butters to take me back to our spot. When she did the woman in red let go a torrent of abuse to Lady Hester, who put on her domineering mask. The woman calmed down but I could feel tension and mistrust in the air.

'I told her Lily is your sister, Harry,' Lady Hester said.

'Almost, anyway, ma'am. Thank you. Bit of a let-off.'

'Most men would have taken advantage,' Magda grinned. I was glad to see her back to normal. I nodded and glanced at the grille, wondering if Butters had mentioned anything about my true age. It wasn't important.

'Attention!'

The woman listening at the door hissed out a warning and we all scrambled to our places. The woman in the red dress squeezed my hand but I took it as encouragement and no more this time. The key turned in the lock.

The door was pushed open more slowly and I rose on the balls of my feet waiting to spring. But no one entered. I allowed the door to swing round fully. In the corridor a German guard stood with his rifle levelled. He snapped out something and jerked his head towards the stairs.

No one moved. He repeated what he'd said, with an angry gesture. Lady Hester asked something in German. He answered her in a more level tone. She asked something else and he nodded assent.

Lady Hester explained what it was all about to the Belgian women. It brought smiles and the odd cry of delight though neither she nor Magda looked pleased.

'What did he say ma'am?' Butters asked and got a 'Shh' for her pains. Lady Hester glared as if to stop any question from me. I nodded my understanding. Giving away we were English might not be wise.

After a further exchange with the women Lady Hester stepped back and the women began to file out. She mouthed 'later' at me and indicated that I should follow. I did so, keeping my eyes down as I passed the guard.

The women had gathered at the top of the stairs, under the anxious gaze of an older German. When we were all there lady Hester and the first guard engaged in more discussion in German. The only word I caught was 'waggon'. So we were being taken somewhere?

We were ushered out of the rear entrance, where I was surprised to see the Wolseley and ambulance still there. Lady Hester gave me a shock by pointing me out to the guard. Then I realised she meant I was to drive. This seemed to cause an argument before the guard gave in. He obviously didn't trust my driving because, having ordered the women to fill the ambulance and back seat of the Wolseley, he made the older man climb in the back of the ambulance. He shouted what sounded like threats to the women behind me then joined Lady Hester in the Wolseley.

To my dismay the woman in the red dress installed herself between Butters and me. She wrapped her arm round mine and I had to gesture roughly that it was dangerous to interfere with my driving.

'Ah, dangereuse,' she laughed and chattered away.

'D'you have a clue what's going on, Lil?' I called across her. The question only brought another laugh.

'I think you've made a conquest.'

'Don't say that. I mean, where are we going?'

'I don't know.'

'It seems to have cheered them up.'

'It does, doesn't it?'

'But not the ladies?'

'Magda whispered to me that she thought we were being transferred to an officers' house.'

'What difference will that make?'

'Not much, for us, I suppose that's why Lady Hester isn't pleased. These others think it's an improvement.'

As if to agree the woman blew me a kiss which nearly made me swerve off the road. I tried to concentrate on the driving. We seemed to be continuing to the rear, passing tented encampments and through marching troops going up to the Line. Nobody appeared that worried about an attack.

There were also ambulances going in our direction. At one place an ambulance had broken down. There seemed to be enquiries directed at the Wolseley as to whether we could take some of its load. We refused and began to move off. Angry shouts tried to make us stop. Then, when the women in the back of the ambulance were seen, there was a clamour to get to them. I slammed my foot down on the accelerator pedal and shot off.

Once we reached a place free of troops the Wolseley stopped and Lady Hester was sent back to have the tarpaulin fastened shut to keep the cargo from greedy eyes. As usual we'd almost learned too late. And how wonderful, I reflected, surveying the dull, flat landscape relieved only by the vast military machine imposed upon it, the contribution I was making to the war effort. I just wasn't sure whose. As to any future contribution, that looked to be increasingly unlikely.

Eleven

The woman managed to extract my name from us and convey that hers was Marie-Claude. This led to her resting her head against my shoulder and cooing 'Arree, oh, Arree.'

'Can't you get her off me?' I grumbled at Butters.

'I don't know the French for "Stop child molesting".'

'Very funny, I'm sure.'

'If Carstairs was in your place, he'd think he was in heaven.'

'I'd rather drive the Wolseley.'

'You're a good boy, Harry.'

'Ah, Arree, Arree,' Marie-Claude cooed in my ear.

'Don't call me a boy.'

'Sorry, sir… er, ma'am. Ha, ha, ha.'

'I wish I could find something to laugh about.'

'Yes, it's not easy for us, is it?'

'Do you regret coming?'

'I've told you before, what choice was there? We just have to get on with it, don't we, and hope for the best?'

'The way this lark is going, I can't see it ending for the best.'

'Make sure you don't propose to her, then.'

'I'm more likely to suffocate from her perfume.'

Marie-Claude put her hand on my thigh and in my shock I smacked it, hard. She cried out and whimpered, not entirely in pain, I reckoned and began the "Arreeing' in a plaintive tone. I was about to shout at het to leave off when the Wolseley turned sharply left and I had to follow. Up ahead, in the trees, loomed another chateau, larger than the one we'd left. I breathed out, heavily. From the number of cars, horses and men outside, it also appeared to be much more important and heavily-populated.

Very important. My gaze was taken by the array of cars. I

recognized an Adler and a Beckmann. And, of course, the Mercedes 37/95 – several of them. Were things looking up?

I was so absorbed by these delights – I remembered seeing a Mercedes at the House once a few years before the War – that a shout alerted me to the fact the Wolseley was turning into an archway in the centre of the building's facade. I pulled the wheel round just in time to miss a German sentry and followed it into a courtyard enclosed by the four sides of the chateau. Iron gates swung to behind us.

We halted in front of a doorway at the top of several steps on the far side of the square. A shrew-faced older woman dressed all in black appeared and shouted out in German. The guard sprang into life, herding the occupants of the Wolseley up the steps then stumbling to us and unloosing the tarpaulin. With much shouting and complaining we also were shoved up the steps and into a damp, white-tiled hall with a high ceiling and sinks down one side. It smelt like a laundry.

Bolts were drawn across the outside door and shrew-face disappeared through an inner one, locking it behind her. We were imprisoned again. At least this cell was above ground but we still hadn't been fed and here there was no privacy. I threw myself down against the wall and shut my eyes. I tried to visualise the Mercedes again but Marie-Claude had joined me, pressing close and murmuring 'Arree' in my ear. I kept my eyes closed. Then I realised Lady Hester and Magda were arguing.

'Outrageous,' I heard Lady Hester say. 'I refuse to put myself in such a situation.'

You already have, I was tempted to call out. Magda's reply made it clear what she'd proposed.

'Only by playing along with them, do we have a chance to overpower one.'

Oh, my Lord, I thought, overpower one of what? What did Magda think they were made of? And what was this 'playing along'? I soon understood.

'I refuse to allow myself to be undressed in order to get my hands on a man's weapon.'

My eyes shot open. I could see the horror on Lady Hester's face.

'You might not have to.'

'*Might* not? I hardly think a gentleman visiting these... ladies expects to be engaged in polite conversation.'

'You admire his sword, or pistol, and ask to examine it.'

'And he'll be fool enough to let me?'

Quite. It was only the latest in a series of mad ideas.

'You'll have to convince him,' Magda said.

'And if I fail..?'

Magda looked away. I think she realised her plan was wild. Lady Hester kept on at her. 'If it succeeded, the result would be worse. What do I do, shoot him? Run him through with his own sword? And what about Harry, here?'

I clamped my eyes tight. I was becoming the convenient excuse for everything. What *about* me? I never found out.

Magda gave a sigh of defeat. 'No, you're right, Hester, we'll have to think of something else.'

The inner door opened and shrew-face re-entered, followed by a German NCO and two soldiers with rifles slung on their shoulders. She called out something in German. Only one or two women responded, by getting to their feet. Lady Hester motioned to me and Butters so I pushed myself up the wall, detaching my arm from Marie-Claude's grip. We were standing ranged round the walls. It seemed like an inspection. I fixed my eyes on the floor and hoped the bonnet was tied tight. My hair wouldn't pass scrutiny if they took it off.

A cry made me glance up. The NCO was tipping up the chin of the woman in the green dress to examine her face. Then she was pulled by a soldier to stand by shrew-face beside the inner door. My heart sank. It was a selection. Or more probably, for me, a detection.

The NCO came nearer. He passed over two and then barked at Marie-Claude to move. I daren't look up. My chin was seized between a thumb and forefinger. I gave a little cry, as much from shock as pain. Cold grey eyes stared at me. I pinched my face. The eyes appraised my body. I waited for the shout of discovery.

Instead he grunted and moved on. He passed by Butters. I breathed in relief. He chose another then came back to Butters and tapped her shoulder. She started. He barked something and she shuffled to join the others who'd been selected. I forced myself to keep still.

He stopped in front of Magda and Lady Hester and stared at then before turning to shrew-face and asking something. She shrugged. He shook his head at Lady Hester and did the same to Magda but looked again and waved her to the chosen group. I caught Lady Hester's eye but it was blank.

I thought at first he was selecting the prettiest ones but then I saw he must also be picking ones he found interesting. In my confusion of worrying what was to happen to Butters and Magda I hadn't paused to think what they'd do with the rest of us. If this was the place for the important figures, would we be sent back where we'd come from?

I shivered and felt suddenly weak. The helplessness of it all was draining away my will. Couldn't I just sink down and forget all about it? Let it be over?

The NCO came to a halt a few women from the end and tossed a question at shrew-face. She ran her eyes over the chosen group and answered him. He appraised the remaining women and nodded one out. Then he flapped his arms to motion us unchosen ones to the far end. I dragged myself along, head still bowed. God, I thought, are they going to shoot us? The tiles would make cleaning up easy.

A German cry of alarm made me jerk round. One of the soldiers had his rifle raised. At a woman in a grey dress tearing at the bolts on the outside door. Two of them slid back with a bang. The German shouted 'Halt!' but she reached for the top one. It was almost too high. Her fingers fumbled at it. A shot rang out, followed by a gasp. A red blotch stained her back then she twisted and sank down to the floor.

For a moment there was silence. A woman beside me shrieked 'Helene, Helene,' and ran and threw herself on the victim. I glimpsed the soldier take aim again but the NCO barked an order and he lowered it. The NCO said something to shrew-face and the other soldier. She gestured to the chosen ones to follow her and they began to trail through the inner door. Marie-Claude gave me a lingering look as she waited in line.

Lady Hester called out in German. Our captors stopped and stared

147

at her. She carried on. The NCO rasped out a command that stopped her, following it with a barrage of questions. She indicated me, which made me shrink back, and pointed to the chosen group. The German said nothing. He went up and stared at her. I prayed he wouldn't give me the same treatment. A second appraisal wouldn't fool him. Though as Lady Hester seemed to be giving away our deceit that might only be a matter of time whether he checked me or not.

He gave a snort of contempt, snapped out something, turned and gave an order that had the departure continue, he following his soldiers out, slamming the door behind him.

The women rushed to Helene, being cradled now by the woman who'd run to her. Lady Hester commanded them to stand back and made an examination. She stood up and shook her head at the comforter. 'Morte.'

That set off a burst of wailing. I retreated to the end wall, my thoughts racing. Had Lady Hester thrown herself on their mercy? It hadn't sounded like it. Nor did it seem as if she had had any success. I glanced at where the dead woman lay. Mercy, here as outside, was absent.

The wailing died down into whimpering and prayers. I wanted to ask Lady Hester what she'd said but hadn't the will. She looked drained. After a time the inner door was thrust open and we all huddled back fearing the worst. The soldier who'd shot Helene strode in and stood with a leer on his face, his rifle slanted across his chest. One woman muttered something. He tensed, his expression hardening.

However, a thin, pale woman struggled in carrying a metal bucket from which a tin mug on a chain rattled. She set it down and scuttled out. The soldier said nothing. Another, similar, woman edged in with a basket of bread, which she placed on the floor next to the bucket.

The soldier gestured at the bucket and laughed as he said something before strutting out. There was a rush for the bread. I waited for the fight to start. Lady Hester brought them to order. She counted us and had two of the women break the bread into a piece for everyone. Then she made us queue for the water. The bucket was soon empty but the relief of my dry throat was overwhelming.

The bread was coarse and hard. I gnawed at it, choking in trying to swallow it too fast.

'Careful, Harry.'

Lady Hester's admonition may have been intended to be gentle but it irked me. Was this the place to worry about good manners? Especially as she seemed to have tried to give us away. I was more concerned about practicalities. I pointed to the bucket. 'Did he say that was all there is?'

'About the bucket? No. I'm afraid he was being rude…'

Rude? Heck, the water hadn't been poisoned, had it? My panic was momentary. Of course not, Lady Hester would have stopped us drinking if she'd heard him say that. Then I guessed what it might have been. I blushed. The bucket was for two purposes. I chewed on the bread to savour its bitter roughness. Anything to take away the thought of what the bucket had had in it before the water.

The hardness of the bread at least saved me from being told off for bolting it down. With hunger and thirst assuaged depression began to settle again. What was happening to Butters? And Magda. Magda had made it sound as if she could stand up for herself but I didn't want to think too closely about what they'd be standing up against. Whatever it was, resistance didn't go down well in German eyes. Or succeed.

I saw again the bodies in the village and the Belgian wounded the Uhlans had shot. The dead woman by the door had a pallor the colour of her dress now. I tried to shut it out but images from the hospital flooded back on me. Having time to think was far from an advantage. Perhaps I should offer to bury Helene. Anything but thinking.

I didn't get the chance. Three more soldiers came in, one carrying a stretcher. The mourners were shooed away, Helene was rolled onto the stretcher and one opened the outside door, letting them carry the body out. The women protested. The third soldier raised his rifle. Most of us shrank away. One who didn't received the barrel on her shoulder. She collapsed screaming.

The soldier shouted something and bolted the door. Two women comforted the injured girl. He went to lift the dress of one of them

149

with his rifle. An angry growl came from the rest. They moved forward. He jerked his rifle at them but the growling continued. With a snort he stepped back and to the inner door. He must have decided being outnumbered was too much of a risk.

We were left to brood again. I made myself think about the Mercedes. I'd read about it in a newspaper in the spring. Ninety-five horsepower. Claimed to be the most powerful production motor car in the world. A four-speed gearbox with the gate change shifter mounted on the outside of the body. What a beauty. With a car like that no wonder the Germans could do what they liked. If they were going to shoot me, would they grant me a last wish to have a drive in it?

I decided that with thoughts like that I must be losing my mind. Although if that brought forgetfulness of everything else, it would be no bad thing. Renewed complaining made me look up. The women were berating Lady Hester over something. She came up to me. Looking awkward.

'Harry, the Belgian… women want you to turn your face to the wall.'

I stared at her, stumped at what offence I'd given.

'Some of them… want to use the… relieve themselves.'

'Oh, why didn't they say?'

I waved to them and swivelled round to sit facing the tiles. What if I suddenly turned back? I wondered but we were well past the point where practical jokes would help. I leaned forward to rest my forehead on the tiles. The peak of the bonnet held me off them. I nearly did turn round in frustration. I sensed Lady Hester still there.

'This must be difficult for you, Harry… No, don't turn round.'

I wasn't sure what was supposed to be difficult so I just shrugged, hoping she'd go away. She didn't.

'I do regret bringing you.'

'I wanted to come. No one forced me.'

I remembered Helena's accusation and wondered where she was now. She had seemed to have got over her reluctance once she met Guy.

'Nevertheless, I feel responsible. And I've not been able to do anything to save us from… this.'

The self-flagellation was getting on my nerves. A shout from down the room broke in.

'Ah, you can turn round now, Harry.'

I swung back with a grunt. The sight of Lady Hester's face cooled my irritation. She *was* down in the dumps. I searched for something to break the awkwardness. 'Is that what you tried, before they went out?'

She didn't look at me. 'I told them we were English ladies, from an ambulance… and were merely caught up with these… others.'

'Didn't he believe you?'

She gave a sigh. 'He said all women are the same.'

That sounded like a Carstairs remark. Very different to his view of motor cars. I decided Lady Hester wouldn't appreciate the comparison so kept quiet.

The inner door opened to spare us more silence.

It was the NCO, followed by half a dozen men. Was this the firing squad? One of the soldiers unbolted the door, three trooped outside and the others motioned with their rifles for us to move. Not in here, anyway. I hurried to hide myself among the others. Lady Hester took her time and earned an angry shout.

Outside, the three Germans formed a cordon to usher us into the back of a lorry. In alarm I looked for our vehicles. Of the ambulance there was no sign. But on the far side of the courtyard the Wolseley stood with its engine running. And a German chauffeur in a peaked cap sitting at the wheel. A mist swam in front of my eyes. I could feel myself swaying. This was robbery.

I realised the other women were in the truck. A German voice was barking at me. A hand shoved me, hard, on the shoulder. If I'd been a woman it might have knocked me over. I forgot where I was and went to resist. The sight of a German officer descending the steps to the Wolseley stopped me. High-ranking, by the look of him and the way the chauffeur jumped out and skipped to open the door. I almost laughed. I'd never seen my dad move that fast for anyone he drove.

The resentment surged back. How dare he steal the Wolseley. The

German soldier spoke again and I blinked and looked in his face. He was giving me a strange stare. I turned away and he pushed me towards the lorry. I stumbled, clutching for the tailboard and heard him rap out an order. My boots must have become visible as I slipped. I stood up, the faces of the women in the lorry staring at me, and waited. The man was saying something to his NCO. A shout made me jump.

'Joachim!'

I wrenched round. It was Lady Hester.

'Joachim!'

She shouted something else in German, at the Wolseley and took a step towards it. The German soldier blocked her way with his rifle. I made a move towards him and a rifle barrel dug into my stomach. My guard made gestures driving me back. I was forced up into the lorry.

Lady Hester kept up the cries. The NCO barked out orders. The guard seized her arm to drag her to the truck and another rushed to take her other arm. She kicked out. I had to look away. Had it been one of my sisters, even Lady Helena, I'd have laughed but this was too much. To cap the indignity the two guards heaved her up into the lorry and she'd have sprawled on the floor if a couple of the women hadn't caught her. We certainly were no different to them now.

Outside the lorry most of the German soldiers shouldered arms. One of them used his rifle to gesture us to move away from the end and as we did so four of his mates climbed aboard and sat at the rear, rifles at the ready, their stocks resting on the floor.

Lady Hester had her breath back and called out that name again. 'Joachim!' followed by more German I couldn't understand. The NCO shouted at her and she shouted something back at him. She seemed to have lost her mind. The NCO must have rapped out an order to his men because two of them leapt up, pushed the other women aside and seized hold of Lady Hester. They began to drag her to the back of the lorry.

I know I should have helped her but I couldn't move. I was too embarrassed by the show. This was no way to save us from being taken away. They'd lock her up in an asylum if she didn't stop raving.

Another thought stunned me. Without her I couldn't communicate with these women. Or the Germans. I was going to be left here on my own. The two soldiers jumped down, holding Lady Hester between them. The landing did jolt her into silence. My move came too late. I stood up and made for the back of the lorry. The remaining two guards barred my exit with their rifles and motioned me to retreat.

I stood where I was, my eyes on Lady Hester. The NCO slapped her face.

'You animals,' I shouted and barged at the 'gate' in front of me, my hands grasping the barrels and forcing them apart. Next thing I knew my cheek was cutting into the gravel of the courtyard and a weight pressing on my back. I was pinned to the ground. The one thing I could see through a gap where the edge of my bonnet had bent, and stretched out behind me where my dress had ridden up, was my right trouser leg.

All I heard was a roaring sound in my ears. Then laughter close to as I was hauled to my feet. My eyes wouldn't focus and everything swirled. My gaze cleared and the noise calmed. Lady Hester stood three yards away from me, side on. What didn't make sense was that the high-ranking German, who'd been about to get into the Wolseley, was not only talking to her, but holding her hand.

I glanced at the guards, who seemed to be as puzzled as me. The conversation was in German so I could tell nothing, other than that Lady Hester and this German appeared to know each other. There were even smiles. So she'd recognised him, had she and that's why she was calling out? 'Joachim.' It must have been his name. I thought she'd meant she was choking! Looking back, I think it was around that time that I decided I did need an education. But at the moment all I could feel through the confusion and fear of detection was a stirring of hope. Was our luck about to change?

My hopes sank at once. I was wrenched roughly to my feet. The high-ranking German was ushering Lady Hester away. *Her* luck might be changing. Mine could be taking a serious turn for the worse. One of the German soldiers was lifting my dress to show off my trousers, to guffaws from his mates. These were cut by the NCO's growl. Whether he'd guessed my secret – my shouting out in English should have alerted him – or was just annoyed that one of his prey had escaped, he seemed intent on revenge in the shape of humiliation. I didn't need the language to understand that he was ordering his men to strip my clothes from me.

The thought of resistance flashed through my mind but I was too slow. Strong arms gripped mine. The leer on his face told me I was in for it. He snatched a handful of dress from my flat chest. This must have confused him because instead of tearing he paused. I saw the same contempt in his eyes that he'd shown Lady Hester inside the room. He was going to enjoy this.

'Halt.'

We gaped at each other. He let go of my dress and turned to salute his superior, who was studying me. Lady Hester spoke in his ear. I pulled the sides of my bonnet closer and looked down. Why they hadn't just pulled off the bonnet, I couldn't imagine. I suppose they wanted more entertainment. Lady Hester said something that didn't sound German but I was too lost in bewilderment and took no notice.

'Harriet.'

I glanced up. She was motioning to me. I'd forgotten my name! I nearly spluttered 'Yes, ma'am' as I shuffled to join her. Was I free, too? One of the other women called out. I looked round. She was asking Lady Hester something.

I noticed our captor NCO's face. It was like thunder now. What his superior said didn't lighten it.

The other women were ordered off the lorry and herded back inside the building. I didn't try to think what that meant. All I could do was let it wash over me. I was past caring what happened. We were led across the courtyard. For a moment I expected to be ushered into the Wolseley. At that I remembered Butters and Magda. Had Lady Hester forgotten them?

We passed by the Wolseley. It had been given a clean and the brass work polished. So these Germans weren't all bad. Then I was inside the building. In a place far different to the other side. A corridor with a high ceiling, dark wooden panelled walls and patterned tiled floor. I almost reached to remove my boots. I hoped they wouldn't leave marks on the floor. This might still be a servants' entrance but it was some degrees higher than that across the way. Hemmings wouldn't have minded strutting about in here.

The reminder of him, and home, disconcerted me further. This made it feel close but I knew it was chasms, let alone a sea and war, away. I hardly noticed that we were ushered into a sitting room, just me and Lady Hester, standing there like stuffed dummies staring at each other.

'Oh, Harry,' she said, reaching out to take my hands. For a horrible moment I thought she was going to embrace me. The sudden relaxation of tension turned my legs to rubber. Tears came into my eyes.

'Sit down,' she went on, guiding me to a settee draped with a rich red material. Far too good for me. 'I couldn...' I tried to say but my legs gave way and I sank into it. She shook her head and went to sit in an easy chair opposite me. 'Do I look as exhausted as you do, Harry?' she asked. She looked awful, like a washerwoman.

'I'm mainly... I wish I knew what was going on, ma'am,' I managed to splutter. 'Not knowing German, or French or anything.' I felt helpless and inadequate and too young rather than tired, though now I was wrapped in the softness of this settee I could feel the tiredness welling up and swallowing me. I'm not sure if she did explain it.

If she did, I missed it because the next thing I knew Butters and Magda were in the room. Butters *did* embrace me. Her soft warmth felt pleasantly strange. Then I remembered. I disentangled myself and looked her over. 'Are you all right?'

'We were given baths,' she laughed, though it looked rather forced to me. I wasn't sure what that meant, either, but nodded, avoiding her eyes.

Magda smiled at me, the light back in her face. 'So here we all are, together again. How did you manage it, Hester?'

'I recognised Joachim...'

'Joachim?'

'As we were being taken outside. He was across the courtyard, getting into the Wolseley.'

'The Wolseley?'

'That's another story.'

My ears pricked up at this. What other story? But Lady Hester went on. 'He'd been a frequent visitor before the War, and fortunately I succeeded in catching his attention.'

I didn't butt in to say how. Butters and Magda listened intently. 'Once he understood our situation, he ordered us released and brought in here.'

I wanted to know about the Wolseley but something else had forced its way into my thoughts. 'Why were the other women sent back inside, ma'am?' I asked

'I told Joachim it would repay their support for us if they could all be kept together.'

So, no escape for them, then, though they'd seemed content enough to be with the officers. I was reassured that Lady Hester hadn't simply forgotten about them. Without their help we wouldn't be here now.

'What's going to happen to us next?' Magda asked. 'Are we to be saved for higher things still?'

'I hoped he might return us to our own side but he thought that might prove a little difficult.'

That was one way of putting it. I don't think Lady Hester ever fully appreciated the nature of the war as it was being fought on the ground. Our lucky – or unlucky – slip through the gap in the lines had reinforced her idea that you could go where you wished.

'Where's the ambulance been taken?' I asked.

'They had intended to make use of it for themselves, but I think Joachim will arrange for it to be returned.'

She sounded evasive. And there was still the 'other story' of the Wolseley.

'You're not sure, Hester?' Magda put in.

'I offered him the loan of the Wolseley if he did.'

So that was it. A loan? She'd never see it again. What was he supposed to do, drive it back when he'd had enough of it? Sir Brydon would be furious. Then it occurred to me that that might have been why she did it. An even worse thought occurred: if we were down to one vehicle, who would be doing the driving? My one experience of being driven by Lady Hester had been quite sufficient.

'Will we have to stay in this place much longer, ma'am?' Butters asked. After the excitement of reunion she seemed afraid of something. I forbore to ask what. In the event we remained less than an hour.

The NCO who'd been our captor bid us come outside. Compared to his mood when we'd parted he appeared in good spirits. Too good, I felt. My misgivings grew when he announced that he was to be our escort the first part of the way. They grew further when we were outside and I saw a German in the driving seat.

'We can't let them drive us,' I whispered to Lady Hester.

'Will it matter?'

'He could take us anywhere.'

'Very well.'

There followed an argument in which both sides reverted to type: the German's scowl returned and Lady Hester gave him the full broadside of her frostiness. It was the first time I admired it. The outcome wasn't in doubt, in my mind. There was, however, a price for me to pay.

'I've insisted that I must drive,' Lady Hester said. My face must have shown my disappointment because she added 'You'll have to sit beside me and tell me what to do.'

This prospect didn't cheer me up until I saw that two Germans were stationed in the back of the ambulance with Magda and Butters. I'd be free of too-close scrutiny. Butters expressed disquiet about the guards but Magda put her arm round her and kept herself between them.

The NCO led off in some small staff car I didn't recognise. I got us started and coaxed Lady Hester into setting off without a lurch. Once out on the flat straight stretch we'd turned off I was able to relax.

Until the staff car took a right turn when I'd expected us to go to the left.

'Ask them in the back where we're going,' I said to Lady Hester. She did and one of the guards came forward and poked his head between us. I understood nothing, as usual. Finally he laughed and his head vanished. Lady Hester looked pensive.

'Is this the right way, ma'am?' I asked.

'He said it's a quicker way home.'

From the increased number of tented encampments it seemed to me it was a quicker way to the German Front Line. Is that why the German officer had appeared so unnaturally cheerful before we set off? There'd been rumours in the newspapers before we left of the Germans using women and children as human shields on their advance into Belgium. The prospect didn't fill me with cheer, I can tell you.

Twelve

'Shouldn't you demand to know where they're leading us, ma'am?' Butters asked.

'Perhaps they are going to send us through the Lines.'

And perhaps we're going to take tea with the Kaiser, I thought. It wasn't for me to disagree with her so I kept quiet. Not that my mind did. All sorts of other tricks our friendly German might play on us scuttled to and fro, none of them comforting. The booming of guns grew louder, which confirmed my suspicion we were approaching the Front, though still several miles off. It had been difficult enough dodging shells in the dark when we knew roughly where the batteries were. Being sent out into who knows where in daylight would raise the odds on being hit no end.

However, in the early afternoon we came to a halt in a village that seemed largely intact. There were still civilians about in the streets, looking cowed but going about their business. We must be further back from the Front than I'd thought. Or perhaps we *weren't* approaching it. It was all very confusing. As was why we'd stopped.

Our escort backed off the road and the NCO waved to us to do the same. Lady Hester got out. I knew why.

'Would you reverse it, please, Harry?' she whispered and went to the car while I lined us up parallel to it then resumed my own seat.

'There's something we have to see,' Lady Hester said on her return. 'What, he refused to say. I suspect a trick.'

'Is this your friend's doing, ma'am?'

'Certainly not. Joachim is a gentleman.'

I expected quite a lot of Germans were but it hadn't stopped some of the horrors we'd seen. Again, I decided silence was my wisest course.

All we saw for the next hour was a stream of marching troops, filling the road and all heading towards the Front. Some of them looked no older than me but I suppose they must have been. Magda and Butters watched with us for a while until they got bored. Butters said she was going to sleep. 'I didn't get much last night.'

Her comment puzzled me but the marching Germans had the same effect as counting sheep. I dropped off, too.

Then I was wrenched awake. Being ordered out of the ambulance. Our escort had lined up at attention and we were instructed to stand in a line in front of the ambulance. Were they going to give us a medal? All around us the road was crammed with troops, also drawn up at attention. I wondered if Lady Hester's friend was going to make another appearance. It might be helpful if he did.

The sound of a brass band became louder and then it marched into sight. It was impressive, with a drum major twirling his baton high in the air and ceremonial uniforms that I'd not seen before over here. But what it all meant, I still hadn't got a clue.

A troop of Uhlans followed the band. I shrank back but they, too, were in resplendent uniforms and not the lot we'd encountered. Following them were infantry, also in fine regalia. They must have been a German Guards regiment; there were no young lads among them. Then there was a gap. Is that it? I wondered. What a privilege for us to suffer all this. Are there no elephants?

My answer was to see a staff car appear, an Imperial pennant limp on its bonnet. For a moment I thought it was the Wolseley then breathed a sigh of relief. Would this be gentleman Joachim?

I'd also become aware, as the noise of the band faded, of loud cheering from further back in the parade. Maybe there were elephants. I even started to feel some interest. Though not in this staff car, a Beckmann, which only contained a couple of whiskered old men. They did get some cheers from the troops but the source of the real enthusiasm remained unseen.

It was another car. A silver Rolls Royce. Now this was worth waiting for. The volume of cheering rose. I was ready to cheer myself.

'I always wanted to meet Cousin Willy,' Magda whispered. I glanced at her. She was smiling. An order was barked at us so I made no reply.

The Kaiser? Oh, lor, what had I said earlier? And the Rolls was stopping. Was he going to offer us tea?

I risked a look. Our weasel NCO stood by the car and was pointing to us. My eyes dropped to the ground, not before I saw the weasel striding towards us. I held my breath. What *was* all this about?

My head jerked down as the bonnet was ripped off. I blinked. Angry, shocked faces greeted me. Then strong arms gripped me from behind and thrust me forward. A tearing of cloth had the dress slipping down in a heap at my feet.

Weasel strode to me, grasped the collar of my shirt and tore that aside. My exposed chest chilled me but made me blush. I soon forgot that. A cry of outrage broke from the crowd. Some troops to my right swayed towards me. My thoughts whirled but I was held too firmly to move, even though I sensed they wanted to tear me apart. Even though the ladies beside me were in the line of attack.

A curt shout stopped them. Weasel. He must have a worse fate in mind for me. I was past caring. My body began to shake. I was grateful for the vice-like grip of the men holding me. Without them I'd have crumpled to the floor and whimpered. Back to the child I was.

The Kaiser stepped down from the Rolls and stood gazing at us, while Weasel muttered something to his aide who passed on the message. I glimpsed the Kaiser's withered arm, cleverly obscured by a purple sash across his shoulder. What was he being told? What did they want with us? Was Weasel telling him about Lady Hester's friend? A fine mess *he'd* got us into.

And my exposure, why had that been done here? Had Weasel known all along? Had Joachim known? Was he behind all this? When I recalled some of the toffs who stayed at the House, it wouldn't have surprised me. Lady Hester always had been too trusting a person, behind her frosty exterior. We'd become an entertainment for the Kaiser.

Weasel was addressing us. I stared at him blankly. Just get it over, I told him in my head. Stop playing tricks on us.

'Oh!'

Lady Hester's gasp was followed by a torrent of protest in German.

Weasel screamed at her but she didn't stop. Two soldiers grabbed her from behind and flung her to her knees. Her head banged on the ground. I tried to wrench myself free but the grip on my arms tightened and I winced with the pain. Lady Hester knelt with her head still resting on the floor. She'd stopped shouting.

'You sad, twisted little misshapen ape,' Magda said in English in a loud voice, staring at the Kaiser. Weasel stepped forward and slapped her face, hard, knocking her back. She held her head high and he went to hit her again.

'Bloody coward,' I shouted. 'Hitting women and…'

I got no further. His fist crushed the breath out of me. My stomach felt as if *it* was tearing apart, like the cloth of my dress had. Waves of pain merged into one pit of agony that surged up into my throat and felt as if my insides were spewing out. Lights flashed and roared inside and outside my head. The arms let go of me and I sank down, curling into a ball to try to shelter from the agony, my eyes clenched tight as if not seeing would make it go away. But a sharp flare of pain also erupted in my back. I uncurled then thrashed back into the coil. There was no escape anywhere. Is this how German royalty likes its entertainment, flitted across my brain. Weasel must have kicked me.

'Stop this! Stop,' Lady Hester shouted and an order in German seemed to agree. I screwed up my eyes to see what was happening. The occupants of the Rolls were getting back in. I caught sight of the Kaiser's face. He didn't seem to be enjoying it any more than me. Was he going to miss seeing us being shot?

The car drove on. I waited for some more kicks and winced at a touch. It was only Butters.

'Can you stand, Harry?'

'Hold me,' I said. Comfort was what I needed. She put her arms round me, kneeling so she could rest my head on her knees. I let it sink against her and took deep breaths. The pain dulled a little. It no longer drove up into my throat so the retching feeling eased.

This heaven was abruptly cut off. My eyes jerked open as Butters let go of me and was pulled away. I was jolted to my feet. I staggered but hands, women's hands this time, steadied me. We were bundled towards the back of the ambulance. Someone ordered the ladies to climb in. I leaned my arms on the tailboard, without the will to lift myself. Rough hands grabbed me and slung me inside.

The waves of pain surged back. I lay still, hoping they'd wash over me. Instead, hands gripped me again and shoved me forward. I must have been blocking the space for the German guards to sit.

The ambulance started and the bumping renewed the torture. I hunched onto my side to find relief but it had little effect. Butters knelt by me again. Once more her presence soothed. I decided I could get used to this.

'You'd be better lying on a stretcher,' she said after a bit. I demurred but with the help of one of the German guards, whose face surprised me by showing concern, she and the others manoeuvred me on to the bottom stretcher. However, the reduction in discomfort was slight. I thought of the poor wounded who'd suffered through my driving in this kind of ride.

'Could you understand what was happening back there, Hester?' Magda asked after a while. 'Had that all been planned?'

Lady Hester glanced over her shoulder. Weasel sat in the front with the driver.

'I don't think so. I think our friend was trying to catch the eye of his master.'

'By showing off English ladies?'

'English spies.'

So that was it? My unmasking had been to prove his point? No wonder the Kaiser had got out to study us and looked so unhappy. Would we have sown doubt in his mind? Would he change his plans because of us? These musings were soon cut short.

'Spies, ma'am, why would they think that?'

'Me,' I muttered since Butters received no answer.

'It's not your fault, Harry,' she said.

Not half, I thought. Who'd slipped onto the ship in the first place? Who'd been so mad keen to come? If it *had* only been women, they'd have been spared all this.

Then I recalled that if it hadn't been me, it would have been my dad. But he wouldn't have allowed himself to be dressed as a woman, would he? No, the argument swung round and knocked me back, he'd be lying there dead with those Belgian wounded. Maybe Lily had a point. It was a consoling idea. Once more, to be followed by a rude shock.

'If they think we're spies, where are they taking us, Hester?' Magda asked. There was no answer. I craned my neck to see why. Lady Hester was looking down.

'Hester?'

'They're going to shoot us.'

'No?' Butters screeched.

A jolt of pain shot through me. Magda tried to smile. 'In which case, I'm glad I told the Kaiser what I thought of him.'

I couldn't find much consolation in that. It didn't answer the question of where they were taking us, either.

'Why didn't they finish us off in front of the Kaiser, when they had the chance?' I asked.

'It wasn't public enough.'

'It seemed crowded to me.'

I bit my tongue. I was pulling up Lady Hester again. Then I realised how stupid that was. If we were going to be shot, did it matter that I forgot my place? Lady Hester didn't seem to mind.

'You're right, Harry. I think more formal is what they mean.'

'If they put us on trial, surely we can make them see sense?' Magda said. 'Though, then again...' Her face clouded. Perhaps she was remembering her suffragist trial. I doubt if anyone listened to her there.

Lady Hester hesitated. 'No, not a trial. The Kaiser is here to review his troops, up ahead. They're going to launch a big attack, one they say will smash through to complete the conquest of Belgium. Tomorrow or the next day the Kaiser will proclaim that fact in the ruins of Ypres, once they have captured it. Before that, we are going to be shot in front of the waiting German troops as an example of the perfidy of the enemy. To inspire the army for when they go into battle.'

There was silence after she said that. If they thought we were spies, telling us that sounded a bit reckless to me. I supposed they believed nothing could stop them now so it didn't matter. I could believe that, as well. I listened to the noise of the engine. It needed some servicing. In all the hectic to-ing and fro-ing I'd not given it much attention. So much for my boast on the ship. Would a breakdown help us now? Probably not. If they needed us for their big show, I'm sure they'd find a way.

For some strange reason the prospect of the final conquest of Belgium filled me with more despair than that of being shot. All our friends to be prisoners of this inhuman war machine. And what of the doctors? Would they be classed as spies for coming to the aid of a small nation daring to defy their invaders? These reflections didn't lighten my mood. And the increasingly bumpy road didn't ease my physical pain. Being put out of my misery had a kind of attraction.

'Come on, Harry, cheer up,' Magda said.

'Give me a reason.'

'They might grant us a last wish.'

'I can't say I've noticed much generosity so far.'

'You could say you wish you could go home.'

Remind everyone I was child? No, thank you. I'd prefer to be shot with the rest of them. That made me think.

'Lady Hester, why won't they believe we're not spies?'

She frowned at me. 'They claim your disguise...'

'But we know why that is.'

There, I was correcting her again. This time Magda jumped in to my aid. 'You didn't try to tell them, Hester?'

'Of course I tried. You heard how he screamed at me. And then...'

'I'm sorry, I should have known...' She touched her own cheek where it still showed a red mark from the slap.

I noticed that Lady Hester's forehead, which I'd assumed had just been scuffed by dirt, was showing the discolouration of a bruise.

'Perhaps you could tell them again when we stop, ma'am,' Butters said, with some hesitation, I could see, but nevertheless with boldness. This war was certainly pushing us into questioning our betters. 'And say how young Harry is,' she added.

165

'Seventeen,' I put in quickly.

'You know you're not, Harry.'

'Shh…' I glared at her. 'I am.'

'No, you're not.'

I went to retort but she cut me off. 'And your stupid insistence will get us all killed.'

'How?'

'Because if you're nearly old enough to fight, you're old enough to be a spy.'

Her logic sounded as stupid as my 'insistence', as she called it. Before I could set her straight the intervention I feared broke up our dispute.

'Harry, what is this?' Lady Hester said. In the "Her Ladyship" voice.

'Nothing, ma'am,' I tried to mumble, without any confidence it would work. It didn't.

'How old are you? Truthfully.'

I cast around for some escape from this. Sixteen? It wouldn't get me off. Butters would tell them.

'Harry?'

'oou –een,' I coughed.

'Pardon? Say it out loud… Now!'

I took a deep breath and looked at her. 'Fourteen, ma'am…'

Her face went white. The blue bruise on her forehead stood out stark through the grime. Her voice was a strangled cry. 'Fourteen?'

'Nearly fifteen, ma'am.'

'Oh, my sainted giddy aunt.'

I heard Magda laugh. *Her* face shone. 'Don't do things by halves, do you, Harry?'

'Sorry, ma'am,' I muttered.

'Sorry?' Lady Hester cried. 'Sorry! I asked you, on the boat, and you told me… an untruth.'

'Yes, ma'am.'

'Fourteen.'

It wasn't a question. I wondered if being shot would be worse than this. If we lived, I'd be cast into the outer darkness for ever. Together with anyone associated with me. My parents would be looking for a new home. Although, it then occurred to me, my dad would be anyway, after his cowardice. That made me bold.

'I only wanted to help, ma'am.'

'You had no right to lie.'

'No, ma'am.'

'But if he hadn't, we wouldn't be here now, Hester,' Magda said.

'I'm fully aware of that. If only we weren't…'

'I meant, Hester, that we would never have got beyond the quay in Ostend. We'd have had to return home.'

'For short while.'

'You know that's not the case. The military authorities would have sent us back there and then if we hadn't driven off. And if we had been sent back, by the time of a return they'd have made sure we never boarded a ship in the first place. We all wanted to be here. We've all manipulated the truth. How has Harry done anything different to the rest of us?'

I glanced at Lily. She hadn't wanted to come in the first place. But she nodded in agreement with Magda.

'I shall certainly make sure they hear about this,' Lady Hester said.

'Will it make any difference, ma'am?' Butters asked.

'What do you mean, child?'

"Child": I felt better, hearing her call Lil that.

'Well, ma'am, back at that village, among the people who'd been shot, there were children…'

No one had an answer to that. And there was more.

'Besides, ma'am, Harry…'

'What about Harry, Lily?'

I almost let out a groan. What had I done now?

'He doesn't look fourteen, ma'am.'

That should have cheered me up but their faces reflected the practical problem we faced. My unscheduled departure meant I had no papers. No means of proving my age. What had been an advantage so far now could become a death sentence.

We sat in silence and pondered this dilemma. I say "silence" but in

167

our gabbling we'd not noticed the upsurge in the noise of artillery. And not all German. A shell exploded to our left and a jagged piece of shrapnel tore through the side tarpaulin, missed us all and clanged against the far stanchion before spinning slowly to the floor. I went to reach for it but one of the guards barked something. Next moment we were careering off the road and slewing to a stop. Had we been hit?

Weasel shouted something back to the guards. They shrugged at each other but made no move. Was this an avoiding action? It didn't make much sense to stand still. Maybe we were in the way.

We were but instead of traffic passing us on the way to the Front, the rush of vehicles was to the rear.

'The Kaiser is returning to his headquarters,' Lady Hester mouthed.

'Maybe somebody slapped *his* face,' Magda laughed. That gained her a disapproving glare from Lady Hester.

'Careful, Magda, we ought not to provoke them.'

Shouting came from in front. Weasel shouted back but it didn't sound like an argument. The ambulance began to reverse and then pull round to the right. The driver knew how to handle her, all right, I had to admit that.

The front tarpaulin parted and Weasel's head appeared. He rapped out something in German to Lady Hester. He didn't look pleased but when he finished he gave a snort of contempt. We looked at Lady Hester for enlightenment.

'He said the Kaiser has finished reviewing his victorious troops and has no time to watch an execution today...'

'You mean our artillery has put the wind up him?' Magda said with a grin.

'Quite possibly. Instead, in honour of the forthcoming victory, we will be shot in the Square in Ypres tomorrow.'

We spent a fretful night in a room in a cottage in the undamaged village. However, the village was steadily becoming less undamaged. I took some comfort from this: it must mean that our side knew an attack was on its way but as nearby buildings took direct hits it was difficult to avoid trembling. All the cellars were reserved for the

Germans. Escaping execution by being blown up by your own artillery didn't feel much of a consolation.

Lady Hester's attempts to explain our situation made no progress. Nobody seemed interested, their minds either on the shelling or tomorrow's triumph. The only result of her pestering was some food, a bowl of water and soap.

'It wouldn't do for them to shoot women who were dirty,' Magda said with a laugh as she dried her face.

'Success might make them magnanimous,' Lady Hester replied.

'Nothing else has, Hester. Don't raise your hopes.'

'I won't. If it's a full ceremonial occasion, though, maybe Joachim will be there.'

That seemed to ease the mood. I wasn't convinced. His last intervention had only been an out-of-the-frying-pan affair. I couldn't see him being able to set the Kaiser straight, especially in public. If they'd just conquered Belgium they'd all be less likely to listen to reason anyway.

The barrage lifted after a while and moved off elsewhere. All that did was create more space for thinking. No one wanted to talk so I felt pushed back inside myself with my own private fears. And plenty of public ones, too. So much for helping out poor little Belgium. We'd made a complete mess of it. Over by Christmas? It looked that way.

When I reflected on the officiousness that had held us up in Ostend and then let us make a run for it, I wasn't surprised. Had the rest of the army gone blundering in with the same blind arrogance? Right from when Lady Hester had been told to go home and sit still, the assumption that they knew best had been belied by the results, like the endless stream of disillusioned wounded we'd met at Victoria.

I just hoped they'd put up a good show tomorrow. The Belgians themselves had whenever I'd been close to them. Time after time, when you expected their Front to crumble in the face of overwhelming assaults, they'd rallied and held back the monster. Who knows, it might also be them in front of this offensive. With luck.

Yet the Germans appeared not only confident but prepared. Not much had delayed them for long so far and those ranks of troops moving up looked fresh. I kept picturing a courtyard similar to the one at the prison chateau and being lined up against a wall. I couldn't visualise what the others were doing. I wondered at what point we'd be blindfolded. Would there be any last wish? And where *was* the Wolseley? That concern must have shown in my face.

'I can't really say "Don't look so worried, Harry,",' Magda said as she sat down beside me against the wall.

'Thank you for sticking up for me, back there,' I mumbled.

'That wasn't difficult. I admire you.'

I could feel myself go bright red and couldn't have mumbled thanks even if I'd wanted to. Then it got worse.

'In fact, you're probably only the second man I have admired.'

I wanted to ask what had happened to the other one but my face felt paralysed. She must have read my thoughts.

'And the only one living,' she said.

She looked sad at that. I remembered the little girl who'd been with her when I first saw her.

'Probably just as well,' she added, 'given the situation we find ourselves in now.'

I was going to mention the little girl but thought better of it. I grasped for something to change the subject. 'Were you really prepared to die, just for votes?' I asked. That did lighten the mood.

'I hope you're showing your age, Harry,' she laughed and then put in quickly 'rather than your prejudice.' I don't know whether my face showed any reaction to the reminder of my age but she sighed, 'I'm sorry…'

'It is all my fault, this, though, isn't it?' I said. 'If I hadn't been such a kid, I wouldn't have been so desperate for glory that I'd…'

'You only did what everyone else did,' she cut me off. 'And for a better cause.'

'It was just wanting to see action, really…'

'Well, we've certainly managed that. I hope it's been worth it.'

'It's horrible, isn't it? And still my fault we're in this mess.'

'Yes, it is horrible and no, it isn't your fault we're here. It's thanks to you we *are* still here. Without you I doubt if we'd have gone much further than Ostend. That's not meant as a criticism. I wouldn't have missed this for the world.'

The praise must have numbed my fears because when the sudden cacophony of massed artillery woke me up I ached all over. I'd fallen asleep hunched over and stiffness dulled the pain of my injuries. Magda was awake and the other two groaned in a similar manner to me.

Flashes of flame lit up the room as a nearby battery unleashed its power. No wonder the village was being targeted last night. From the thunder of those guns, the intended target hadn't suffered much damage. I groaned.

'Here we go again,' Magda smiled at me.

'Maybe they'll forget about us,' Butters said.

'Some hope,' I yawned.

'Let's not give up hope,' Lady Hester reproved me. She was back to normal, then, was she? I stretched and kept my thoughts to myself. The waiting was going to be the worst of it. Dawn hadn't shown yet. Wouldn't it be afternoon before we were moved up into Ypres? The Kaiser's victory parade would need to follow not only the capture of the city but the securing of some distance beyond. Quite a long distance to ensure his triumph wasn't ruined by an enemy shell.

That did give me some hope. Surely our lot would manage to dig in somewhere further back and limit the Germans' gains?

You fool, I told myself at once. If they want to shoot you as a spy, they'll find a place. And if the great triumph doesn't happen, won't their frustration need some other outlet? Either way, the outcome for us "spies" looked bad. Something occurred to me.

'Why do they think you three are spies?' I said, to no one in particular.

Butters looked puzzled. 'Because we're with you.'

'Exactly. But you're what you say you are – women, ladies with Lady Hester's ambulance.'

'Driven by you,' Magda put in.

'Yes, but that doesn't make *you* spies.'

'By association.'

'Not necessarily.'

'I think you'll find that makes no difference, in their eyes.'

'Well, it ought to.'

'If they were minded to bother about such niceties, Harry, I suspect we'd all be safe.'

'Can't Lady Hester try to tell them?'

'No,' Lady Hester called.

Her verdict brooked no objection. I stared at her. That brought me another lecture.

'If you think, Harry, that I will attempt to save our own skins by convincing the Germans of something regarding a fourteen year-old boy which is a flagrant untruth, you have sadly misunderstood my nature.'

'No, Lady Hester, I only meant…'

'The answer remains "no".'

I gave a deep sigh and closed my eyes. Someone, Butters, I think, patted me on the shoulder.

'Sorry,' I muttered. When I opened my eyes Lady Hester was looking down, her hand rubbing her chin. Then she nodded and regarded me with a frown. I waited for a further onslaught.

'I appreciate your thoughtfulness, Harry,' she said. 'Don't think I don't.' She glanced at Magda. 'We all do. But we came into this together and we shall proceed through it together, however it may transpire. We may not be able to influence events outside our control. We can, however, influence our own conduct in response to those events. And that, I am determined, we shall do.'

I could feel tears welling up behind my eyes. Don't cry, I urged myself, don't cry, you'll only show yourself up. I forced myself to think about Lil, who, I reminded myself once more, hadn't chosen this and was being yoked into these noble sentiments. I shrugged at her.

'We couldn't leave you behind on your own, Harry,' she said, taking my hands and pulling me up.

'No,' Magda added. 'We may need to reverse the ambulance.'

So the day dragged on. During the morning the nearby batteries ceased firing. Did that indicate that their own troops were now occupying the limit of the guns' range? Perhaps they were even now limbering up to move forward? The rumble of battle maintained its steady roar. At what distance, it was impossible to tell. Our guards kept a stony silence, refusing any question about progress. When I remembered that we were spies, any hope the thought that there was no progress gave me also drained away.

'Perhaps we should offer to fetch the wounded,' Magda suggested.

'British casualties?' Lady Hester queried. 'I could ask.'

She did. It only brought abuse, by the sound of it. Should she offer to transport *any* wounded? That didn't appeal to me. Being blown up saving Germans would be an unfortunate joke. Besides, I guessed that they'd view any attempt on our part to be let out of here and up towards the fighting as a trick. The kind of deceit you'd expect from spies.

They did bring us food, plenty of it though Magda and Lady Hester didn't eat much. Some sort of cabbage soup and black bread. I was too hungry to care. That must have made it around midday. From earlier on streams of wounded and prisoners had moved past the windows to the rear. It was obvious many were in a bad way but the guards still refused to allow us out to help. It seemed to me that there were more wounded than prisoners but that might mean anything. Including, when I remembered with a shudder the uhlans in the village, the possibility that the Germans weren't taking prisoners. Still the sound of battle raged.

Later in the afternoon the door burst open and an angry-looking German barked orders to our guards. One dashed out, the other ushered us to the door. Hardly were we outside when we had to squeeze against the wall to let a column of prisoners pass. Most of them looked exhausted, their eyes staring and sightless, many were walking wounded. A few, however, glared at us. One spat in our direction. I caught ' – king German whores.'

'I'll have you know we're English,' Lady Hester called. He stopped and gaped at us.

'You're on their ferkin side, then, are you?'

'We're prisoners, like you. And due to be shot.'

A guard shouted at him and forced him on with the butt of his rifle. He threw a laugh back at us.

'Ha, ferkin ha. It was your ferkin class what got us into this mess. Serve you ferkin right.'

This outburst upset Lady Hester, I could see. And that it made Butters as uncomfortable as it had me. To be shot as spies while being regarded as traitors by our own side gave this whole thing an even more horrible twist.

The ambulance drove up and we were bundled in the back. A new NCO or whatever he was and one of the guards accompanied us. The driver was alone in the cab.

We set off towards the Front but progress was slow. The road was clogged with ambulances and wounded coming back and from time to time we had to pull aside to let reinforcements through. The cheerfulness of yesterday had cooled down and the number of extra troops seemed less.

We pulled off the road again and the driver cut the engine. Something strange struck me. It took a few moments to realise what it was. The rolling noise of battle had ceased. There were sporadic explosions like passing thunder but that was all. So, was it over?

Yet I could see out of the back of the ambulance that we were still in countryside. This wasn't Ypres. Were we awaiting an all-clear before entering? In amongst the lines of walking wounded I noticed squads of battle-weary troops, marching to the rear. I couldn't make out an air of triumph about them. And they weren't large groups. Had they taken the brunt of the attack? If so, they weren't going to share in the victory celebrations in Ypres.

I expected us to continue but we were again ordered out. Up ahead a huge pall of smoke smothered the landscape and stretched either side as far as I could see. Not the conditions for a pageant. Would we have another stay of execution? A different thought succeeded that. Would it be worth making a dash for that smoke? Hoping our guards might be distracted by the chaos around us and allow us to commandeer the ambulance? But how could we make a "dash" when the road was so clogged? There was also the small matter of evading the guards, too.

You're thinking like a woman, I told myself and then felt ashamed. Our best hope was a delay. Since dusk was falling maybe they'd wait and shoot us at dawn.

Like all my hopes that one also had a short life. A staff car, an Adler, this one, came from the rear and screeched to a halt. Out climbed Weasel. From the rear, I noted, he wasn't first into the breach, then? If that deprivation had disappointed him, he certainly showed it.

He marched up and down before us, shouting into our faces, spit flecking his mouth. The word I kept catching was 'kindermord', sometimes repeated two or three times, accompanied by a stamp of his foot. If his fury hadn't induced such terror in me, I'd have been tempted to laugh. Lady Hester made no attempt to argue with him so I guessed it was no laughing matter. Had their own high hopes, it occurred to me all of a sudden, also been dashed?

At last he ran out of energy, spat on the ground at Lady Hester's feet and stalked to his car. We all took the chance to gather our breath. At length Magda spoke.

'Killing children, Hester, is that what he meant?'

Oh, lor, not ranting about me again, was he? Why the song and dance? What had I done to him?

'I th-think so. I don't think we'll be going to Ypres.'

'You mean, they haven't taken it?'

My eagerness didn't seem to be shared by Lady Hester. She shook her head. 'From what I could gather – and you might guess from his tone that he wasn't entirely coherent – the attack failed. Quite disastrously.'

I must have smiled because she shook her head again.

'It hasn't changed the outlook for us, I'm afraid.'

My supposition that disappointment at losing their triumph would merely change the motive for shooting us sounded as if it had been correct. So were we going to be the consolation prize?

'But what was the "kindermord" about?' Magda asked. 'He made it resemble some terrible offence. Surely we hadn't resorted to shooting children to hold up their attack?'

'That's what he said.'

'I can't believe we'd descend to that. It's too fantastical.'

'He meant *their* children.'

'Their children? But we've seen no children anywhere near the Front.'

Apart from dead ones, I thought, and they were Belgian.

'Ma'am,' I ventured. 'a lot of the soldiers who marched past us yesterday towards the Front looked very young.'

'As young as you, Harry?' Magda smiled.

I didn't. Why did they have to keep bringing up my age?

'You could be right,' Lady Hester said. 'If they threw in those young men believing it was going to be easy, they could have suffered terrible casualties.'

That should have been a consolation. But from Weasel's reaction, if Lady Hester's surmise was correct, they'd be wanting revenge. And who were the ones nearest to hand?

Thirteen

We stood outside as it grew dark. And cold. Weasel climbed into the Adler and sat immobile. The flow of ambulances never stopped. More weary troops trudged past towards the rear. There was much scurrying to and fro of men who must have been messengers. By and large we were ignored. From the grim faces that was probably just as well.

My teeth began to chatter. I consoled myself by thinking that if this was the extent of their revenge, it had its merits but I suspected its real intention was to humiliate us before the bitter end. Then a flurry of messages woke up Weasel and the Adler lurched off – towards the Front. Once it had gone, our guards drove us back and inside.

One began to smash up an old dresser set against the wall. I shrank back as splinters flew. Then I realised this violence wasn't to cow us: his mate gathered the pieces and piled them in the grate. They were making a fire.

The warmth calmed my shivering and since the whole situation was beyond comprehension, I gave up trying to puzzle it out and fell asleep.

When I awoke the sky was grey. The fire had died. No one else, guards included, was awake. Had we missed being shot at dawn? I tiptoed to the window. The absence of traffic surprised me, so did the relative quiet. The Germans weren't going to resume the attack today, then?

As I turned away from the window a car did appear. The Adler, but from the rear this time. I shuffled back to my place then had a thought. Stepping round the ladies' bodies I kicked the sole of the nearer guard's foot. He shot awake, swinging his rifle round on me with a vicious cry. I pointed to the door. He caught on and kicked his mate, who grumbled as he opened his eyes. The first guard hissed something and he, too, was galvanised into life. I resumed my position. The ladies stirred.

The door flew open and Weasel's gaze swept the room. His mood hadn't improved. He barked something at the guards, waved us up and strode out of the door. The guards bustled, herding the still-groggy women outside. I followed. The urgency bemused me. *Had* we missed the dawn?

The first guard ran off and returned driving the ambulance. What was coming started to hit me. This must be it. But where? The ambulance stopped and the driver got out. His mate went to the Adler. The first guard regarded us and I wondered if they were going to shoot us here. If so, why bring the ambulance? Had they lost their nerve about an execution and were going to make it look like an accidental shooting in the ambulance?

The second guard returned from the Adler. Carrying a white flag on a pole, which he jammed into the side of the seat on the passenger side. He bid us climb in the back. As I did so the first guard tapped my shoulder with his rifle. I stopped and stared at him. He nodded and motioned me to continue. Was that thanks? If Weasel had found them asleep, we wouldn't have been the only casualties.

That didn't ease my bewilderment. Nor did the fact that after the guard climbed in behind us and gestured to us to sit he closed the tarpaulin. We were in the dark in every sense. I gritted my teeth to stop them chattering and pulled my knees up to my chin.

'Where are they taking us, ma'am, can you tell?' Butters asked. Lady Hester's reply sounded strained.

'No, Lily, they're all very agitated but about what they gave no indication.'

They weren't alone in their agitation. I tried to guess which way we were going. To the Front? That didn't make much sense but the ambulance hadn't turned round at the start. We seemed to swing once though that might have merely been a bend. The uneven road slowed us down.

Again my mind pondered making a break for it. There was only the one guard. If we overpowered him, we could slip off the back of the ambulance without the driver noticing, perhaps. Could we overpower him without the driver becoming aware of that, though?

And if we did, what would we be slipping out into? If they were going to shoot us, the risk would be worth it. But what if the original plan to repatriate us had been re-instated? Attempting to escape would seem to confirm our guilt.

The road became rougher and we bumped slowly on. If we were headed to the rear, shouldn't the road surface improve? At least at this pace jumping down would be manageable. On my bottom I edged closer to Lady Hester.

'Lady Hester, should we try to escape? If we overpower him, we could slip...'

'Overpower?' In the gloom I could sense her shudder.

'But there's only the one g...'

'Shh. I won't hear of it.'

'What are you proposing, Harry?' Magda asked.

I mumbled, not wanting to annoy Lady Hester. She saved me the bother. 'Harry proposes "overpowering" the guard and fleeing.'

'I'm game if you are,' Magda said.

'I'm not.'

'Why ever not? It doesn't sound like you, Hester.'

'I don't believe Joachim will have let us down.'

I groaned to myself. More blind faith. Where was the evidence? Joachim had disappeared off the face of the earth. It was Weasel who was determining our fate now.

'Besides, escape from the middle of the entire German army... Where do you imagine we are, Magda? It's simply not a practical proposition.'

That pronouncement ended the discussion. Not a practical proposition? After some of Lady Hester's earlier fancies, when I weigh up the odds, I'm dismissed as not practical?

A sudden jolt to a stop cut off my complaint. A voice shouted outside. The driver's replied. I looked towards Lady Hester but couldn't make out her response. If we had company out there, that did put paid to any bid for freedom.

The tarpaulin parted. I glimpsed a plank road behind us, piles of debris to one side. A German soldier blotted the view and the flap closed to. The glimpse left me no wiser.

The German soldier thrust a piece of white cloth at me and did the same to the others. He issued instructions that meant nothing then indicated his eyes.

'We're to blindfold ourselves,' Lady Hester said.

My stomach, empty though it was, lurched. Blindfold? That could indicate only one thing. The meanness of it almost brought tears to my eyes. Not even a last look at the sky? Did they insist in refusing us any last little drop of compassion?

'Do we have to?' Butters asked.

'I think we'd better.'

I saw no logic in that. What penalty could there be for not complying? The German soldier snapped out more orders.

'If they shot us in here we wouldn't need blindfolds,' I muttered. That gained me another bout of what sounded like abuse, right in my face.

'No speakee hogwash,' I retorted. He raised his fist.

'Just do as he says,' Lady Hester said.

I got the impression the others were doing so, so stretched the bandage out to wind it round my head. 'I'd like to have seen the sky before they...'

'Don't say that, Harry,' Butters gasped.

'Don't say what, Lil, it's not blind man's bluff, is it?'

'I know, but I don't want to think...'

'Me neither,' I relented. 'I just wish they'd get a move on.'

'It'll certainly stop us making your dash for freedom,' Magda said.

'We didn't need any hindrance for that, did we?'

I hadn't intended to snap at Magda and bit my lip for having done so. No one had the chance to respond because the German soldier began speaking again. A hand gripped my arm and jerked me to my feet.

'We're to get out of the ambulance,' Lady Hester said.

'Be easier without the blindfold,' I retorted. A hand in the middle of my back propelled me forward and in two steps I was treading air.

My right knee jarred as my foot hit the ground. I flung my arms out and bent my left leg as it made contact, hoping to steady myself then crashed against a solid body that smelled of sweat. Hands grasped my arms and pushed against me, holding me upright. Warm sour breath on my face made me catch my breath, but the words uttered in it didn't sound harsh. I guessed the guard I'd helped had caught me.

Any feeling of gratitude was lost in my shaking.

Where to now? Or did we just have to wait for the shot?

Would we even know? That would have been consoling if the uncertainty wasn't so agonising. What were they playing at? There seemed to be a discussion going on but even if I'd understood German it was too far off to catch.

'Perhaps if I started singing, they'd get a move on,' I said. That only brought a 'Shh' from Lady Hester. 'Sorry, Harry, I'm trying to hear what they're saying.'

Being apologised to! I wanted to ask what she thought but kept quiet. Was Weasel there? Had someone found a conscience? If somebody didn't do something soon, I was going to run off shrieking and let them do their worst.

'They're disagreeing about times and places and don't seem sure about what they have to do,' Lady Hester said. 'But to do with what, I can't understand.'

Was she deliberately ignoring the obvious? Maybe she wanted to spare us more distress? If so, her good intentions weren't working on me. And anyway, that wasn't Lady Hester's style.

A car drove up. The Adler? I wasn't sure. Orders followed. Brisk, urgent. Here we go, I thought. Footsteps hurried nearer, orders. To do what?

'Lady Hester..?'

'We're to climb back into the ambulance.'

'I would if I could see it. Can we take these off?'

'He hasn't said…'

I pulled mine down and saw the ambulance to my left. A volley of abuse hit me at the same time as a hand wrenched the bandage up across my eyes. I slipped backwards, flashes of grey uniform, blazing eyes and sky reeling into darkness as, his knees pressing my chest, the guard used both hands to tug the blindfold tight.

The weight lifted off me and I gasped to breathe. A noise of shouting seemed distant. Hands yanked me up, dragged me and heaved me up onto the roughened planks of the ambulance floor. I reached forward to break my fall and heard the engine start.

The jolting bumped my head so as my breathing steadied I crawled into a crouching position and shuffled towards the sound of the engine.

'Harry…'

I didn't need Lady Hester's admonishment. 'I know, I know..,' I said. Then remembered. 'But I saw something.'

Maybe they hadn't heard because nobody asked what. I didn't notice that at first because another thought had struck me, one that both confused me more and gave me hope. 'It's why they're so keen we wear these blindfolds.'

'It sounded much more than "keen", young man.'

'You didn't take yours off, Harry?' Magda said. 'Is that what all the fuss was about?'

"Fuss" was one way to describe it but I was taken aback by the "young man". Was I growing up at last?

'What did you see, Harry?' Butters asked.

'The Front Line. We're just behind the German Front Line. That's why they they've blindfolded us.'

As I said it I realised it might only be an additional reason. Had they brought us here to shoot us in view of our own side? To show them the penalty for sending spies? If so, why the need for blindfolds so soon? Would we have seen the extent of their casualties?

Again, nothing added up. We bumped onward. Very slowly now, on a road, if it was a road, whose surface felt worse than any we'd passed. A log road? Then we stopped.

The engine cut. The driver climbed out. I heard our guard stand, the swish of the tarpaulin and the thud of his boots on clay. I pulled down the blindfold a touch and saw we were unguarded. Footsteps approached and I shoved it back up. The tarpaulin was dragged aside and a voice said: 'Four, then? Yes, four.' An English voice!

'What?' I screeched.

'Hold your horses,' the Englishman said. 'Not long now.' The flap slapped down and the sound of voices faded. I could hear loud breathing beside me.

'Oh, stick this, I'm going to find out...'

'No, Harry, do as...'

I'd gone no further than seizing the bandage when I was thrown down by the violent lurch of the ambulance as it shot forward. A new driver, anyway. A speed merchant and on a road that felt like a ploughed field. If he wasn't careful, he'd kill us all.

'I wish I knew what was happening to us, ma'am,' Butters said. Her plaintive tone echoed my own feeling.

'I think we've been handed over to the British,' Lady Hester said. If I hadn't already been wearing a bandage, I think everything would have gone black.

We were exchanged, it turned out, which explained all the agitation over time and place. And the reason for the blindfolds, after all. The relief was almost too much. My shoulders shook. I couldn't help myself. The tears flowed from my eyes. Lily hugged me and I hugged back for all I was worth, just wanting to feel something solid for once.

As ever, it didn't last. The bombardment, which must have been curtailed for the exchange, started up with renewed vigour. That was accompanied by the dispiriting information that our own side hadn't set out to free us: we were merely the makeweight for a couple of captured German officers, don't ask me why. And we were suspected of being German spies!

'I think we can take these off now,' I said as we bumped up onto cobbles, where the driver slowed down. The ladies were holding on to the stretcher stanchions. I struggled to the partition behind the driver and moved the tarpaulin aside.

'Get the fuck back out of it,' shouted a British sergeant in the passenger seat. I did so from shock more than anything. The language had stunned Lady Hester.

'What was all that for?' Butters asked me. I shrugged.

'Welcome home,' Magda said. 'That greeting reminds me of Holloway. An education in so many ways. You know it was only in prison that my sense of humour failed?'

I went and drew back the rear tarpaulin. We were on a straight road once more. But one without poplars. Or rather, mainly with the stumps of poplars. Either side of the road was a sea of mud and debris, the occasional shattered farmhouse here and there. Fountains of earth spouted willy-nilly amongst this. A landscape no different from the one we'd journeyed through from Furnes to Dixmude in what seemed an eternity back. Except that nothing fell close to the road here. And we had no clue where we were going. Straight to hell as the speed accelerated again.

Then we swung left on to a wider road. And did slow, because of the traffic – human, straggling along on both sides of the road, horse-drawn and motorised – that took up most if it. But not going our way, by and large. Yet we seemed to be heading towards a Front again, not away. The wagons, many almost touching one another, that unfolded as we passed, carried wounded, not reinforcements. There weren't many ambulances and it occurred to me that we might actually be going to help.

I should have known better. Before long the ambulance swung left into the forecourt of a white chateau. Well, it had once been white. The signs of shelling lay in a chimney collapse at one end and craters on the lawns. Several staff cars sat outside. I glimpsed a Wolseley and my heat thumped until I realised it wasn't ours. So much for Lady Hester's generous 'loan'.

'OK, get down but don't move from here,' a military policeman appeared at the back and called in to us. He waved a pistol to illustrate his order. Charming. Crossing the lines hadn't reduced my confusion. I began to feel that our chances of being shot may not have receded at all. At least Lady Hester felt at home. 'You, man, kindly explain what is going on.'

'All in good time, lady.'

'Do you know who I am?'

'Matter of opinion, that, ain't it?' he said.

'My name is Lady Hester Dunranald.'

'Mine's Charlie Chaplin, how'd y'do.'

'And my son is a captain here in the Life Guards.'

This appeared to be worth more than lady Hester's title. He man looked taken aback. 'Is he, by gum? He'll not thank anyone for a visit from his old mum.'

Lady Hester's face darkened, whether from being referred to as an 'old mum' or from the man's manner, I couldn't tell but she shut up. You're probably more right than you realise, mate, I thought. I doubt if James would have been overjoyed to see his mother anywhere.

The MP strode into the chateau, leaving a private with a rifle to guard us. Magda tried to engage him in conversation. 'Would you mind telling us where we are?'

'What's it to you?'

'We've been held captive by the Germans, accused of being spies and threatened with execution.'

'So you say.'

'Why would we make up a story like that?'

He nodded towards the chateau. 'I bet that's what they're trying to figure out, too.'

'Good Lord, *they* don't think we're spies, as well, do they?' Lady Hester cried.

'Tricky beggars, these Jerries.'

'You hardly need to tell us that.'

'Oh, for bloody hell's sake, mate,' – I ignored Lady Hester's snort of disapproval – 'I'm no more a German than you're the Grand Old Duke of York. Just tell us where we are.'

He glanced behind him as if to see he wasn't being overheard then came to attention. A British officer was striding from the chateau. The sentry's secret froze.

'Lady Hester?' the officer held out his hand, unsure which she was. Lady Hester offered hers. He regarded her with some trepidation. 'Captain Willoughby de Canville, 2nd Life Guards. I don't believe we've met?'

He looked younger than her but older than James.

185

'My son is with the First...'

He flinched. 'Er, yes...'

'I don't expect to see him – unless he's somewhere close at hand, of course. We really just want to know what is going to be done with us.'

'Quite. The First have been in some pretty sticky stuff... I understand that once it's clear you are who you say you are, you'll be taken into Ypres, back to Boulogne and then home.'

'We're near Ypres?' I spluttered.

'It's a mile or two back there.' He jerked his head. 'Up the Menin Road.'

'Do you have news of my son's regiment?' Lady Hester butted in.

He looked uncomfortable. 'As I said, they'd been in some...'

'We gathered that the Germans had launched a massive attack. They expected to break through to Ypres and declare Belgium conquered...'

'As you can see, they failed in that. At huge cost. They threw in inexperienced reserves to the north with no regard for casualties...'

'"Kindermord",' Magda said.

'I beg your pardon?'

'Murder of children, that's what they called it.'

'They were hardly children...'

I recalled the youthful reinforcements passing our prison. No, they weren't children and I knew where the fault for their slaughter lay, too.

'Is that where my son's Lifeguards were?' Lady Hester pursued. The officer again became evasive.

'No, er, they were down there. Gheluvelt.' He indicated the direction opposite to Ypres.

'And did they hold, man?'

'They did, but...'

'But..? But..?' Her voice rose. 'What are you hiding from me? Tell me.'

He looked back at the chateau then at the trees.

'Not before they had been overrun. Your son did not desert his post. He did his dut...'

'He's dead?'

My body felt rigid. The officer nodded. 'Captain James Dunranald was killed in action two days ago…'

Lady Hester sank to her knees. I shrank away from her sobbing. Magda stood with her hands on Lady Hester's shoulders. Butters looked at me with tears in her eyes. I glanced aside. The captain's embarrassment was plain. But I couldn't stop seeing the last time I saw Lady Hester with James. Were these tears sincere? I wondered how my mum would react if she heard I'd been killed. I didn't remember much reaction when little Percy died. Maybe it was different if the son was only two.

The captain coughed. Lady Hester looked up at him. 'Was he buried where..?'

'I believe so.'

'Then I want to go and see his grave.'

'Ah, I don't think that will be possible…'

'I demand to see it.'

'The Front Line is somewhat fluid at…'

'I don't care. Go and get me permission.'

He hesitated. A couple of shells landed behind the chateau. I heard glass breaking as I flinched. Another shell hit the back of the building. Smoke blew out from the front door. Captain de Canville gave a cry and ran towards it. The private tore after him.

'I think permission might be a little difficult to obtain, Hester,' Magda said. 'If you want to see James's grave, this is probably the only chance we'll have.'

Lady Hester stared at her. 'You mean..?'

'Did you expect an escort? Harry…'

I ran to the cab and jumped in. Everything seemed as it had been. Magda pushed Lady Hester into the passenger side and squeezed in beside her. I got the engine to fire first time. People were staggering out of the chateau. Someone raised an arm as if calling for us. I turned the wheel and screeched away, shutting out the cries I heard but the accusing voice in my head pursued me: you weren't much help to little Belgium, were you and now you're abandoning your own side.

At the main road I swung left, against the stream that seemed thicker than ever. It struck me that we had no idea of our destination. Towards the Front. Which was 'fluid.' If we blundered through into the German lines again they *would* shoot us for spies. Though from the steady increase in shelling that might be the least of our worries.

Once, an officer flagged us down.

'We're going up to the Front,' Magda shouted and he called out 'Well done.' That didn't ease my shame. But shame soon gave way to a growing dread. The stream passing us was no longer just wounded. These were retreating troops and not lingering about it. The Germans might have been held yesterday – 'not before being overrun', the Captain's comment forced itself on me – but none of these men appeared to believe that could happen again. And we were heading straight for the maelstrom.

Or it was heading straight for us. I wrenched the wheel hard over and slid along the ditch, missing the onrushing horses of a gun carriage by little more than their whiskers, it seemed. How I steered us back onto the road, I don't know. But thumping with my blood was the thought: they're saving the guns. Glorious pictures in a book my dad had from the South African war ensured I knew what that meant but close up there was no glory. This spelt defeat.

Three huge fountains of earth erupted in the field to my right and two to the left. The thought registered that these shells were now coming from ahead, no longer from the left. Our own retreating troops weren't what we'd confront soon. And we were looking for a grave? The idea was so preposterous it almost swept away my fear.

However, what replaced it drowned both. The noise swelled as it had in Dixmude, with the rattle and crash of every kind of gun, while the road ahead vanished in a cloud of smoke and dust. I slowed. It was fortunate I did. A figure materialised in front of me, directing us to go left. Had I not been braking I'd have mown him down.

As it was, I swung into the drive of yet another chateau and followed it round to the right then out onto the front lawn, directed by a further pointing arm. I glimpsed prone bodies, piles of abandoned equipment and a couple of shattered guns then ducked under a hail of shrapnel that spattered down all along the passenger side.

I heard a cry beside me but another shout penetrated the din. A soldier was waving at me to drive towards two stretcher bearers stumbling from the boundary hedge. I engaged the gear and bumped across the lawn. A second stretcher appeared. Grave-hunting would have to wait.

'Harry, wait. It's Magda, she's been hit.'

Lady Hester's voice stopped me in mid-stride as I set off to the stretcher bearers. I stumbled round the front of the ambulance. Magda was half-twisted as if trying to step down from the seat. The length of her left thigh throbbed in a red mess, the side of her dress ripped off completely. The sight of naked flesh stunned me but Butters was there, seizing Magda's arm to hold her up.

'Harry, lift her,' she shouted in my ear.

I swept Magda up and staggered to the back of the ambulance, my left hand drenched but my fear now that I couldn't do more than shove Magda onto the floor of the ambulance. She gripped my shoulders with her right hand which eased her weight. I strained to raise her.

'I'm glad you're carrying me over the threshold, Harry,' she whispered in my ear. Except I wasn't. Then I was pulled backwards, the weight gone. Butters had run out a stretcher and a soldier held one end while his mate laid Magda on it. I looked at my arm, soaked in blood, and then at Magda's side, the blood also pooling on the stretcher. I felt my own will draining out.

The soldiers lifted the stretcher into a rack and Butters swabbed a dressing on the wound. It turned red at once. Magda's face was turning grey.

'Here, give us an 'and, boyo,' a voice grunted. Its owner bade me lift one end of the stretcher they'd laid down to help Magda. A sergeant with one leg gone lay unmoving on it. We heaved that up and then two more.

'Now get the hell out of it,' the man who'd first beckoned me across shouted.

'We can take two more,' I shouted back through the din, 'and a couple of walking wounded.'

'We're all fucking walking wounded, just go.'

I realised he was, his other arm limp. Lady Hester had trailed after us and stood stunned, peering into the ambulance, where Butters had now wound a bandage round the bloody mess.

I went to touch her arm for her attention but a cry of 'Down!', a furious whining screech and a thump as my head hit the ground was followed by a cartwheel of flying earth and a thunderous roar. The ground rose and fell.

I seemed to wake from a sleep but I think it could only have been momentary. I lay on my back. The one-armed soldier sprawled across me and from his moving mouth looked as if he was alive. I could feel nothing and hear only a dull roaring. But I could smell something that wasn't blood or pus, smoke or cordite. The name eluded me. My eyes skittered trying to find its source.

Lady Hester lay unmoving a few yards away. My brain ignored her. Two more shells erupted across the lawn. Oil. It was oil. I stared between the rear wheels of the ambulance at the thick black mess between the front ones. A steady drip was slowing. I peered at the engine block and thought I detected a sag. If a pipe had been split, it might be salvable – though where I'd find oil here, heaven only knew – but if shrapnel had smashed the engine, we were stuck. A tree on the edge of the lawn was decapitated in a whirl of shrapnel. This place was a killing ground and the Germans had the range.

Then I remembered Lady Hester. I crawled over, praying I wouldn't see indignity but she sat up and glared at me.

'I have done it, now, haven't I?'

One-arm was on his feet and the two stretcher bearers jumped down from the ambulance. One pulled me up and the other Lady Hester.

'You'll have to get in the trench,' One-arm said.

'I need to check the eng…' I began.

'It's bloody fucked, man,' he replied. 'Dropped its guts, it has.'

'What about the chateau? Isn't that safer?'

'We're needed in the trench. You, too.'

'But the wounded…' Lady Hester said.

'They're fucked, too, now, aren't they, lady?'

She made to remonstrate but he waved her away. 'And we'll be joining 'em soon, don't worry, so no need to get shirty with me.'

'I'm not leaving Magda,' Lady Hester said.

'You won't have to, ma'am.' Butters stood on the back of the ambulance, with tears streaming down her face. 'She's gone.'

Fourteen

At a crouching run the soldiers dragged Lady Hester, Butters and me to the hedge line, where we tumbled into a shallow trench. Only two men occupied it, both sitting with their rifles pointing out over a low parapet. One had a bandage round his head, the other's face looked grey.

'Keep your bloody heads down,' One-arm said. 'They're gathering for the next push but somebody may fancy a go if he sees you.'

A rifle was thrust into my hands.

'Know how to use it?'

I shook my head.

'Jehovah bloody wept. Get down next to Joey, he'll show you. Fifteen rounds a minute it won't be but beggars can't be choosers. I'll get you a tunic. If you're captured say the rest of your uniform got burnt.'

I gaped at him which he must have taken for a question. 'Because if you're not in uniform the fuckers'll shoot you. You're Royal Welch, now. First battalion.'

I did as instructed. Joey took me through the routine. Curly's wooden rifle it wasn't but I thought I understood.

'Sorry, ladies,' One-arm said. 'I should have sent you into the house but it's too late now. Tell 'em that's where you're from when they overrun us.'

'I'll tell them that we're what we are,' Lady Hester replied, 'Women of the ambulance.'

One-arm went to retort but Joey said 'Sarge. They're coming.'

'Shit,' he said then called to what I now saw were similar trenches to either side, with two pairs of men in each. 'Steady. Wait for the order.'

That gave me some irrational confidence. We weren't quite alone. But the grey wall emerging from the wood beyond this field reminded me how outnumbered we were. And with no sign of reinforcements.

'What the fuck are you doing?'

It was One-arm's voice. I glanced round. Lady Hester was loading a rifle. 'I used to amuse myself working out how these things worked when my husband left them lying around in the stables.'

One-arm looked at her as she'd gone mad.

'I know how to shoot, too,' Butters added. They often said her dad was a poacher so maybe she did. She took up a position beside Lady Hester. The wall was slowly coming nearer. A solid mass. They were either crazy or so confident we posed no threat. Perhaps they knew.

Even so, we weren't likely to miss bringing a few down out of that formation. I remembered the kindermord. If *they'd* come on like that against lines of seasoned regulars, it was no wonder they'd paid for it. Now, I watched with a sinking feeling: all we were likely to do was give the buggers retreating more time to get away.

'My son was killed near here with the Life Guards,' Lady Hester said. 'You wouldn't happen to know where, by any chance, would you?'

I expected to hear a stream of abuse from One-arm. 'Not here,' was all he muttered, then, 'Wait for it. Wait... Now! Ten rounds rapid. Aim low.'

Joey had his ten off before I'd done three. Through the unbroken roar I saw whole swathes of grey collapse. The wall paused in its forward movement.

'Again!' One-arm shouted. As the cacophony ceased this time the wall broke and floundered back into the trees. I wanted to whoop but Joey muttered, 'Just testing to see our strength. They'll be back.'

'Not like that, they won't,' One-arm said. 'It'll be the artillery next. We're getting out of here.' He called out to the sides. 'Back to the house. Or they'll blow us to hell. Grab what you can.'

I hesitated for Joey to move. Then saw he couldn't. I froze.

'No, go on,' he said. 'I'll cover you.'

I stumbled up in a daze and scampered after the others. The crack of Joey's rifle from the trench told me he was as good as his word. I couldn't grasp the enormity of it. He was staying behind to sacrifice himself so we could escape? Even though that sacrifice was also likely to be in vain?

As I ran past the ambulance I saw what One-arm had meant. A huge piece of shrapnel had sheared through the side of the bonnet and stove in the engine. That wouldn't be driving anywhere any more. I thought of Magda lying dead inside it and my heart lurched. Was that what Lady Hester was thinking when she said 'I have done it, now, haven't I?'

There wasn't time to brood. I helped a limping man to the shelter of the stables on the far side of the chateau. There could only have been a few dozen of us. Many were in a bad way. I joined the rest in manhandling carts to form a barrier, aware as I did how insubstantial it was. Then I saw its main purpose was to funnel the attackers into a narrow gap. Facing that, men took up positions behind the low walls of pigsties and water troughs. I wanted to ask what if they outflanked us, but decided I'd be advised to keep my mouth shut.

The German bombardment grew in sudden intensity. As One-arm had predicted, our vacated trenches disappeared in a mass of smoke and flame. I closed my eyes, thinking of Joey. We might not amount to much where we were but if we'd stayed put, we'd amount to nothing by now. I marvelled at One-arm's grasp of tactics. This wasn't Curly's headlong flight. But it seemed likely to be as futile. I presumed these must be the regulars of whom we'd heard nothing since they'd crossed the Channel. So this is what an 'orderly retreat' felt like? Being massacred by slow degrees.

For ten minutes you couldn't hear a thing. It ceased all at once. Without any telling, the men who weren't in cover took up defensive positions. They did it as a matter of course, like they were doing an ordinary job. One-arm ordered *us* inside a stable, in the walls of which his men had knocked out some bricks to make firing points. From where I was the stable half-door gave me a view across the lawn. I'd be able to watch the full line of the advance.

'Is he your commanding officer?' I asked the curly-haired man next to me, indicating One-arm.

'Who? Dewi?' he chuckled. 'Yesterday he was only a corporal. Mind, if he gets through this, he probably will be tomorrow. There's nobody else left, is there?'

A cry alerted me to the fact that the German advance had reached the lawn. Still in close order, rifles at the ready, their pointed helmets now also clear. Their pace had quickened, their confidence apparently justified by the lack of resistance. Before Dewi could give an order volleys of shots rang out from the German front rank. I flinched back but nothing came our way. They were shooting at the chateau, not realising it was unoccupied.

'Fire!' Dewi shouted, aiming a revolver in his good hand, and the crash and smoke obliterated thought. I fired into where the lawn had been, the stock of the rifle jarring my shoulder. The whistling and pinging of bullets off the brickwork told me we hadn't driven them off this time. Then the firing on both sides paused. I dared to hope but through a gap in the smoke I saw the nearest attackers were merely gathering behind our barricades. They weren't panicking, more probably weighing up how best to neutralize us. I guessed it wouldn't take them long. The rest on the lawn had pulled back out of sight. Or were they even now outflanking us?

'You ladies, get to the back of this, you hear?' Dewi said. 'You don't want to be at the front when they break through.'

'Don't I?' Lady Hester called. Butters also stayed at her post. I think I'd have taken the choice but no one here appeared to believe me too young.

'You've not got time to argue,' Dewi snapped.

'I'm not arguing,' was her response.

'Oh, sod you, then.'

I glanced to see how she'd take that but she kept her gaze fixed through the loophole. I took another look outside. Those Germans behind the barricades were making no move. I wondered what they were up to. Dewi – and an outbreak of firing to our rear – provided the answer.

'Oh, shit, they're behind us.'

A clutch of men across from us, crouched behind a stone trough, went down face first as they were hit from the rear. Another was bowled over backwards as he leapt to switch his cover. The fire was coming from both sides.

'In the doorway!' Dewi shouted.

I was too slow. He and two others stood side by side at the half door and blazed away. One turned aside to reload and crumpled in a heap. I shoved in and took his place. Germans went down everywhere but the mass moved forward in a solid wedge. Our first defensive line just vanished.

Then I froze. In bewilderment. The attacking Germans were themselves being taken in the rear. All I could see was chaos. And now, panic. They were turning away, trying to make for the lawn. I looked at Dewi for an explanation.

'Fire on them!' was all he cried and as they broke we did. Then 'Cease fire!' rang out in my ear. 'Cease fire!'

The flight across the lawn was khaki. But these were chasing. And shouting. Dewi jerked the door open.

'Check the bodies,' he snapped. 'If it has a weapon and moves, shoot it. You hear?'

I did but hardly had the strength to comply. My shoulder throbbed. The scene of carnage stunned me. I wasn't the only one. A big German stood with his hands above his head. I motioned him against the wall. Several stirred on the ground but none seemed inclined to resist.

Butters touched my arm. 'You all right, Harry?'

I nodded. 'Dunno what all that was about, though. Were did they come from? I'd never seen any reinforcements coming down here.'

'Worcesters, ma'am,' a clipped voice said. I swung to my left. A hatless officer was addressing Lady Hester, who must have followed Butters out. 'Major Hankey, Second Battalion.'

'Thank you, Major. In the nick of time, I think.'

'Pleasure,' he said, saluted and ran to follow his men.

'Never thought I'd believe in miracles,' Dewi said, returning to us. 'You got any medical supplies in that ambulance?'

'I'll go,' I replied, following Major Hankey's route round the end of the chateau. The lawn was strewn with German dead. That wasn't what stopped me in mid-stride. In front of the hedge they lay in piles. Huge mounds. Some way off I heard the chatter of a machine gun. The Worcesters' charge, that had seemed to come from mid-air, must have been more calculated. They'd had a machine gun set up to catch the fleeing Germans from the flank.

I remembered my task and approached the ambulance with trepidation. I didn't want to see Magda's body but I had to make sure she was all right. When I peered inside all I could see was a bloody pile. I turned away and retched then looked again. Her body *was* undisturbed. Before it lay the shattered mess of one of Dewi's casualties, whose body had been flung out of the upper stretcher rack.

Deciding the priority was to help the living I gathered as much bandage and dressing as I could carry from the rear of the cab and trudged back to the stables. Steady firing came from beyond the trenches where we'd left Joey but none of it came this way.

We did what we could for the wounded, who seemed to bear their fate with much less noise than the men we'd dealt with at Furnes. The line had been re-established in a sunken road beyond where our first glimpse of the advancing wall had been. Unlike the area around Furnes this was more wooded and rolling country so the distance you could see was limited.

Another company of Worcesters arrived and were sent to bolster the new line. Because of the limited field of vision the Germans must have felt they were threatened by massive forces – in reality there were not much more than a few hundred – since they'd shown no desire to stand and fight. Maybe these troops were more of the 'kinder', too and didn't take a fancy to further 'mord'.

I made a closer examination of the engine but it was hopeless. Lady Hester procured two of Dewi's unwounded men to help me dig a grave for Magda. Butters fashioned a rough cross. We also found Joey's remains and covered him and several of his mates with earth in the trench where he'd died. Dewi had his men scour the battlefield for rations carried by the dead of both sides so later in the afternoon we sat on the straw inside the stables and gorged ourselves on bully beef and biscuits for the first time. Once things had settled down I began to feel quite shaky. I'd actually been in a battle. I thought of Curly. This was an experience I'd craved back in England and wished I'd be able to boast about. The reality of it I now just wanted to forget. Doing so wasn't that easy.

The clatter of hooves on the stable yard startled me out of my daydreaming. I clambered up and looked outside, thinking it might be a horse-drawn ambulance. I had a further shock.

'Ma'am,' I called, 'you should see who's outside.'

Lady Hester came to the door. 'Douglas,' she cried.

General Haig was handing his horse – a white horse – to an aide. He turned and a look of incredulity crossed his face.

'What are damned women doing here?' he said to Major Hankey, who'd gone to greet him. 'Get them out of here.'

I breathed with relief. He hadn't recognised Lady Hester. And we had no Wolseley to jog his memory. Lady Hester told me to stay where I was and strode towards him. That jolted me. Then I recalled why we'd come down here in the first place. I watched with a sinking feeling.

I couldn't hear what was said but it gave *him* a jolt. He was shaking his head. Lady Hester seemed to be insisting. It made no difference. He grew red in the face. With a flurry of orders he marched off, followed by Major Hankey and his aides. They disappeared round the side of the chateau. A private blocked Lady Hester with his rifle from following.

'A charlatan,' she fumed as she returned to the stable. 'The man's beneath contempt. Don't I have any rights at all?'

'You're lucky he didn't have you shot,' Dewi called.

'All I want is to see the grave of my son.'

'And all I want is to see the evening showing of the can-can at the Folies Bergere,' Dewi laughed.

'This is *not* a joke!'

Dewi showed not the slightest sign of being abashed by Lady Hester's fury. 'Too right, it ain't, but I've got more chance of walking to Paris by tonight and doing the can-can than you have of finding a grave anywhere in all this mess. By rights we should all be in our own by now.'

It was Lady Hester who backed down. 'I'm asking the impossible?'

'You are, ma'am. For two reasons. First, who knows where the grave is – behind the German lines, in No Man's Land? There are no maps here, it's all shifting sands. And second, you seen the effect of artillery back where we were? Even if you find the site, what you find there may no longer be a grave. We have to make do with our memories now, in this lot.'

Lady Hester said nothing. I wondered if she longed to find the grave to obscure her memories. As for me, what I'd seen in the last month would probably blot out all my earlier life. The picture in my mind of Magda's grave certainly brought no consolation.

As it grew dusk a succession of lorries and ambulances arrived to load up the wounded. Haig had ridden off without another word but Major Hankey informed Lady Hester that the two of them – she and Butters – were to leave for Ypres with the wounded and from there to accompany the worst cases to England at the earliest opportunity.

'The three of us, you mean, Major,' Lady Hester said.

'Three?'

She indicated me. Major Hankey frowned. 'I assumed him to be with the Welch. He's wearing…'

'He's my driver, with the ambulance…'

'Ah. I'm sure we could find…'

'And under age…'

Oh God, here we go again. Back with the 'kinder'.

'He looks old enough. How old are you, my lad?'

I stared at him, unable to speak.

'He's fourteen,' Butters said.

Major Hankey turned pale. 'Good Lord.' He backed out of the stable. 'Very well, ma'am. I wish you all well.'

When the time came I was sad to leave. I offered Dewi the tunic. 'Don't think I'll be needing this any more.'

'You keep it, boyo, you earned it. Bring it back with you in three years when you *can* join up.'

'You won't still be here in three years?'

'We won't be here tomorrow.'

'What?'

199

'We're pulling back after dark. Shortening the line. Today was a bit too close to it being over by Christmas. But the Welch'll be hereabouts, you can be sure of that. And Jerry's not going to give up in a hurry.'

'But the graves?' Lady Hester put in.

'Memories, didn't I tell you?'

'We can't just leave…'

'That's what it's all about. We're always leaving some place or other.'

The journey back to England was the most disconsolate of all the ones I'd made. Despite everything, the last few weeks had been the headiest of my life. And it wasn't just regrets I was leaving behind: the Wolseley, the ambulance and above all, Magda, I'd never see again. Memories, Dewi had said. They were all we had. And what lay before me? Once Lady Hester remembered what he'd done, I couldn't see my dad still having a job. Which meant no home, either. Where would we go?

That side of it was soon pushed aside. Not least by something that hit me with a shock: I was unwounded. We'd become used, I suppose, to being eyed with suspicion since the Germans captured us so the glares from some of the casualties on the troop train to Boulogne didn't seem odd. Lady Hester and Butters sat beside me, asleep or pretending to be so in order to forestall the banter the sight of a woman had attracted on several occasions already. One of the walking wounded in our carriage broke off complaining about his discomfort – he only had a bandaged arm – and eyed me with scorn, I thought.

'Should be ashamed of yerself,' he muttered.

I took no notice, not realising he was addressing me.

'You. Too big to speak to a wounded man, are you?'

'Sorry, mister, I didn't think you…'

'It's not for ones like you to be proud of yerself.'

I stared at him, without a clue what he was referring to. I glanced to my right but neither of my companions stirred. He must have taken my silence for contempt. It roused his. 'Whyn't you back there where you belong?'

I shook my head in incomprehension. That stirred the man beside him, one eye covered by a bandage, to jump in.

'You got the heeby-jeebies? Windy? That why you're scarpering back home? Or are you in the women's army, now?'

They both laughed. The third man with them gave a glassy grin: his bandaged jaw made anything more beyond him. I began to wonder if their brains had gone, as well.

'I don't know what you mean,' I protested.

That only caused more laughter. Its viciousness cut into me. '"I don't know what you mean,"' my first accuser whined, his imitation piling on my shame.

'He'll have one soon enough to show the girls,' One-eye opined. 'Reckon we should help him out there, Jim?'

'He'd fancy his chances against a wounded hero, wouldn't he?' Jim – my first accuser – sneered.

I tensed, alert for any movement and then it struck me. Here I was, on a troop train full of returning wounded, and I stood out because I had no wound. They glared at me. I clenched my fists and waited but they made no move. My mind sought for some way to explain but the words that formed sounded feeble even in my head.

Butters' voice made me start.

'How long were you lot in the Front Line?'

'Front Line?' One-eye asked.

Butters snorted. 'Harry's been both sides of it. We all have. And some of those with us are still there – buried. We're only here now because we were ordered back by General Haig in person.'

'Oh, yeah..?' Jim began.

'Yes.' Lady Hester had come awake, too. 'And had my ambulance not been smashed beyond repair, I'd have also given *him* a piece of my mind. With scratches like yours the Belgian troops were staying at their posts until they could no longer stand. Kindly keep your crassness to yourselves.'

The rest of the journey passed in silence. As we waited to board the steamer across the Channel I became conscious of the lines of men limping or being helped on board.

'Can you support me, Harry, I feel faint,' Butters said when our turn came. I gaped at her in surprise. She grabbed my arm and thrust herself against me before I could ask what was the matter. We struggled up the gangplank with her weight unbalancing me. Lady Hester had been given a cabin and directed me to help Butters there.

Once inside I eased her onto a bunk and stepped back to appraise her condition. She gave me a broad grin. 'Done like a true gentleman, Harry,' she said. 'I was going to suggest you put on a limp but that didn't seem right.'

I forced a smile of thanks. However, the recollection of the jibes I'd faced on the voyage out didn't cheer me. Lady Hester told us both to stay in the cabin so I escaped further torment but the prospects of the train journey to London depressed me. The closer we got to home the less I felt I belonged anywhere.

Fifteen

After we landed my confusion increased. On English soil Lady Hester's status re-asserted itself. She was expected and a carriage reserved for her. An escort led us off the ship ahead of its main cargo. Butters had me support her but made less of a show of being on the point of collapse. Again I enjoyed the feeling of closeness. When we reached the First Class carriage I had my first reminder of the realities of English life.

'Not you two. Servants to the guard's van,' an officer with a red hat-band barked at us.

'Oh,' I said and set off the way we had come, towards the rear of the train. I could see the walking wounded by now streaming into the carriages. Should I limp?

'No, they're with me. I need their help,' Lady Hester called and motioned us to return.

I stumbled aboard, conscious of the disdain of the railway officials. We mumbled thanks to Lady Hester and took our seats at the opposite side of the carriage. This was another aspect of the old life that had come as a shock. I wondered why she hadn't sent for a car to collect us. Was there no one to drive? Had my dad already been dismissed? What of Hemmings, had he given in and joined up? Lady Hester must have read my thoughts.

'I would have preferred to return home directly by car but our Army friends clearly did not trust us with an automobile in the port. We have to be given clearance in London before being permitted to re-assume civilian life, I'm afraid.'

I wondered if that explained Lady Hester's invitation to share her carriage. Her formal-sounding reply to Butters' light-hearted response to that further reminded me of the distance re-asserting itself between our worlds.

'Didn't want us to go in the first place, did they, ma'am? And now they don't want to let go of us.'

'No, indeed, Butters,' Lady Hester said. That was the end of "Lily" then? I waited to be addressed as "Butler" but there was no more conversation on our way in to Victoria.

On arrival we were taken to an office to obtain the papers for our release. Once more we came from the train ahead of the wounded and I was conscious of the gaze of the crowd waiting at the barrier. Lady Hester marched with her head held high – a bit different to our last departure from here – and shuffling behind her seemed to confer protection.

Of course she knew the old boy in charge and after signing on our behalf asked us to wait for her outside as she wanted a word with him.

'Another one for a roasting?' I asked Butters when the door had closed behind us. Before she could answer something was thrust into my hand. I felt it jab and started. A white feather. I looked up at the back of a young woman walking away.

'Here, what's this?' I called after her.

She turned and looked me up and down. I was reminded of Lady Helena, though this one had never got her hands – or her face – dirty. She gestured towards the train. 'Ask them. They're not cowards.'

I held the white feather up for Butters to see and shrugged in bewilderment. Butters snatched it off me, flung it to the floor and stamped on it. 'Nor is he,' she shouted. She also pointed to the train. 'We've just come off that.' Then she pointed at me. 'And he's under age.'

'Lil, no,' I began. The shame of being called a child was worse than baseless accusations of cowardice. Butters cut me off. 'He's only seventeen.'

I gaped at her. She was glaring at the young lady. The latter seemed about to reply but gave a haughty shake of her shoulders, turned and stalked off.

'Thanks, Lil,' I mumbled. 'Good to be back, isn't it?'

When Lady Hester came out she didn't look very pleased, either.

It never occurred to me that what we'd been through in the last six weeks might turn out to be the easy part.

As homecomings go, I can't say we made a splash – not that we wanted one. No one expected us and no one was waiting. I don't know why Lady Hester still didn't telephone for someone to come and fetch us. Maybe she feared what she'd hear. She commandeered a taxi-cab. You can tell what state I was in because I didn't even notice the make. The driver regaled us with how hard life was with the war on. We all pretended to be asleep.

In my case, not until we'd left the centre of the city. If London was suffering from the War, it hid the fact very well. Everywhere was still plastered with recruiting posters and boasts of patriotism, while the hustle and bustle sounded undimmed. Perhaps it's all war-preparation, I told myself but those sauntering along in uniform seemed the only ones with time on their hands. I yearned for the horror and destruction of Dixmude: that, at least, was real life.

Of course, when we arrived at the House we had no English money. I was sent inside to find someone – through the front door! The place was cold and empty. Afraid to call out, I peeped in one or two rooms before I remembered there could be no one here. I ran downstairs and burst into the kitchen.

You'd have thought I was a squadron of uhlans. Cook, who was sitting at the end of the table facing me, swayed and looked about to pass out. Hemmings, lounging against the mantelpiece, shot upright. 'You get the buggery out, you hear, you thieving...'

'It's me, Harry.'

He stopped still, his mouth hanging open and gaped at me.

'It never is?' Cook said. 'Harry, you gave me a right turn. What you doing, coming in like that? From there.'

You'd think I'd merely come down late from polishing the silver. Convincing them of my errand made protesting I wasn't a spy to the Germans appear like a game. Then they claimed to have no money to hand. I was all a lather, thinking of Lady Hester outside being accused by the taxi driver of trying to diddle an honest tradesman.

'The baker's tin,' I cried out.

'You can't touch that,' Cook screeched but I'd already grabbed it and unscrewed the lid. Seeing it contained some notes I set off for the door. Hemmings blocked my way.

'You ain't running off with that,' he said.

I shoved him hard with the flat of my hand and dodged aside. 'Then run after me,' I called, taking the stairs two at a time. If this was a fair taste of civilian life, the sooner I was old enough to join up the better. And things only got worse.

I thought my own home had been abandoned. No smoke came from the chimney and there were no sounds of children. Had they already been evicted? Surely Lady Hester would have said. Weeds were showing through the flagstones on the path. I peered at the windows as I approached the door but could make out no sign of life.

I expected the door to be locked. However, the latch lifted and the door creaked open. The sight that greeted me made me catch my breath. It *did* look abandoned – as if they'd all been carried off in mid stride. No fire burned in the grate. A newspaper lay strewn across the floor. Unwashed pots covered the table. The smell of rancid cheese wafted up from it.

I covered my nose. 'Hello?' I called out. Silence.

I climbed the stairs slowly. The children's bedroom had been left unmade. I pushed open the door to my parents. There was no sign of my mum. The bed in there also looked a mess. I shivered.

Bending low I squinted out of the back window. And started. My dad, at least I think it was him, sat slumped on the bench under the apple tree. Asleep? I couldn't tell. But where was everyone else?

I went to rush downstairs then stopped myself. What was I going to say? I'd half-expected a warm greeting from the children, perhaps even from my mum. My dad's welcome I'd not been able to guess. Would he blame me? Would he feel guilty? Would he try to give me a leathering?

'Oh, it's you?' was all he said when I'd managed to wake him. He was unshaven and I could smell drink. He offered nothing else except a coughing fit. Then his eyes closed again.

'Dad! Where is everyone?'

He gaped at me as though the request was incomprehensible. I repeated the question. He avoided my gaze.

'Have they gone out? Away?' I asked.

He still didn't reply. I shook his shoulder. 'Dad!' Then realised what I'd done – laid hands on him. I started back but there was no reaction. He mumbled something that I didn't catch. Had the whole civilian world become stupid?

'I beg your pardon?'

'Dead.'

For a moment my mind wouldn't work. 'Dead?'

He made no move to contradict me. I stared at the one side of his face I could see. His hair hadn't seen a comb for longer than mine. He continued to look away, refusing, by the set of his pose, to face me. My brain made some sense of what he'd said but couldn't clarify the enormity.

'What, all of them?' I managed to gasp.

He shook his head. That only gave me another jolt.

'Then, who?'

Again he mumbled. I lost my rag.

'Who!?'

He swung round on me. 'Your ma.'

It was my turn to look away. I stared at the apple trees. The fruit hadn't been picked. The ones on the ground were well-rotted now. All I could think was:

'When?'

He gave another maddening shrug. I realised I was breathing heavily. I couldn't stand it but I couldn't repeat the question. Then he broke the silence.

'Not long after you gone.'

That shook me more. Was it my going away, then, that killed her? I daren't ask. My eyes stayed on the rotted apples. Why hadn't the children made short work of them? They usually did. I tried to think where they'd be.

'Dad, where are the others? The nippers.'

Again, he flapped his hand in a vague gesture. I followed its direction and saw the church spire. But he'd indicated that only my mum had died. They couldn't be in the churchyard. I let out a sigh of exasperation. His anxious face glanced round at me. 'Workhouse.'

Exasperation gave way to anger. 'You put them in the workhouse? What were you thinking of?'

'I couldn't manage… After she gone. You wasn't here…'

The attempt to blame me blew my top. I beat at his shoulders with both fists. 'Don't you lump it on me, you worthless coward,' I screamed, the blood pounding in my head. 'You ought to be ashamed of yourself.'

He made no attempt to resist, made no sound. All of a sudden he slid off the bench and lay curled over on the ground. I froze with my arms raised to strike. Had I killed him? No, I could see him breathe. But what I'd done hit me just as hard as if I had. I'd attacked my dad. Hit him. Hurt him. Is this what the War had made me into? Some ambulance man I'd turned out to be.

Gasping apologies, I tried to sit him up. Now he did resist and shook me off. He eased himself to sit with his back against the bench, his face set away from me, saying nothing. I could only stare at him, my body starting to shake. Then I saw his shoulders convulse and heard the sobs. I turned and bolted.

By the time my anger had given way to shame and that had eased, it was growing dark: too late to try the workhouse in town today. I knew I couldn't stay in that cottage but it was too cold to sleep out.

I went back to see if my dad had gone inside. He was sitting on the bench, slumped again. I took his arm, heaved him up and dragged and pushed him through the back door. My fears about how I'd get him upstairs were stilled when he threw himself into the armchair beside the dead fire and closed his eyes. This I took to mean that all conversation was over.

I salvaged a coarse blanket from upstairs and spent a fretful night in the church porch. I'd grown used to being able to sleep whenever I had the chance, whatever the level of discomfort, and the porch was both hard and cold, but it was my thoughts that disturbed my rest. My mum had never been a strong presence in my life. Now she was gone I felt her absence more than when she had been present. Even her grave which, with its wooden cross, wasn't far off, didn't bring her close. My dad I regarded with both anger and guilt: anger at the way he'd let things fall apart alternating with guilt at the way I'd laid into him when I recalled how broken he seemed.

Then there were the kids. The workhouse. How could he? Workhouse kids. My shame on their behalf swung the balance back to fury at his feebleness. His "I couldn't manage" made me grind my teeth. Jessie was twelve, Sairy eleven, they could easily manage the house if he'd shown any gumption. The little-uns, Wilf and Eddy, weren't babies any more, they could fetch and carry.

Sometime in the middle of the night I woke from a doze wondering if money had been the problem. With Lady Hester away my dad would have had no job. And whose fault was that? I told myself. Besides, with so many men gone to the war, it shouldn't have been difficult to pick up work. If you tried. It was still no excuse.

My intention had been to go straight to the workhouse and get the children out but I woke up so stiff and famished I hesitated while I tried to get my brain in order. 'Just like your old man,' I heard myself think.

Sticking my head under the pump did clear it but only sharpened the hunger. I hovered near Pa Billings' bakery, the smell from which drove me crazy. As I was plucking up my courage a thin-faced man in an apron, who I didn't recognise, came and stood in the doorway. He eyed me up and down. I slunk away. Begging from strangers was something I couldn't face. There was only one place left.

This time I didn't catch Cook unawares. She caught me.

'Harry, you poor love, you look half-starved to death. Sit by the fire while I rustle you summat to eat.'

I'd expected a frosty reception after yesterday but you'd have thought I was the prodigal son. She prattled on about how good it was to see me back safe and sound. Then Butters came in and I realised why. Cook beamed at her, too. 'Our Lil's been telling us all about what you been up to, young lad. Fair gave me a turn, some of it.'

'You all right, Harry, you look awful?' Lil asked. I shrugged then realised I was imitating my dad and turned to face her. 'I'm OK. My mum died. My dad's sent the kids to the workhouse. I'm going to fetch them when…'

'Not before you've had some of this,' Cook said.

She waved me to the table and I threw myself on the pile of food she laid there. I felt hers and Butters' eyes on me as I crammed it into my mouth.

'Lor, Harry, ain't they been feeding you up over there in that France? Slow down.'

'Sorry,' I spluttered with my mouth full. I changed the subject to evade my embarrassment. 'How are you, Lil? Back to normal?'

She gave a glance upstairs. 'Oh, you know. Not easy, is it, when you have time to think?'

I remembered the empty rooms I'd found when I ran inside yesterday. Lady Hester didn't even have the comfort of a grave, for what it was worth. And Helena, would she ever see her again? Yet I already sensed the pain would be more than physical separation.

Hemmings came in with a breakfast tray. The sight of me made him start. I clenched my fists but he gave a snort and carried on through into the pantry. I noticed Butters shrank away from him.

'Want me to come with you?' she asked.

I peered up at her, not sure what she meant then realised and shook my head. 'No, thanks, I'll be all right.'

All right I wasn't. At the workhouse they refused me entry. I couldn't see the children because they were in the schoolroom and couldn't be disturbed. I said I wanted them out. That brought the matron to the door. Who was I to ask? Their brother? Could I prove that? Did I have their parents' permission?

I lost my rag at that. Didn't she know my mum had died? Ah, she remembered. But my father had said he couldn't cope. The rector had backed him up. Was my father able to now? He didn't need to, I fumed, I was back from Belgium, I could take care of them.

'Belgium?' She looked me up and down. Her lip curled.

'In the Army? You don't appear to have been wounded. Won't you soon have to go back? Leaving us to pick up the pieces once more?'

'I'm not in the Army. I'm not going back. Just give me my brothers and sisters.'

Her eyes narrowed. What had I done now?

'How old are you?'

'Seventeen.'

A supercilious smile played across her face. 'Then they can't possibly be handed over to your care. You are not of an age to assume the responsibility.'

I could have hit her. I blustered, telling her I'd coped with things the like of which she couldn't imagine in Belgium but that just hardened her stance. She was typical, really. It was why you gave up trying to convey what it was like over there: the reality was beyond people's imagination so they disbelieved you. Keeping quiet was the only way to keep faith with those who'd suffered and died. That's what I thought then.

The upshot was I found the door closed in my face, with her final rebuke echoing in my head. 'Look at the state of you. You think you could take care of anyone else?'

What could I do? Force my dad to come and get them out? He'd be less impressive than me. Plead with the rector to help? I could visualise how patronising he'd be. So I tried Lady Hester.

She wouldn't see me.

'Why?' I asked Hemmings when he came down with the answer to my request. He looked down his nose at me. 'What makes you think her ladyship needs a reason?'

I turned away. So much for what we'd shared in Belgium. I wasn't going to add to Hemmings' smugness by trying to explain. Normal service certainly had resumed.

'There is one thing,' Hemmings added. I swung back, hopeful until I saw his sneer. 'There's a load of wood wants chopping out the back.' He must have seen my scowl because the smile on his face broadened. 'Not fancy the chance to earn a few bob? Didn't make much pay on the field of combat, did you?'

Commonsense cooled my fury while chopping wood certainly provided an outlet for it and closed off the frustration of trying to think. There was two months' worth of timber to saw and chop up. In our absence Hemmings hadn't found it becoming to soil his hands with such work.

By the end of the day, despite being 'a few bob' better off, I'd made no headway with the problem of the children. The only solution that offered itself was drink. I jingled the coins in the palm of my hand. It was a waste, I knew. I also knew that I hadn't much head for it and I'd only make a fool of myself – or worse. What the hell.

'Harry.'

Butters was at the scullery doorway.

'Cook's just put some dinner out for you.'

I shook my head and turned to continue through the gate.

'Please.'

I glanced round. Something in her tone reminded me of the times with the ambulance when I'd thought she was scared. I went back. In the kitchen Hemmings sat with his back to me, eating. I could see only one other plate on the table, across from Hemmings.

As Butters bustled in he reached out his left hand. 'I told you, no need to sit over there, Lil,' then he saw me and his face darkened. 'Oh, the outside help, what you want?'

'His dinner,' Lil said, pushing me into the chair. 'You start, Harry, I'll just get mine.'

The exercise had sharpened my appetite and the sight of Hemmings' discomfort didn't blunt it. I hadn't realised until I pushed him out of the way yesterday how slight he was. Is that how he'd avoided being pressed into joining up? A white feather might knock him down.

'Getting a bit smoky here,' he said with a nod at the fire, blazing away now thanks to my labours. 'Think I'll finish mine in the den.'

The den was the butler's but Mr Saddleworth had gone to London with Sir Brydon and hadn't been replaced. Except in Hemmings' eyes. Butters brought a plate of bread and cheese and sat next to me. The colour had come back to her face. And being thrown into that

212

helter-skelter world had done wonders for my powers of observation.

'He bothering you, Lil?' I asked.

'Just don't feel comfortable when there's only him around, that's all.'

'Where's Cook?'

'Gone for a lie down. She said she didn't feel too bright.'

'She feeling the strain, now Lady Hester's back?'

'There's a lot to do. She was having to chop the wood until today.'

Not something she'd over-exerted herself with, I reflected.

'Where's everyone else?' I asked.

Disappearance seemed to be becoming a feature of my homecoming.

'An ammunition factory's been opened in town. As there was no work here once we'd left, they all went and signed on there. Better pay as well.'

'You're not going, too?'

She glanced at door through which Hemmings had left. 'Not sure. Her Ladyship's been in a foul mood since she came back…'

'Is she? She refused to see me…'

'The divorce has come through. And she's been going through Mr James's things.'

'I thought it was just me.'

'From the state of you, it would have been if she *had* seen you. But what did you want to see her for?'

I explained and was touched by her concern. Being close to her brought back the warmth and comfort I'd felt a couple of times in Belgium.

'So what are you going to do now?' she asked when I'd finished.

'Get drunk.'

'Oh, no, you're not. I'll tell you what you're going to do.'

She dragged me after her to the servants' quarters round the side and flung open the door to a narrow room containing a bed, a chest of drawers and a table and chair. I wondered what I was letting myself in for.

'Your room,' she said. 'Fred's gone and joined up. But that's not all.'

She rummaged in the drawers then held up a pair of trousers and squinted at me. 'Hm, these look a bit small. Never mind…'

'Never mind? I'm not wearing them.'

'Of course, you're not,' she fussed, bundling me down the corridor.

The white tile of the bathroom gave me a jolt. It reminded me of our prison. And Magda. I stood and gaped while Butters turned on the taps. Steam rose.

'Right,' she said, thrusting a big towel in my hand. 'Get those smelly things off and pile them by the door…'

'Not while you're…'

'Yes, while I'm finding some clothes that might fit a bit better. Get a move on before it goes cold.'

She shut the door behind her. I hesitated. She was right. Only the dirt was holding some of my clothing together. But would she come back in?

I stripped off quickly, one eye on the door and listening for footsteps. The water stung at first but I sank into it, the warmth delicious. There wasn't any of this in Belgium. After I'd set to with the block of carbolic a dark scum covered the surface of the water. I felt a weight lift off me, which in a sense it had.

The door opened and I ducked down, getting scum in my ears. Butters' voice called 'Good, thanks. Put these on until yours are washed.'

When the door shut I peeped out to see a pile of clothes by the door. I looked from them to the greasy scum around me. I must have been a filthy little wretch. When I had my new clothes on it wasn't to the alehouse I went, it was home. I swept out the kitchen, made up the fire and washed all the pots, while my dad made out he was asleep. Having finished, I shook him, pointed out how different it looked and said I'd be back to check he kept it that way.

From then on I seemed to become part of Lady Hester's household. I'm not sure if she knew. Cook found me plenty of jobs to keep me busy and Butters had taken on a mission to strip all the absentees' rooms and have them ready for a new intake. I couldn't imagine when that might be. I fretted about the children but could find no answer. Once, I thought Cook and Butters were deep in discussion about them though both denied it was any such thing.

With all this I hadn't had the time to think about cars. Until Hemmings came hurrying into the kitchen garden, where I was clearing its two months of neglect for Cook.

'Here,' he called, as if I was a dog. I ignored him.

'Her Ladyship needs your help,' he added, coming nearer.

I looked up in surprise. I didn't know she knew I was here. 'Mine?'

'She wants to go out… in the Model T…'

'She wants me to drive?'

'Course not, but it's been laid up. I can't get it to… It won't start.'

I stared at him. 'Helping Lady Hester?'

'Helping her out, like.'

'Oh, right,' I said, laughing and jamming my fork into the ground. 'In that case…'

'Cheeky little bleeder, ain't you?'

'Not in front of Uhlans.'

'What?'

I left it at that. Two months ago the idea of speaking my mind would have sent me scampering back into my shell. Now, I'd taken to telling myself 'They're not Uhlans' and carrying on.

The sight of the Model T jerked back the picture of Magda lying in the ambulance. But I was glad to get my hands on an engine again. Two months' idleness hadn't suited the Model T. She'd been covered in a dust sheet which now lay in a heap. That also produced a jolt of memory about Magda. Don't think about it, don't think about it, don't think about it, I repeated to myself to drive out the pictures. Then I felt guilty for doing so but I couldn't face them.

I wondered if Hemmings had tried to use the car himself while we were away. If so he hadn't succeeded. The oil had gone sludgy and the timing was out. I gave Hemmings the details.

'I'll need to try it out when I'm done,' I added.

'Just give me a shout,' he called as he went off.

I was soon immersed in the engine, other cares forgotten and before long she was purring. For some reason Carstairs' "Treat her like a woman" crossed my mind and I looked round to see if Hemmings was lurking. He wasn't so I decided I'd have the pleasure myself.

She rolled off without a hitch and I congratulated myself on not losing the knack. I decided a circuit of the House would serve as a fair test. What astonished me was the smoothness of the ride. Then I realised we were on gravel and not those Belgian cobbles. Wherever it was, I was in heaven. Until a shout made me brake.

I expected to see Hemmings cursing me but it was Butters, waving to me from the front door. She stepped aside and Lady Hester swept down the steps.

'I thought I told you two o'clock? I've been waiting... Oh, Butler?'

'Sorry, ma'am, Mr Hemmings couldn't get her to start so I've been...'

'Never mind that. You know the way to..?'

'Yes, ma'am.'

'I'm expected at two-thirty.'

The town wasn't far. I wondered at all the song and dance. And whether she really realised it was me. 'You don't want me to let Mr Hemmings..?'

'Just take me to town.'

I stumbled out and held the rear door open for her. She shook her head 'I'll join you in the front. But I don't wish to talk.'

That suited me. I wanted to enjoy the trip. I had no sense of what time it was but decided putting my foot down couldn't go amiss. After hurtling through the dark to dodge shells, this travel was magical.

'Not quite so fast, please.' Lady Hester broke into my daydreams and I slowed right down. It was lucky I did since round the next corner we came up on a lumbering hay wain. At my previous speed we'd have gone through the back of it.

'Over there, behind that big car,' Lady Hester pointed as we rolled up the High street. "That big car" was a Wolseley, I noted with a start. If you gave them away, I don't suppose you bothered too much about the make.

I pulled to a halt behind it. I went to get down and run round to help Lady Hester out when the sight of a figure emerging from the Wolseley made me stop. It was Sir Bryden. He strode up to us. His first words didn't ease my shock. 'Damn you woman, I have a meeting at the War Office at four.' Nice way to greet your wife. I flinched but Lady Hester's recent experience had toughened her.

'To discuss how many more innocents you can send to the slaughter?' she piped up. 'And don't tell me I don't know what I'm talking about because I've seen more of this War in the last few weeks than you ever will.'

Sir Brydon's eyes popped and he went red. I struggled to keep a straight face.

'There's no cause to take that tone,' he spluttered.

'No cause? I thought there was every cause?'

'I am trying to do the decent thing.'

'And failing.'

Out of the corner of my eye I saw him offer his hand to help her out but she brushed it away.

'I was entitled to keep the House,' he said.

'Perhaps, but we both know at what cost, don't we?'

They may have done but I didn't. They went into the office that proclaimed 'Hamble, Jeavons & Martin, Solicitors & Commissioners for Oaths' across a wide opaque window. I let out a deep sigh. The world had changed, inside and out, since August.

Before I could settle to gather my wits Lady Hester was back out and climbing in beside me. For a moment I was too startled to react. Lady Hester spoke sharply. 'Take me for a drive on the Downs. And not too fast. We're not in Belgium now.'

This acknowledgment of our comradeship eased the sharpness and I did begin to relax. Lady Hester said no more. The sky had cleared and there was a weak November sun. This certainly wasn't Belgium. Soft undulating country with winding lanes. And no shells. I think we may have passed the place of our clash with General Haig in July but when I glanced at Lady Hester she gave no sign of recalling it.

'Stop here,' she said as we crested a rise. In the distance the shapes of ships dotted the flat sheen of Channel. I turned so we faced them.

217

Lady Hester sat and stared straight ahead. I don't know what she was thinking. Did she have regrets? Both her children were over there. Were they both dead? They might as well have been.

And then there was Magda. All sorts of pictures skittered through my mind but Magda always imposed herself. Lying in the back of the ambulance. The injustice of it brought a lump to my throat. But hers was merely one in the whole panoply of slaughter. And the other figures I'd never see again would flit past.

At length Lady Hester bade me take her home. Again we drove in silence. At the front steps she did allow me to help her down. And thanked me. I felt at ease. My eyes followed her, remarking the heaviness in her step. Then, halfway up she turned and called to me.

'Butler, your father...'

'Yes, ma'am?'

I wasn't sure if she'd think I was staring but the mention of my dad gave me more of a shock.

'Tell him I want to see him. Tomorrow morning at ten. Sharp.'

'Yes, ma'am.'

I climbed back in the cab in a dream. Fearing a nightmare. Lady Hester must have remembered what he'd done. If she wanted to see him, it could only be for one reason.

Sixteen

But it wasn't. I was dumbfounded, even when Butters, who'd been present at the interview, told me what went on. 'She laid into him about his desertion. Said if he ever let down those children again, she'd have him thrown into gaol.'

'Let them down again? It's too late for that. He can't do a proper job any more and without that…'

'He's to manage the kitchen garden…'

Reason went out of the window when she said that.

'But the kitchen garden's mine! I've brought it back to life. I've done all the hard work. He'll not bother…'

'Lady Hester threatened him about that, too.'

'I don't believe all this. I'm going to tell her what I think…'

Butters blocked my way, seizing my shoulders and pushing me back. It was her closeness that took away my will. I felt more of an urge to pull her to me than to shove her aside. I did neither, just looked down, panting. She made me sit and poured a cup of tea.

'It was because of you, Harry,' she said.

'Me?'

'It's her thanks.'

'But he let her down. Nearly ruined the whole thing.'

'And you saved it.'

'So now I lose for it?'

'Not really. She's giving Jessie a place here, as a scullery maid.'

Those words also stunned me. 'Jessie's out of the workhouse?'

'They all are. That's why she's given him the job, made him take the job. And promise not to let it slip. It's so he will be able to get the children back.'

That did put a bit of a different complexion on things though it still irked. Then a suspicion crossed my mind.

219

'Lil, you didn't tell her…'

'I was there when she tore a strip off him.'

'That wasn't what I asked.'

'What's it matter how it came about? They're all coming back home.'

'I still feel miffed. I know it's selfish but…'

'I think she has other plans for you.'

'All I want to do is drive cars.'

'When you're old enough.'

That did bring on a sulk. However, the children returned before I could go off in a huff and my grumbles were forgotten. Jessie and Sairy seemed to have grown up faster than I had while I was away and soon had the cottage, and my dad, under control.

So things settled down. I even felt sorry for my dad and helped out with the heavier digging in the kitchen garden. My biggest gripe was that while I was permitted to maintain the Model T − all the other cars had gone − Hemmings took over the driving.

'Not got a yellow card, have you?' he sneered when I protested. 'You're too young.'

'I wasn't too young to drive in Belgium.'

'Yeah, well, I'd keep quiet about that, if I were you.'

'Why should I?'

'You'll get others into trouble.'

I stormed off without listening to what he said. When I'd calmed down I did sound out other people whether I was too young. Nobody's view encouraged me to push for permission. I'd have moped more than I did had it not been for the need to help restore the household. And remembering the dead made me count my blessings.

Nevertheless, the winter months were grim. The War had ground to a halt, the newspapers reported. Despite all their morale-boosting stories, I could understand what that meant for the men over there. Dewi's 'The Welch will still be here' came back to me. Yes, cold and wet and still being shelled, I guessed.

Soon I wouldn't need to guess. After Christmas Butters told me that Lady Hester had decided to let out most of the House as a convalescent home for the wounded. We'd be learning what it was really like by seeing the casualties. If I wasn't too young, of course.

Then everyone's plans went awry. We were famous. That is to say, Lady Hester was. Whether it came about through the plan to open a convalescent home, I didn't know at first, but a journalist discovered our adventure in Belgium. There wasn't much good news to report early in 1915 so her heroic mission to help 'gallant little Belgium' made a good splash.

Had it ended with that there'd have been no mess. She wasn't the only lady who'd evaded the cumbersome military machine and gone over to 'do her bit.' It wasn't a secret. Unfortunately someone tracked down Helena, who, it appeared, had retreated to Dunkirk to care for a wounded Lieutenant de Brokelen.

Only at that point did the journalists get a sniff of secrets. So where were the other members of the ambulance? When had Lady Hester pitched up in Ypres? She refused to speak to the Press and Butters and I had no wish to court publicity so we kept our heads down.

It was their discovery of Magda's death that fed the flames. The noble self-sacrifice soon gave way to awkward questions about why a woman had been allowed so near the Front. And the military authorities soon displayed their talent for sacrifice – of others.

The gallant Lady Hester became 'reckless', ignoring the Army's wise counsel and dragging her companions into danger. With the predicted results. 'Gallant little Belgium' was forgotten – again. 'Just let us get on with the job and don't interfere' became the military refrain. There was even a hint that Ypres had nearly fallen because we were in the way.

Lady Hester then made the mistake of talking to a reporter. He was supposed to be sympathetic. I suspect Sir Brydon might have pushed her into it. And given the journalist information that could be used against her. Why do I believe this? If the spotlight came too near to him, his own affairs might not bear that much close scrutiny. Unveiling more scandal about the ambulance diverted away that danger.

Otherwise I couldn't see where else our capture by the Germans would have come from, if not from the details of our exchange for the German officers. That, of course, gave the story fresh impetus. Behind the lines, capture, exchange, caught in the near-disaster before Ypres. These details racheted up the risks Lady Hester had taken that led to Magda's death. Oh, and flung in a few suspicions about how far we were helping the Germans. The fact that no mention was made about our proposed execution confirmed to me how the story must have come from our own side. But that wasn't the biggest bombshell.

I was.

'You'll have to go away, boy,' Sir Brydon said.

I squirmed. When Butters had told me Lady Hester wished to see me, I hadn't expected him to be there. Of Lady Hester there was no sign.

'G-Go away, sir?'

'To the family's estate on Arran.'

I shook my head, not knowing where Arran was. It might have been near Dixmude, for all I knew. He must have taken that for a refusal.

'You can't refuse. Lady Hester's reputation depends on it.'

Fine care you took for Lady Hester's reputation, I thought. Did she know about this? Sir Brydon might have shared some characteristics with a uhlan but I wasn't going to give up without a fight.

'There's my brothers and sisters to look after. My dad can't...'

'They'll be taken care of.'

'Not in the workhouse again?'

'Don't you dare speak to me in that manner.'

'I'm not going to be forced to abandon...'

'I said be quiet. If you refuse to agree, your father will be dismissed and you'll all end up in the workhouse.'

'Does Lady Hester know about this?'

'It's not your place to ask. Get out!'

Two days later I was on Arran. In a cottage on the west coast, lodging with an old couple whose speech was incomprehensible to me, digging peat. What a miserable two months. The ground was half-frozen for much of the day and driving winds and rain blew incessantly from the sea.

That was all that drove with any power. Motor transport didn't appear to have penetrated this far north and west. If it had, it would have sunk into the dirt roads in no time. The Belgian pave seemed like a lost paradise.

Hemmings had been deputed to drive me up to the ferry on the Scottish mainland, a task he undertook with his characteristic bad grace, although he cheered up whenever he remembered my banishment. He took a delight in not allowing me to appear in public so that when he stopped for a drink I had to remain in the car and when we stayed the night in an inn near the Scottish border I wasn't permitted to come out of the room. Had there been an alert journalist within ten miles he'd probably have smelt something fishy. Unfortunately there wasn't.

I say that, although from a newspaper that Hemmings bought on the second day, Lady Hester was in enough trouble as it was. 'Forced a Fourteen year-old boy to the Front' was the headline. The article gave my name but no more information. I wondered how much of that had come from Hemmings himself or long it would take them to track down my dad. Or one of the girls. Mind you, they didn't know much. And if Hemmings wasn't careful, his own inglorious part in it all might rebound on him.

I'd tried to see Lady Hester to beg to stay but Butters said she'd been sedated. I suspect Sir Brydon there, again. It only occurred to me after I'd landed in Arran that if a journalist had caught up with me, he'd see that I wasn't the 'small child' Lady Hester stood accused of transporting into danger. And I could have explained my own part in it.

But before I could think, I was marooned on Arran. Half a day's walk to the ferry and with no money anyway to make an escape. Once the snow fell in mid-February even leaving the cottage became too much of a struggle.

No one had told me how long I needed to hide. Sir Bryden refused to see me. Hemmings claimed he'd been told it was until the War was over. I didn't believe him but I couldn't find anything from my captors – the old couple with whom I lodged – either. They weren't a bad sort: our communication improved thanks to the practice in sign language I'd had in Belgium and as I picked up some of their expressions. But trying to ask what they knew would have been futile. They didn't ask questions, just did as they were told. So I settled down and came to like the space and peace out there.

However, inner peace took some time. The War didn't end for another four years, of course and mine kept coming back. At first, to say it took me by surprise would be an exaggeration. I'd far from forgotten what I'd seen but always assumed I could cope with the memories. Then one day the smell of death overwhelmed me.

The smell was real enough. I was out with the sheep – the old couple had a small flock – and sauntering along beside a drystone wall when the stale, cloying stink drove up my nose. I knew what it was: that wasn't the first time I'd come across a dead sheep out there. But somehow on this occasion the smell wouldn't leave me. And it called up the image of a trench outside Dixmude that we'd been sent to one night.

Our casualties weren't that badly wounded – though one died from the shock of being transported – but the trench they'd held for a week was filled with their own dead. They seemed immune to the stink: it made me, and Butters, sick. I'd forgotten it until I stumbled by the dead sheep.

After that similar images would be triggered without warning. Sometimes I could shake my head and they'd disappear; sometimes they'd last for days. On more than one occasion I woke up screaming. Or covered in sweat.

One morning I tried to apologise. The old lady patted me on the shoulder, her eyes filling with tears. I gathered that I shouldn't worry about it. In my normal way, it was only months later that I realised that must have been what she expected: whether they'd been told about the reason for my being sent to them or whether she thought they were merely childhood nightmares, I never discovered.

After that – and again I didn't really notice at the time, just put it down to the arrival of spring and summer – I seemed to be worked less hard. I was sent off to watch the sheep – and that was all they needed, watching. Or told to go and roam on the mountain. Gradually the nightmares eased off.

I'd been told to make no contact with home so didn't expect the letter that arrived in the autumn. I opened it wondering if my exile was over. It was from Butters. She thought I should know that Lady Hester was still under severe strain, helped neither by the abandonment of her 'friends' nor by a breach with Helena, who'd returned to England and been re-united with her father. Helena had also provided more fuel for the condemnation of her mother by relating in detail how she was forced to accompany her to Belgium.

This letter knocked me back. News of the family was good, Jessie was doing well and even my dad seemed to be meeting his obligations. However, the prospects for my return appeared dim. Worse, I felt I'd been forgotten as, by Sir Brydon, no doubt I had. I sank into a depression, not helped by the autumn mists that rolled in here for days. Another dark winter loomed ahead of me. The thought of being trapped indoors with the smoke and gloom filled me with dread. Had it not been for the autumn sheep market, I don't know how I'd have survived.

Pa Grant, as I'd come to call him, wanted to go to Brodick, the main town on the other side of the island, to sell six sheep in order to reduce the size of his flock, something that gave me hope they didn't expect me to be around for all that long. 'Go' meant on foot so the sheep had to travel the same way. Ma Grant persuaded him to take me to manage the sheep and save his legs. Although barely a dozen miles, it was a slow trek, taking two days. For Pa Grant it was a well-worn trail and we spent a night on the way in a shepherds' hut.

I had looked forward to seeing the bustle of life again but the noise and crowding of Brodick – a small place anyway – battered my senses. I could feel the rolling thunder of the guns at Dixmude waiting to intrude. While Pa Grant concluded his business I sat on the beach and stared across towards the Scottish mainland. On the way out I'd wondered if an urge to escape would seize me and I'd make a run for the ferry, not that I had any money for a ticket. Now, all I wanted was to retreat to isolation.

Whether that would have been in my best interests I never found out. Returning to meet Pa Grant at the market I came on a scene of chaos outside its main gate. A lorry – yes, there was one here – had broken down and was blocking the exit. The bonnet was raised and several heads hovered over it, arguing, by the sound of it, but otherwise doing nothing. From the back of the lorry, the bleating of sheep punctuated the row.

I couldn't understand a word of the discussion, shook my head and found Pa Grant, to whom I expressed my scorn for the ineffectual efforts I'd passed. He asked me something that I guessed amounted to what did I know. I shrugged and indicated that I couldn't tell without looking. He grabbed my arm and drew me through the crowd.

His authority among these people astonished me. An old man from an isolated croft he might be to me but the people here knew him and made way. My cockiness evaporated. His reputation could be about to suffer a big knock on my account. I hadn't looked in an engine for a year. And this was a lorry. I'd had a peek inside one or two at the convent at Furnes but never worked on one.

Now I'd talked myself into doing so in front of an audience with no knowledge of an engine but plenty of opinions. And I lacked the means of communication to indicate to them that all I could do was take a look. I tried to gesture this but it only appeared to stir their impatience.

Giving Pa Grant a despairing shrug I bent over and peered in. At that point I realised I should have asked the driver what had gone wrong. It was too late. The crowd who'd done nothing but talk now wanted action. Let it be something simple, I prayed, while expecting that if it had been simple, they'd already have discovered it.

It was so obvious I almost missed it myself. The mounting on the end of the clutch lever had split. The lever had slipped out and hung without a connexion. When the driver engaged a gear he'd be driving thin air.

I straightened up. The crowd hushed.

'Cannaye foux it, laddie?' a voice said, surprising me that I understood it. The owner was dressed in a dark suit, which perhaps explained the nearness of his acquaintance with the English language.

'Not by myself. It'll need a blacksmith.'

There was no mistaking the individual who was propelled out of the crowd. He frowned at the bonnet.

'We need to push the lorry out of the way,' I said to my interpreter. 'The work will take time.'

Provided with an outlet the crowd pushed the lorry out of the entrance and down the road. Just in time I reminded the driver to get in: he might need to brake – as he did since the enthusiasm of the pushers would otherwise have launched the vehicle down the slope into the sea. It occurred to me that they might have removed the blockage earlier had they thought about it. But I then saw that their efforts hadn't just been blind sweat. We'd reached the blacksmith's.

He understood what was needed and set to. While he hammered out the replacement piece my linguist took me and Pa Grant to his place, which seemed to be some sort of estate office, for a cup of tea. Pa Grant, never the most communicative of men, again appeared to be well at ease with this man. Since they dived into a discussion about some matter of finance that was beyond me, I picked up a newspaper lying on the desk.

'Victory at Loos' the headline read. 'Advance of more than a mile.' But what caught my eye were the casualty lists. The heading 'Heavy casualties' came well down the report. I gathered the battle still continued so wondered how much of the report was wishful thinking. I remembered our 'victory' at Ypres. It seemed the fighting there had intensified. The Welch featured a lot in the casualty lists and I wondered if the names included Dewi but I'd never asked his full name so couldn't tell.

'You know about motor cars?'

I hadn't noticed the man was addressing me. When I said I'd learned about them from a chauffeur in England, he asked me if I knew how

227

to drive. His eyes lit up when I mentioned the Model T: I kept quiet about the ambulance version.

When the blacksmith came to say he'd finished the part Pa Grant was deep in conversation with the man, whose name I found from the blacksmith was Gourlay. The new bracket looked good and it didn't take us too long to effect the repair. My nerves were on edge as the driver climbed into the cab. She jerked a bit when he engaged the clutch but that was him; the part worked like a dream. The lorry moved forward.

I refused the offer of a half crown from the driver and indicated that the blacksmith had done the work. That's your passport to a ferry ticket gone, I told myself but I'd done nothing to deserve payment. The thanks of the locals were more gratifying to me.

I went back to Mr Gourlay's with a smile on my face. When I saw him and Pa Grant standing outside the door waiting for me, my face clouded. But Mr Gourlay smiled.

'News travels fast here,' he said. 'You did well.'

I shrugged. 'It was fairly obvious.'

'Do you want a job?'

I blinked and glanced at Pa Grant, who seemed unruffled by the request. 'Er, I'm working for… I'm not sure I can…'

'It's no problem for Malcolm, he's willing to release you. He's worried you might be missing out, being stuck out there with them all winter.'

Pa Grant indicated his agreement by nodding. I was bemused by the turn of events and couldn't find words.

'You'll be wanting to know what's involved,' Mr Gourlay said.

That hadn't occurred to me. I was still weighing up how much to confess about my exile. Would I run the risk of exposure – and add to Lady Hester's troubles – if I agreed to whatever this entailed? My grunt must have been taken for acquiescence.

'The estate is taking delivery of a Model T Ford of its own, mainly to allow me to pay closer attention to the land in the north. I need someone to drive and look after it. The fellow we had in mind went and joined up. Would you be able to do it?'

My face lit up. 'Of course!' Then I recalled Hemmings' sneering about my lack of a yellow card and getting people into trouble; there was also the small matter of my banishment. I glanced at Pa Grant again. 'I'm not sure that…'

'I told you, Malcolm has no objection. He'll be recompensed for your time. And I won't need you every day.'

'It's not only that. I don't have a card…'

'No cause to worry about such things here.'

This was proving hard work. 'And… I was sent here, to P… Mr Grant's.'

'I'm sure Sir Brydon will have no objection…'

'You know Sir Brydon?'

'I manage his estate. What he doesn't know won't hurt him.'

So I came to drive for Mr Gourlay. And lodged with him two or three days a week, which gave me access to his library. He not only encouraged me to read but made recommendations. Looking back, I think he was pushing me but he had no need: I devoured everything I could. That winter, far from being the gloomy prison I'd feared became an opportunity to immerse myself in reading.

I was aware that it wouldn't take much for Mr Gourlay to learn to drive himself and, even though I'd be putting myself out of a job, I demonstrated the rudiments to him.

Again my foresight was correct but my fears were groundless. The next year – the year of more glorious headlines after the first day on the Somme – I was sent to the technical school in Glasgow. By then the catastrophic loss of life had pushed any concerns about Lady Hester out of sight. I'd forgotten about her myself, if I'm honest; only later did I learn that all this had been her doing.

In 1918 I should have been called up but as I had no papers the War ended before they caught up with me. Strange that four years earlier I couldn't wait to get over there. Instead, I agreed to go to the university in Edinburgh. But it wasn't me. The academic life left me cold. I left after a year. There were other things, too. The girl, Jeannie, that I'd met in Glasgow, died of the influenza. I longed for the peace I'd found on Arran but felt that I couldn't face the people who'd been so good to me after falling out of the university.

I ended up on Rannoch Moor, handyman at the manse of a minister who also had a vast library. The damp and gloom suited me, I thought, but it weighed me down without my noticing. It's also where I got this limp. Slipping off the roof of an outhouse as I tried to fix the slates. Not a bad injury but the hospital was too far away for me to be bothered and so it never got fixed either.

Two years on, when the minister died, I drifted into Pitlochry and found work on the dam. That ended and I pitched up at last working where I'd always hoped: in an automobile garage in Perth. I threw myself into it. Yet something nagged at me. Whenever a Model T came in the memories came with it. I began to wonder if I hadn't been glad to be sent away. If I hadn't wanted to escape.

As times worsened the garage had to let me go. I felt myself drifting south. Time spent in the Durham coalfields showed me further evidence of what all those who died had really won. Their families weren't under bombardment but the desolation they lived in had an atmosphere more chilling than anywhere at the Front.

I suppose I sensed that my life was drifting, too but that just seemed to be the way of things. It was the same for everyone. At twenty-five I should have been in the prime of life but the men I felt I belonged with were the cripples. Young men who'd become old. Who were only fit for the scrapheap now. Who could see no future.

Ten, eleven years earlier the future didn't matter. The rush was to grab the present before it slipped away. Should I have stopped to think? My excuse was my youth. Wasn't that the excuse of all of us? But our leaders weren't young. Shouldn't they have calmed us down? Lady Hester wasn't young. Yet her intentions were good. Perhaps all our intentions were. To help gallant little Belgium. If I'm honest with myself that was an excuse. I wanted to see action; where it took place was secondary in my mind. I ended up doing whatever good I did by accident.

Didn't it all come down to accident, to luck, to being in the right or wrong place at a particular time? If my dad hadn't lost his nerve, if I hadn't been on the ship... you could go on for ever. Why had I survived and hundreds of thousands of others hadn't? Like Magda. Luck. It was where the shell burst that mattered. Anything you did yourself or tried to do, your own efforts, counted for nothing.

So life was a downward drifting path. It seemed the same everywhere. Pinched faces, struggle but still helplessness against the massive forces that pressed down on your circumstances. It may have been different down south and for the upper classes – though there must have been more families like Lady Hester's that had been torn apart by the War – but in Scotland and the North the fruits of victory were small, bitter and shrivelled on the trees.

A Durham miner I got talking to said he was going to Africa. South Africa. There was work in the gold mines, he claimed. A skilled man could make a new life. Someone else had gone off to West Africa but he'd come back cursing the climate. 'The white man's grave,' he called it. Or Canada, Australia. After their own losses in the War there were plenty of openings. A new life, a new opportunity.

Why didn't I take one? Perhaps if it hadn't been for the War I would have. But the spark had gone. What was the point? A sense of unfinished business – what sort of business, I hadn't a clue – hung over me and held me back. Even cars held no attraction for me any more. Nothing did.

I'd also lost touch with everyone. Jessie used to drop me a line now and then but after leaving the university I couldn't find the will to reply. When I was in Glasgow a letter from Butters had found me, saying she was going to go to Australia. She'd met an Australian ambulance driver and they were to be married. I was pleased for her but even then I couldn't bring myself to write back.

The glimpse she gave of Lady Hester suggested the scandal had broken her. My part in that didn't ease with time. I could rationalise it all away but no matter how many times I told myself my contribution to her disgrace was minute – after all no one had caught up with me and persuaded me to spill the beans as Helena had done so readily – the dull sense of guilt weighed down on me.

Then I read that she was dead.

Seventeen

The funeral passed me by in a daze. I wasn't the only one absent. The references to Lady Hester herself were brief to the point of indecency. The vicar muttered a few platitudes. Sir Brydon said nothing. I suppose I should have been grateful the hypocrisy was therefore reduced but it didn't assuage my anger. Did I have a right to be angry on her behalf? I was too confused to know. Or care. I just was.

When I say Sir Brydon said nothing, I meant about his former wife. He stood up and intoned how it was a sad day for all of us, then launched into thanks to all those who'd contributed to the war memorial fund, the unveiling of which was due to be held the following day. Some muttering followed by a 'Shhh' made me glance to my right. A man I didn't recognise stared straight ahead, his face set, while a woman shook his arm.

Sir Brydon's self-congratulatory tone let me guess what the man's reaction had come from. It wasn't the dead – including the person who was the reason we were here today – who deserved our thanks: it was the noble local worthies who'd sacrificed a few bob for a slab of stone.

I limped out during the final prayers to get as far away as possible until I found a tree stump in Beech Wood outside the village. Curly's war games had romped through here. I sat and tried to remember if we'd fought – or run away – over this particular patch. It hadn't been important enough to remain in my memory. Had the trees changed or was it just me?

I did recall once overhearing Magda tell Lady Hester that we never come back to the same place. The comment made no sense to me but somehow stuck. I could see its validity now. Lady Hester had wanted to do her bit – and had – yet when she returned all she received was recrimination and, now, impatient near-silence. They couldn't wait to shove her in a grave and forget all about her.

I shook my head at Sir Brydon's encomium to the unveiling of the war memorial. Perhaps Lady Hester would have been better off if she had been killed over there. If the Germans had shot us as spies, what added lustre her reputation would have gained. Maybe we who survived weren't the lucky ones.

Thinking of the dead always meant Magda. I realise now that I wanted the memories to flood back. For all the horror there was also something that I otherwise couldn't reach anywhere around me: feeling. Whatever else it was, it was of an intensity I'd not found since. I began to feel the importance of that time's not being taken away. That's why I lingered for the unveiling ceremony at the war memorial the next day. Would I for once be in tune with public sentiment?

I met another disappointment before then. When I came for the funeral my intention had been not to stay. To call remaining for the unveiling 'curiosity' would be untrue; it was more a sense of responsibility. To see how not forgetting would turn out. Armistice Day had become established by now but its once-a-year switching on of the remembrance tears grated on me. I hoped to see a more permanent reminder tomorrow. If not for Lady Hester then at least for the others who'd shared her fate years earlier.

So I hung on and decided to fulfil another obligation. I went home. It might have been an image of the wider world. My dad didn't recognise me. In my then state of mind I made no attempt force him to. I'm not sure it would have made any difference if I had. Or if I'd have recognised him either had I not found him slumped on the same bench I could picture him on all those years before when I first came back.

'Hello, dad,' I said.

He peered up at me with a frown. His eyes looked vacant and he mumbled to himself. Only his complaining sounded unchanged. 'Where's our Jessie? She come back yet, eh?'

'Er, no, I don't...'

'I told her to get me them. She going to take all day over it? I told her. It's always the same...'

'I'll go and see.'

I slipped away. Who he thought I was, I didn't know. Were the younger lads as big as me now? Whoever it was, he didn't care. Being waited on he clearly believed to continue to be his God-given right. My depression deepened as I thought of this. And Jessie's inheritance of servitude.

Then I met her.

'What do you think you're doing?'

I'd stumbled onto the road, not concentrating on where I was. A young woman in a flower-printed frock eyed me up and down. I suppose I did look shifty.

'Jessie?'

That only seemed to increase her suspicions. She didn't answer my question but repeated hers. Something she'd inherited from my mum. 'I asked you why you were in our house?'

I stared at her but made no impression. Except to confirm my guilt. She tensed. I prepared to be attacked.

'Harry,' I said. 'Your brother.'

She stared at *me*. Her demeanour didn't soften. If anything, my relationship sounded more of a crime.

She gave a snort. 'Come back, have you?'

Her statement of the obvious threw me off balance. The last time I'd seen her we'd parted amicably and she had written to me – without receiving a reply. Maybe that was it.

'I was… passing, so I thought…' I mumbled.

'Generous of you. Passing, eh? Not thought to pass by a bit sooner since, have you?'

I muttered apologies. Coming home had been a mistake. I just wanted to get away and edged past her.

'Couldn't manage the funeral, either?' she asked.

'I was there,' I said, turning in surprise.

'I didn't see you.'

'I was at the back. I slipped out, before the end. I couldn't stand…'

'Couldn't stand much, could you, Harry? Not here when our mum died. Not here when her Ladyship was fading.'

'I didn't know…'

234

'Course you didn't. How could anybody know where to find you? You never replied to letters.'

I gave up protesting. She must have taken my sigh for annoyance because her tone hardened even more.

'I'd invite you in but I need to start packing.'

'Packing?'

'That'll be something else you didn't know. Her majesty Helena's moving into the House and she's clearing out the old servants. Dad's got to move.'

That did stir me. 'And you..? Weren't you..?'

'Don't worry about me. I'm due to be married. We've a farm on Sir Gerald's estate. We'll be all right. There's work for the boys, and Sairy, though she's a bit like you, ideas above her station…'

'Good,' I nodded. 'Good.'

She tossed her head in disgust. I didn't intend to mean I was praising Sairy's ideas above her station. I turned away and limped off, not thinking to ask if dad would also go with her. At least I had no fears she'd be downtrodden by him.

After that dose of emotional flagellation I found a dark corner of *The Bull* in which to hide and reflect. Who else could I bump into to add to my sense of worthlessness? Sir Brydon? Helena? There was nothing either of them could say to shame me. Quite the reverse. I couldn't recall having seen Helena at the funeral although from Jessie's comment I hadn't noticed much at all. Then I heard Curly.

Strange that having barely recognised my own sister, Curly's voice sounded no different from twelve years earlier. I couldn't miss that complacent lilt, with the burr that somehow told you everything you heard was probably a fairy tale.

The voice came from the central part of the bar. I inched round to see, still staying in the shadows. The speaker's back was to me. With a jolt I saw he wore an army uniform, with a captain's pips visible on his near shoulder. A captain, Curly? No, that wasn't possible. Not in your wildest dreams. If Curly had made lance corporal, I'd have been amazed. Was it someone else? The voice was Curly's. He was relating some of his military service. It clearly wasn't recent. I thought I could guess when.

'We rubbed it in all right. Not 'arf. "Do this, do that, at the double now. And say sir when you do." Ha, ha. You could tell they didn't like it but what could they do. They was starvin'. Pathetic. Like beaten dogs. So they shoulda been, as well, shouldn't they? They needed a lesson teachin' and we gave 'em one. We never let 'em forget they was beaten. You have my word for it, we never let 'em forget.

What puzzled me was that I'd heard when I first came back in 1914 how he'd been rejected as unfit. However, when I realised what he was describing I decided he must have got in in the last months, when they were scrabbling round for any material. Even so, a captain? Things weren't that bad, surely? The service he was boasting about had been in the Rhineland: with the Army of Occupation.

After my bemusement eased his exploits took on an air of comedy. Curly on the front line and not running away. But as he continued he began to grate on my nerves. I didn't believe he'd done any fighting yet his use of 'we' in all his reminiscences came across not just as empty boasting but an insult to those who had fought and died. I stood up and limped past him then stopped and looked him full in the face.

'Curly. Well, I never…'

'It's Charles to you,' he said with a glance at his companions, two well-padded individuals in sleek overcoats. Not army surplus by any means.

'Can I help you?' he added, his voice more plummy now than in his military yarn. For a moment I was caught off guard again but amusement cleared my head.

'Harry,' I said. 'You remember, I was in your gang. Before the War. You had us pretending to be soldiers even then.'

His face betrayed some glimpse that he was being insulted but he shook his head with an appearance of sadness. 'I'd like to give you a job, chum, whoever you are but with times as they are, you know…'

Curly, give me a job? I glanced at his companions. Their blank faces showed they weren't accepting his drinks in ignorance of what he was like. But Curly, an employer? So he couldn't still be in the army?

236

'You gone up in the world, then, Curly?' I asked, not trying to hide my surprise. 'Made your money bullying Germans, did you?'

His lip twisted. 'I served my country.'

'After it was all over?'

With Curly you were always able to see his mind working but he could only manage one thing at a time. I could tell he was trying to place me, which was why he uttered platitudes that exposed his bluster.

'I answered the call.'

'Weren't you rejected as unfit?'

I saw that that stung but it must also have jogged his memory. His sneer brightened. 'Oh, I know who you are.'

'Fit enough to run from the Topham gang, though, weren't we?'

One of his companions twitched. I was the one not paying enough attention now. Curly seemed to swell inside his neat khaki. 'You're that kid who got her ladyship into all that trouble.' With a nod of his head he indicated me to his mates. 'They kept it quiet at the funeral, didn't they? He was the one she run off with.'

I'd walked straight into this. Their condescension swept over me. I was the one grasping for platitudes.

'It wasn't like that at all.'

'No? Not half,' Curly laughed.

'It wasn't!'

'Sez you.'

He'd hit on the guilt and I'd have slunk away if one of the others hadn't put his oar in.

'The disgrace was deeply felt round here, as you'd know if you'd been to the funeral.'

'Disgrace? You lot are the bloody disgrace,' I said, too loudly. I sensed conversation stop elsewhere in the bar. It stirred me on. 'She went over there and did more than you ever lifted a fat finger to. She drove up to the Front to bring out wounded. Under fire. And she was captured and threatened with execution by the Hun. Disgrace? The Germans treated her better than you scum.'

That brought silence. I turned and strode out, glaring at the startled faces I passed. In the Square workmen were covering the newly-erected memorial with a tarpaulin. What hit me was a memory of the tarp on the back of the ambulance: we were inside, prisoners of the enemy. It gave me a slap that cleared my head. When I walked out of *The Bull* my intention had been to keep going, to get as far away from there as possible. Now I changed my mind. I'd be back tomorrow. If no one else did, I'd be remembering Lady Hester and Magda at the unveiling of the memorial.

Eighteen

I slept out in the woods. Early June had begun warm and dry so it was no hardship. Before the War we used to do it quite often. Indoors you could feel suffocated during the summer.

Watching the worthies assemble gave me a similar feeling. Together with the smouldering anger as I saw two separate groups form. Had I not known some of the members I'd still have had little difficulty distinguishing them. Even without the wounded – and the number brought out in bath chairs gave me a shock – the spare, upright demeanour of the former servicemen set them apart from the well-padded worthies who seemed to be running the show.

Curly, still in his uniform, belonged to this latter group. His captain's presence alone gave the whole scene an air of obscenity. I guessed the old soldiers, with medals on their civilian suits, would have given him short shrift if he'd paraded before them. Sir Brydon arrived in a Wolseley, which gave me a twinge but I had a bigger one when Lady Helena stepped out. The man with her clearly wasn't Guy.

I made myself get a grip. Why should it be Guy? How long ago was it now, twelve years? He might have been killed, too, later in the War. And hadn't he been married? I was in no position to judge. How much change had I been through in that time? Was I letting myself get stuck in a time that was past? Judging everything by how much its relation to Lady Hester remained unaltered?

But wasn't that what we were here today to try to do? Set in stone the memory of those no longer with us?

The beginning of the ceremony put a stop to my musing. A crowd of onlookers had gathered by now around me, looking on at the two groups of participants – I call them both participants although the old soldiers were reduced, like me, to spectators.

The regimental brass band struck up and when they'd finished some portly chap who looked like a farmer but wore a suit and with a chain of office round his neck said some words of introduction before handing over to Sir Brydon. I wasn't really listening.

My own position had struck me as amusing in a strange sort of way. Here I was with the spectators, no part of what was taking place. I had no right to stand with the old soldiers, though I shared their memories far more than any of the official party could do. Some might take me for a casualty but to claim it would have been as false as Curly's posturing. I belonged nowhere.

Just like Lady Hester did here. Sir Brydon pulled on a rope that released the tarpaulin, revealing the cross that topped the memorial. A chill ran down my back as I realised someone was reading out the names engraved on it.

A deeper chill struck when I heard Tom's name. I'd forgotten I'd not seen him about. I was still taking in that shock when Carstairs' name hit me. Carstairs? But he had a cushy job, driving a big-wig around. Again I told myself not to be stupid. None of us knew how the War would unfold in 1914. It had caught out a good many who'd seemed safe at the start. We'd rushed into it without a thought for the consequences and they'd reaped their revenge.

Of course, there was no reference to Lady Hester. Why should there be, she wasn't a casualty of the War. Nor of Magda, neither, but then she wasn't local. I think I could have accepted all that if it hadn't been for the air of self-congratulation that rose from the official party and stuck in my throat like the smell from those massacred villagers' bodies in Belgium. You'd think they were celebrating a victory.

As the band wheeled and marched off the crowd dispersed and I limped across to the stone to find the names of Tom and Carstairs, as if to hope my fears had been groundless. They were there, right enough. And there was another one. I must have missed the name when it was being read out. George Robards. The firm voice of reason on the eve of war who'd warned against all the hysteria. So, despite his misgivings, he'd heeded the call, too, and paid the price?

I reeled away and bumped into Helena. She gave me such a look of disdain I couldn't hold my tongue.

'Don't worry, you won't catch anything here, specially not a Belgian lieutenant,' I said.

She went pale at that. I wondered if I had hit a wound and made to back away but her male companion butted in.

'Have a care, fellow.'

His tone stung me. 'Oh, I do, chum,' I said. 'I didn't desert her mother when the going got hot over there.'

'Who are you?' Helena asked.

I stared at her. There was no sign of recognition.

'Harry…' I was becoming fed up with having to introduce myself. 'Driver… Remember?'

Was that a flicker of guilt in her eyes before the scorn replaced it?

'Oh, you? You were the cause of all her trouble.'

'Me? I didn't write about her…'

I should have known better than to think I could shame her or affect the self-justifying construction she'd put on everything that didn't suit her. She launched into me.

'You were the one who led her into the whole insane episode. If you hadn't been so eager to persuade her you could drive…'

I tried to protest but she brushed me aside. 'And lied about your age. How could you? That's what broke her heart.'

'I'll tell you what broke her heart,' I began but never finished the sentence. Sir Brydon must have been drawn by the altercation. He broke up my reply.

'It's lucky she's dead,' he said. 'If she saw the state of you, her heart would break again for all that paying for your keep and education achieved.'

I gaped at him, the ground swept from under me. My puzzlement brought a gleam of triumph to his face as he drew Helena away. 'Surely you didn't think I would waste *my* energy on an ungrateful wretch like you?'

I slumped down on the low wall surrounding the monument. So I'd been as ungrateful as all the rest? But how could I know? Sir Brydon had handled everything. He'd refused to let me see her. Should I have realised? I tried to think. I remembered Mr Gourlay, Sir Brydon's estate manager, saying that what Sir Brydon didn't know wouldn't hurt him. Did he believe it was Sir Brydon behind it all?

I shook my head in disbelief. A man standing beside the memorial laughed. I looked up, frowning. He nodded in the direction he must have thought I was staring, though I was actually seeing nothing. Certainly not Curly, at whom he pointed.

'Know where he got that uniform from?' he said. 'Bought it the same time he picked up them army surplus lorries he set up his business with.'

'His business?'

'Hopkins' Haulage. There's men on here…' He indicated the memorial, 'whose boots he's filled, no messing. Where he got the money to start with, well, that's another tale.'

He walked off. I watched Curly get into a big car – another Wolseley, I saw with a pang. For a moment I wondered if he'd confiscated that in the Rhineland.

'Excuse me.'

I looked round. A smart young woman in a two-piece suit stood to the side. I shuffled to my feet. 'Sorry,' I said, presuming she was a relative of one of the names and didn't appreciate my sitting on the stone. But *her* face was apologetic. She held her hand up to detain me.

'I heard you… having words with Sir Brydon and his daughter. Did you work for Lady Hester?'

'Not exactly,' I muttered, starting to move away. Her manner was milder than that of the last two women to harangue me but I feared she might be another journalist, trying to catch me off guard. Especially when she didn't give up. 'No, wait, please. I want to ask you something.'

I steeled myself for the onslaught. It wasn't what I expected. But it almost knocked me over.

'My mother went to Belgium with Lady Hester…'

I felt myself stagger. I must have put my weight down on my bad foot. I struggled to focus. Her hand gripped my arm. 'Are you all right? Do you want to sit down again?'

I was eased back onto the low wall. I sat with my hands on my knees, looking at the ground and took in deep breaths. Having helped me the young woman stepped away. I became conscious I was staring at her feet – the skirt only reached to her ankles – and turned my head away.

'Magda,' I said.

'You knew her?'

The tone was so exultant I swung round. Her face had lit up.

'I went with her... them, to Belgium. I was near... when she died...'

My hand was grasped in hers, in a pair of soft gloves. She knelt on one knee. 'Then you're Harry?'

I could only nod. Not being harangued was confusing enough but the sight of Magda's daughter stunned me.

'She wrote about you several times. She admired you.'

I didn't believe it but it was good of her to say.

'I liked her,' I replied. 'She was good to me. And always had a smile. Her loss was the worst thing that happened to us over there.'

She pursed her lips. 'It wasn't a cause of great joy over here. I was only nine and it made me an orphan.'

Her pained expression gave me a start. 'You don't blame Lady Hester? Because if...'

'No, no,' she smiled, sadly. 'My mother had a mind of her own, as you probably know. She insisted on going. I don't think she'd have settled for a refusal. I don't blame anyone.'

I sighed. 'That's an unusual attitude around here.'

'You can say that again. I introduced myself to her husband...'

'Former husband. He ran off with someone else.'

'... yesterday... Because of what she did?'

'Before. He didn't need an excuse. But he used it afterwards to justify his own betrayal.'

She studied the trees beyond the Square, pinching her neck between two fingers of her gloved hand.

'Did you never hear Lady Hester's version?' I asked in the silence.

'Until two weeks ago I didn't know who she was.'

'Your mother didn't say in her letters?'

'She mentioned her only by her first name, and you and Lily – and that daughter whose main contribution was to flirt with any man she could find. It was only when Lady Hester's obituary appeared that I realised she was *that* Lady Hester.'

'I see.'

'And only when I reached my majority last week and the papers were released did I learn that it was she who had paid for my education.'

Another stab in the heart. 'You, too?'

'Too late to thank her. When I tried to thank her husband after the funeral, he was most dismissive. "Guilty conscience, I expect," he snapped at me and walked off.'

'Something he wouldn't know about,' I said. 'A guilty conscience.' I indicated the memorial. 'They're doing their best to forget she ever existed. Let alone their own role in driving her to an early grave.'

She let her gaze roam round the now empty Square and nodded as if pondering. 'You could help in that respect.'

I looked at her in surprise. 'Me? I let her down as much as anyone. My age was the excuse they used to condemn her for going over in the first place. If it hadn't been for me, your mother wouldn't have been over there to be killed.'

'She'd have found a way.'

'I still don't see what I can do now. As you said, isn't it all too late?'

'Not to remember.'

'I do remember. The memories stay with me.'

'But I have none. Nor does anyone else. Unless you provide them.'

'Me?'

'You were there. Why don't you share the memories?'

'Share them?'

I was conscious of sounding stupid but I felt I was sliding onto slippery ground. How much did I want to expose to this stranger, attractive and sympathetic though she was?

'You could write them down.'

'Are you a journalist?' I asked, the pleasant feeling that her company had brought deflating.

'No, though I work in publishing.'

'Ah…'

'Is that just as bad?'

'You probably didn't read what was said about Lady Hester after she came back. It put me off journalists for life.'

She laughed but without the scorn I'd had from everyone else here. She was her mother's daughter. 'There are one or two journalists who could tell the truth. If you wanted, I could put you in touch with them.'

'I'm not sure I do want.'

With an inclination of her head she indicated the monument. 'Will you erect something like this instead?'

I followed her gaze. What had I said about these things? The names of people I knew on it made me feel a bit ashamed of that reaction. But what did the mere names tell me? What *had* happened to Tom and Carstairs – and the others? Maybe remembering was better than not remembering but without their story how much would still lie forgotten? I could feel myself weakening. She broke the silence.

'It would also be a memorial to my mother.'

'Can I think about it?'

'*I'm* not sure I should let you. You might refuse.'

'Since I came back here yesterday you're the first person who hasn't been on at me – so far.'

That made her laugh again. 'You don't seem the sort to be pushed into doing something you don't want to do, Harry.'

That forced a wry grin. 'Much good it's done me.'

'Would you respond more positively to an incentive?'

'It was an incentive – the chance to drive a car – that took me to Belgium.'

'What sort would you like?'

'You are joking?'

'Sorry. I was hoping. Would there be any incentive, now?'

'To tell? It doesn't have the same appeal.'

'Does anything?'

I looked sharply at her. She had her mother's ability to understand what was gong through your mind.

'Stop or you'll be wearing down my resistance,' I said.

'Good.'

'Good?'

'Who else has the opportunity to restore the reputation of Lady Hester? And remember her – and my mother?'

'Who'd listen?'

'You can't approach it from that angle. If there is no record, how can anyone know, let alone remember?'

I looked away and my gaze met the memorial. George Robards. I saw Magda lying in the back of the ambulance again. Felt the presence of this young woman standing near me and remembered the warmth of Lily's body close to me. My eyes fell on Carstairs' name. What was it he'd said about cars and women?

She did allow me time to think about it – Lena, Magda's daughter. Like her mother would have. Magda treated both Butters and me as if we were her equals. Lady Hester, even when she used our first names, was always up there and we were down below. We knew our place. Magda was different. Ahead of her time, they'd say of her nowadays. Like the daughter she never had the chance to see grow up.

So I did think: that's why I agreed to do this. I came to see it's not just about remembering, any more, is it? Once the Strike had petered out and the miners been driven back to work on less pay than before, it came home to me – I told you I was slow to catch on to things – that the better world people thought they were fighting for is already buried and forgotten. The task for those of us left behind has become more than merely to remember.

As I said, I'd always believed that the act of remembrance, through a Day or a memorial, lacked something vital. It's too passive, too sporadic, too prone to being exploited, like that memorial ceremony, for others' ends.

Remembering can only be a first step. To asking the questions we never really stopped to ask then. Why did we do it? What was it for? What has it all added up to?

I don't know. All I can do is re-tell my small part in it. Something

246

I couldn't face for years. I do know now that there has to be an obligation on us, the ones who came back, to refuse to forget. Otherwise, don't we condemn ourselves, and others, to drift only into repetition? Into more of that bloody waste and mess.